CRYPTID HUNTERS

For the Mandan Public Library —

rolandsmith

Hyperion Books for Children
New York

All new parents should have a book dedicated to them.
This one is for Niki and Derek
—Gramps

Printed in the United States of America

First Edition

1 3 5 7 9 10 8 6 4 2

This book is set in 11/16.25 Palatino.

Reinforced binding

Library of Congress Cataloging-in-Publication Data on file.

ISBN 0-7868-5161-9

Visit www.hyperionbooksforchildren.com

cryp·to·zo·ol·o·gy (CRIP´tuh-zoh-AW-luh-jee) *noun* The study of animals, such as the Sasquatch, the Yeti, the Loch Ness monster, the Chupacabra, and others, whose existence have not yet been proven scientifically. There are thought to be more than two hundred cryptids in existence today.

theterriblenews 1

Marty and Grace O'Hara were twins, but you wouldn't know it if you saw them together. Marty has brown hair, eyes the color of rain clouds, and he is a foot taller than his sister. Grace has black hair, startling blue eyes the color of robins' eggs, and she is a foot smarter than her brother.

The O'Hara twins were at the Omega Opportunity Preparatory School in Switzerland when they received the worst news of their lives.

Marty was illustrating a comic book with his best friend and roommate, Luther Smyth, when his art instructor, Mr. Umber, tapped him on the shoulder and said, "You are wanted in the headmaster's office. Again."

Marty shrugged. He was sent to Dr. Bartholomew Beasel's office at least once a week (sometimes two or three times) for various infractions of the rules (of which there were many). The only thing that surprised him was that this time Luther wasn't being summoned as well. (They were usually punished together, which saved the headmaster a great deal of time and effort.)

"Give my regards to Dr. Weasel," Luther said.

"I will," Marty assured him.

As always, Marty took his time getting to the office. He chatted with friends, went to the restroom to muss his hair and pull his shirttail out (this drove the headmaster wild), and stopped in the kitchen to tell the chef he would be by later to help her roll out the dough for the cheese biscuits. When he finally arrived at the office, he was shocked to find his sister, Grace, sitting on one of the uncomfortable chairs outside the headmaster's door.

"What are *you* doing here?" Little Grace never broke the rules.

Grace stared at him mutely with an expression he hadn't seen on her face in a very long time. It worried him. "When we get inside," he said, "you'd better let me do the talking."

Grace started to respond, but was interrupted by the massive door swinging open, and the tall, skeletal Dr. Bartholomew Beasel beckoning them into his inner sanctum. Seated around his long conference table were the school's nurse, counselor, chaplain, their two dormitory supervisors, and three teachers who had known the twins since they began attending the school seven years before.

Marty looked at the staff's grim, solemn expressions and knew that something had gone very, very wrong. "I didn't do it!" he insisted.

Dr. Beasel ignored Marty's shirttail, his wild hair, and his all too familiar disclaimer. "There has been a terrible accident," he said. "I'm afraid your parents are . . ."

Grace fainted before Dr. Beasel was able to finish. The nurse jumped up from her chair, and together with the chaplain and counselor's help, laid her out on the sofa.

"I'll get my smelling salts," the nurse said, and ran out of the office.

Marty, who had seen Grace's emotions overwhelm her like this before, was not overly concerned. He glared around the room in angry frustration at the fussing adults until he could stand it no longer, then shouted, "Our parents are *what*?"

Everyone stopped what they were doing and stared at him helplessly. Dr. Beasel slithered over and put his long slender arm around his least favorite student's shoulders. "I'm afraid your parents are . . . missing," he said.

Marty sank into the nearest chair. "Both of them?"

Dr. Beasel gave him a sad nod. "A helicopter crash in the Amazon. The pilot was found . . . dead . . . a conflagration . . ."

Marty blinked. "A what?" He didn't know what

3

the word meant, but it sounded bad.

Grace, who had recovered without smelling salts and was now sobbing uncontrollably, said, "A fire, Marty. A terrible fire."

Marty joined his sister in her bewildered despair.

The next morning the news was all over the local papers and on the lips of every student and teacher in the school. The twins retreated to Grace's private table in the back of the school library to escape all the sympathetic murmurs and curious stares. Grace spent more time at this table than she did in the dormitory room she shared with her best friend, Brenda Scrivens. No one was allowed to use Grace's table.

"I have something to tell you," she said, holding her stuffed monkey. At least it was thought to be a monkey. The fabric was covered with patches and stitches that look like scars; its left arm, mouth, and ears were long gone. She'd had it since she was a baby and called it "Monkey." It was never far away from her. Marty referred to it as the "Frankenstein monkey."

He was seated across from her. Scattered over the table were several newspapers, open books, crumpled tissues, Grace's Moleskine journal, and scraps of paper filled with mathematical equations, which looked like Egyptian hieroglyphics to Marty, and made just about as much sense.

"But before I tell you," Grace continued, "you have

4

to promise not to say a word about it to anyone else."

A promise between the twins was a sacred pact that could not be broken unless the one who had promised was released from the promise by the one who had asked for the promise. A promise was sealed by giving Monkey's remaining arm a squeeze.

Marty squeezed Monkey's arm.

Grace nodded and took a deep breath. "Remember those nightmares I used to have when I was little?"

"How could I forget?" Marty answered. "They nearly drove you crazy. Don't tell me they're back."

"They're back."

Marty shuddered. No wonder she'd looked so tense outside the Weasel's door. The nightmares had bothered her from the time she was two and a half years old until she was six. When Grace was a little girl, two or three times a week she would wake up screaming. And when she had calmed down enough to speak, she had virtually no recollection of what the dream was about.

"I thought you'd outgrown all that," Marty said. The nightmares had stopped after the twins arrived at the boarding school.

"I did, too." Grace shook her head. "But they're back."

"Do you remember anything?" Marty asked.

"No, but there's something very familiar about all this. Déjà vu, as if I've been through all this before."

"Well, I haven't," Marty said, feeling as if ants were crawling on his neck. Grace sometimes had this effect on him.

She opened one of the newspapers and spread it out on the desk. "Have you seen this article?"

He looked down at the newspaper. Accompanying the long article describing the accident was a dramatic color photograph of the twins' father, Timothy O'Hara. The photo had been taken by their mother and the caption below it read: SYLVIA O'HARA'S FINAL PHOTOGRAPH.

"Mother's last kiss," he whispered, staring at his father's handsome face, trying to hold back tears.

Their mother believed that taking a photograph was like giving someone a kiss. She had told them if there was no affection as the shutter released, the photograph was not worth taking.

"She must have taken this on Mount Everest," Marty commented. Their parents had reached the summit just before they flew off to South America to write an article about the rain forest.

In the photo their father was smiling at their mother with mild amusement. His oxygen mask and goggles were pulled down around his neck. His face was windburned and slightly paler around his gray eyes where the goggles had been. It was a bright day—the kind of day their mother loved because it gave her photos something she called "depth of field," meaning the background was as sharply focused as the foreground. Their mother was standing next to him, which meant she had put the camera on a tripod and set the shutter to release on its own. Her curly blond hair spilled over the collar of her down parka. Her right hand was bare. (You can't manipulate a camera with mittens.) A light meter hung around her neck.

Marty stared at the photograph so he didn't have to watch Grace cry. A lump the size of a chicken egg lodged in his throat.

"Do you think Mom got our Mother's Day card?" The twins had sent the handmade card to her two weeks early, hoping it would get to her in time.

"I hope so," Grace said, reaching over and taking his hand.

With his free hand Marty picked up a used tissue from the table.

Sylvia and Timothy O'Hara were one of the most famous photojournalist teams in the world. Together they had climbed the highest mountains, probed the deepest caves, and rafted the wildest rivers.

After Marty and Grace were born, Sylvia hung her cameras up and moved into a house in Missoula, Montana, while Timothy continued traveling and writing to support their new family. He was gone more than he was home, and he missed many of the twins' early accomplishments.

At age three, Marty could run faster than his athletic mother. At the same age, Grace had a vocabulary larger than most sixth graders. At four, Marty could unlock the back door and start the car. (Fortunately, his legs were too short to reach the accelerator pedal.) At the same age, Grace could add a long column of figures in her head and pick a lock as fast as a professional burglar. At five, Marty sculpted a statue of their neighbor's aggressive dog out of mud that looked so real his mother called the pound to have it picked up. At the same age, Grace began to learn French, decided she wanted to become a doctor, and started writing the first of many diaries, using blank Moleskine journals from Italy. Six of the blank journals arrived for her by mail every year directly from the company that made them. Her father used the same kind of journal to keep notes for his articles. Grace suspected that he had them sent, but when asked, he would merely smile and say, "They're from a secret admirer."

The turning point for the O'Hara family came when the twins were six years old. Marty decided he wanted to catch a bear. He and Grace dug a five-foot-deep pit in the backyard, covered the opening with brush, and caught their mother, who became as angry as a bear. The twins didn't understand why she was so upset. They had not used the sharpened stakes in the bottom of the pit which the instructions had called for. (Marty wanted the bear alive for show-and-tell at school.)

While Mrs. O'Hara was in the hospital recovering from her injuries, she got to thinking about the direction her life had taken. She missed her husband. She missed her former independence. But most of all, she missed the wild places her cameras had taken her to. If I'm going to fall into pits, I might as well get paid for it, she decided, and soon after her release she took the twins and joined Mr. O'Hara in the field. This did not work for very long. Grace was afraid of everything that moved (and many things that didn't). Marty was afraid of nothing except ghosts, which he had only read about.

For the twins' own safety, the O'Haras decided that Marty and Grace should stay at home. They hired a succession of live-in nannies to care for the children, but none of them lasted long. One by one, these disgruntled women fled the house with hastily packed bags, shouting back at the twins' panicky parents, "Your son is as wild as a hurricane and that daughter of yours is just plain weird."

"But they're only first graders!" Mr. and Mrs. O'Hara would yell back helplessly.

To which the fleeing nanny would shout, "First graders from—"

Well, you get the point. The O'Haras had a major problem with their minors, which was finally

resolved when they discovered the Omega Opportunity Preparatory School while on a magazine assignment in the Swiss Alps.

In many ways, the school had been very good for the twins. Grace was allowed to be as smart as she wanted to be, and Marty had learned to turn some of his wild streak into paint strokes and spices. But of the two, Grace liked the school best. Marty merely tolerated it and tried to curb his wildness so he (and more important, his weird sister) would not get booted out. He liked Grace that much.

Grace and Marty spent several weeks with their parents every summer and saw them on most holidays, which was more than many of the other students saw of their parents in any given year. During the remaining days of summer the twins were sent to camps and courses all over the world. Grace had attended Medical Camp, Physics Camp, Astronomy Camp, Poetry Camp, Shakespeare Camp, and Latin Camp. Marty had gone to Mountain Climbing Camp, Scuba Diving Camp, Whitewater Camp, and Cowboy Camp.

It was not an ideal family relationship, but Grace and Marty had grown accustomed to their globe-trotting parents and accepted them for who they were. Or at least who the twins thought they were.

six months later 2

The magazine that had sent the O'Haras to the Amazon had spent a small fortune looking for them, but to no avail. Timothy and Sylvia had simply vanished and after a few months the search was called off.

Marty and Grace had not given up hope entirely and refused to believe their parents were gone for good. But as the weeks and months went by without any word, their hope began to erode. Neither would admit this to themselves (or to each other), but sometimes late at night, in the solitude of their beds, they feared their parents were not coming back and wondered what was going to become of them.

The answer to this question came in the form of an e-mail:

Subject: Arrangements
From: wolfe@ewolfe.com
To: grace_o'hara@xlink.com
Cc: marty_o'hara@xlink.com

Dearest Grace & Marty:

I can't tell you how sorry I am to hear of your great loss. Your mother and father's accident has had a profound effect on all of us.

I waited to contact you because I had hoped to have better news. Unfortunately, there is still no sign of your parents.

During this sad time, I think it best for you to be with family. To that end I have arranged for you to come here and live with me.

Your headmaster has been contacted and he will assist you in getting here. I'm looking forward to seeing you again.

Love,

Uncle Travis

Grace was totally distraught by the message. She printed it out, found Marty, marched him down to Dr. Beasel's office, and burst through his door without bothering to wait for the secretary to announce them.

"What does he mean, *again*?" she shouted, waving the e-mail before the headmaster's perplexed face. "We didn't even know we had an uncle!"

The headmaster expected this kind of behavior from her brother, but not from Little Grace, the finest student ever to walk the hallowed halls of the school. "Calm yourself, Grace," Dr. Beasel admonished her. "Can't you see that I have a visitor?"

The visitor was a rough-looking man wearing orange coveralls with "Geneva Pest Removal" in French stenciled across his back in large purple letters formed by various rodents and insects. Dr. Beasel motioned the children over to the sofa and resumed his conversation with the burly exterminator.

"What are they saying?" Marty whispered. His French was still not very good, despite seven years of lessons.

"They're arguing," Grace whispered back. "Dr. Beasel insists that there are termites in his office."

Marty grinned, and Grace suspected that her brother knew more about the termites than he should.

"Whatever you're thinking," Grace whispered, "stop. Marty, this is serious."

"What's so serious about termites?"

"That's not what I meant," Grace answered impatiently. "They're about to hand us over to a complete stranger. We don't even know where this so-called uncle of ours lives."

"Well, it can't be worse than this place."

"I mean it, Marty! I want to stay right here. It's the only place I feel safe."

"Oh, please."

"The nightmares are back. You remember how it used to be. I can't live like that again."

"It seems to me if the nightmares are starting to bug you here, you'd want to get away from them."

Dr. Beasel suddenly turned to them. "Did you say something about bugs?"

"No." Marty pointed to the carpet. "I was telling Grace how I always admired your rug."

Dr. Beasel adjusted his hairpiece and gave Marty what Luther called the "stink-eye," then turned his attention back to the exterminator.

"Help me, Marty," Grace pleaded.

Marty looked at his sister and melted inside. The joke between them had always been that he had gotten both their bodies and she had gotten both their brains—a mix-up in their mother's womb they weren't able to straighten out before it was time to go. He was her bodyguard and Grace was his brainguard. "Oh, all right," he said. "But I'm not sure what I can do."

"Thanks, Marty."

Dr. Beasel concluded his conversation with the exterminator, walked him to the door, then turned to the O'Hara twins. "Now, what's this all about?"

"This." Grace handed him the e-mail.

Dr. Beasel glanced at it, then handed it back to her. "Yes, I spoke with your uncle this morning."

"Well, that's more than we've ever done!" Grace said heatedly. "We didn't even know he existed until we got this!" She wadded up the e-mail and threw it on the floor.

Dr. Beasel took a step backward. He had never

seen Grace so upset. Marty was surprised at her outburst as well. He had only seen her lose her temper three times: once when he put a snake in her bed (it wasn't venomous); another time when he took an innocent little peek at her Moleskine; and then the year before when he hid a bucket of cow manure in her closet (it was an emergency).

"Your uncle's name is Dr. Travis Wolfe," Dr. Beasel said.

"Mom has a brother?" Marty asked. Their mother's maiden name was Wolfe.

"Yes," Dr. Beasel answered.

"What kind of doctor?" Marty asked.

"He's a veterinarian."

Marty glanced at Grace. "That's not so bad."

Grace gave him another stink-eye. Marty was wild about animals.

"He doesn't practice anymore," Dr. Beasel continued. "He owns a company called eWolfe. They make computers, software, and communication satellites— a very successful business from all accounts."

"Hmm," Marty said.

Trouble, Grace thought. Marty was also wild about computers. He and Luther had secretly built a computer in their dormitory room and tapped into the school's phone line so they could surf the Net without supervision. They charged the boys on their floor ten dollars a session, which had paid for the computer in less than a week. They were trying to earn money to get their first full-length comic book published.

"So, you've met him?" Grace asked.

"Not exactly." Mr. Beasel looked a little uncomfortable. "But I've spoken with him on the telephone many times over the years. I feel as if I know him."

Weak, Marty thought, enjoying Dr. Weasel's discomfort. "So you and he are phone buddies?"

"I wouldn't exactly characterize it that way. He calls once or twice a month to check on your progress. He's been very generous to the school and I hope he continues his support after . . ." Dr. Beasel cleared his throat. "But, that's beside the point. What's important for you to know is that he's been your benefactor as well as the school's. He has paid your tuition since you arrived here."

"Why would he do that?" Grace asked. Their parents were two of the highest-paid journalists in the world. They weren't hurting for money.

"I assume he wanted to help your parents by paying for your education. It's not that unusual here."

"Why would he check on our progress?" Marty asked.

"Concern, curiosity . . . I don't really know. It never occurred to me to ask. I know that this is a very difficult time for both of you, but as your legal guardian and the sole executor of your parents' estate he thought it best—"

"Legal guardian?" Marty said.

"Executor of our parents' estate?" Grace added. "Our parents aren't—"

"I hope you're right, Grace," Dr. Beasel interrupted soothingly. "There is always a chance they survived. But until this is all straightened out you'll be staying with your uncle."

"When?" Marty asked.

"The day after tomorrow."

The twins stared at him.

"There's still more than a month left of school," Grace said, shocked. "We'll miss our final exams. Don't we have any choice in where we live or who we live with?"

"At your age, I'm afraid not."

The twins had recently turned thirteen. Grace stepped on Marty's foot, which was his cue to say or do something about this terrible situation. Marty, of course, was not in the least upset about missing his final exams. And he was intrigued by his mysterious uncle, instead of being appalled like Grace. Still, he had to say something or else she would be mad at him for the rest of his life.

"Where does Uncle Travis live?"

"In the Pacific Northwest," Dr. Beasel answered. "Near Seattle."

Marty could feel Grace's blue eyes boring into him, but for one of the first times in his life he couldn't think of anything to say.

"Grace." Dr. Beasel squatted down and put his bony hands on her shoulders. "I want you to know that we will really miss you here."

She pushed him away and ran out of the office, sobbing. Marty watched her go, then turned back to the headmaster. "Will you miss me, too?"

Dr. Beasel did not answer him.

Marty nodded, then began staring at a spot just beyond the headmaster's left ear and started moving his eyes around the room as if he were tracking a flying insect.

"What is it?" Dr. Beasel asked excitedly. "What do you see?"

"I don't know." Marty stood. "At first I thought it was a fly, but it's bigger than . . . Look, there it is! Jeez, I think it's a termite." He pointed.

The headmaster looked around frantically. "I don't—"

"There!"

"Where?"

"Over by the window. No . . . now it's by the painting. Wow, it crawled right behind the picture frame. Did you see it?"

"Yes!" Dr. Beasel said. "I believe I did!" He picked up the phone. "Is that fool of an exterminator still in the building? Well, find out and send him back up here!"

Marty reached into his pocket and pulled out a

handful of dead termites. While the headmaster was distracted, he tossed them under his desk, then left the office. There were some things he was going to miss about the school.

He found Grace sitting at her table in the library. She looked up at him through red-rimmed eyes. "You were useless."

"Sorry. But Dr. Weasel wouldn't have listened to me no matter what I'd said."

"I wish you wouldn't call him that."

"Why not?"

Up until their meeting, Grace could have given him a long list of reasons, but now she couldn't think of one. She'd always thought that Dr. Beasel loved having her at the school, but he had caved in to their uncle's plan without a hint of protest.

"Look," Marty said. "I'm sure there's a logical reason why Mom didn't tell us about her brother."

"Like, maybe she was embarrassed about him," Grace said. "Or maybe he's insane, or maybe he's been in prison all these years for murder or worse."

"Oh, please. Where would he get the money to pay for our tuition? And how could he run a computer company from a jail cell?"

"He's the executor of Mom and Dad's estate. Maybe he's after our money. A lot of computer companies have gone out of business in the past few years."

"Maybe." Marty picked up one of Grace's pencils and started rolling it through his fingers. "Do you think Mom and Dad are okay?"

Grace sighed. "I go back and forth, but I think that if they were dead I would somehow know it."

Marty felt the same way. "I think they're okay too," he said. "They've survived worse things than a helicopter crash."

"What are we going to do, Marty?"

Marty shrugged. "What we always do. Deal with it."

the bishops 3

Grace stepped off the airplane in Seattle wearing a gray pleated skirt, a starched white blouse, and a black blazer with the school's coat of arms proudly sewn on the left breast pocket. Marty had on gray slacks, a wrinkled white shirt, a paint-stained school tie, and a black blazer identical to Grace's, except for the tear in the right sleeve at the elbow and a bit of dried yolk on the lapel from the omelet he had just eaten. Dr. Beasel had insisted the twins wear their school uniforms so their uncle would recognize them when they arrived.

On the flight, when he wasn't drawing in his sketchbook, Marty had slept. As he walked toward U.S. Customs with his passport in hand, despite his worry about his parents, he was nearly bursting with anticipation for this new adventure. Grace had slept some as well, but she was not nearly as excited. She had spent all her waking moments writing in her diary and plotting her and Marty's return to the Omega Opportunity Preparatory School, hoping their uncle would listen to reason and was not a homicidal maniac.

As they waited in the customs line, Marty spotted an older couple just beyond the gate holding up a crude sign with O'HARA scribbled on it. He pointed them out to Grace and said, "Uncle Travis must be Mom's *older* brother."

The gray-haired man was wearing a pair of blue jeans, an old sweatshirt with AIR FORCE written on it in faded letters, and a pair of high-top sneakers. The woman was much wider than the man, dressed in what looked like a flowered tent.

"That can't possibly be Uncle Travis," Grace said.

"A dollar says it is."

"You're on." In the past seven years, Grace had won a total of two hundred and eleven one-dollar bills from him, each carefully tallied in her Moleskines. Marty had not won a single dollar.

Marty walked up to the couple. "Uncle Travis?"

"No," the man said. "My name's Phil Bishop, and this is my wife—"

"Bertha," the woman said, throwing her arms around them. "You poor, poor things!" She drew them into her like a famished spider. "We are so sorry about what happened. You're so young. . . ."

She went on and on. Marty thought that Bertha's

dress disguised rolls of soft flesh, but what lay beneath was as hard as bricks. It was like being hugged by an oak tree. He thought he might suffocate before she finished, but managed to wiggle free and get a gulp of air. Grace was not as lucky. Bertha held her in a headlock from which she could not escape.

"So, where's Uncle Travis?" Marty asked.

"He couldn't be—" Phil started to answer.

"He and his crew just got back this morning," Bertha interrupted, "or he would have been here to meet you himself. He's been in the field and he had a lot of things to attend to at home. We offered to stand in for him. I hope you're not too disappointed."

"What crew?" Marty asked.

"His merry band of pirates," Bertha said with a laugh.

"So you're not relatives?"

"No, but I hope you'll consider us family."

"Wolfe will explain everything when you see him," Phil said. "Let's get your bags." He tossed the sign into the garbage and started down the corridor.

"Grace, you haven't said a word," Bertha said, still clutching her.

Grace squirmed out of her grip and glared at Marty. "You owe me a dollar."

Marty reached into his pocket and handed her his two hundred and twelfth one-dollar bill.

* * *

When Phil jerked Grace's bag off the conveyer belt, he nearly dislocated his shoulder. "What in the blazes do you have in there?"

"Books," Marty said. He had told Grace to leave the books behind, but she insisted on taking a two-week supply (or by Marty's estimate, sixty pounds of words), which is how long Grace calculated it would take to convince her uncle to send them back to the school.

"I'll go see if they have a forklift," Phil said. He returned with a sturdy cart and pushed the bags to the parking lot.

Half an hour later they arrived at a beautiful lake in the center of Seattle.

"This is great!" Marty said.

"Oh, this isn't where your uncle lives," Bertha explained. "He's a hundred fifty miles west of here."

"But Seattle's on the West Coast."

"That's right," Phil said, dragging the luggage down a wooden dock to a small seaplane that had seen better days.

"We're flying in this?" Grace asked.

"I know she's not much to look at," Phil said apologetically. "But she can fly." He opened the storage compartment, and a bag of food spilled out onto the dock.

"We are going to die!" Grace hissed in Marty's ear.

Marty ignored her. He was used to her being

afraid of everything. "Relax," he whispered. "I've flown in dozens of small airplanes—some worse than this." He helped Bertha pick up the bread and meat, and said, "This is a lot of food."

"We have two new stomachs to fill," Bertha said. "I'm your uncle's cook . . . among other things."

"No kidding?" Marty said. "I do a little cooking myself." He was being somewhat modest. At school when he wasn't drawing, painting, sculpting, or cartooning, Marty was in the kitchen learning everything he could about the culinary arts. His long-range plan was to support his comic-book business by becoming a world-famous chef. Even Dr. Beasel thought this was a reachable goal. Marty's only regret in leaving so quickly was that he had missed his last lesson on making the perfect broccoli soufflé. He peered into the crammed compartment and was delighted to see several items he could work with if Bertha would let him use the kitchen. "No vegetables?"

"We grow our own," Bertha said. "In greenhouses. And they're all organic."

"Do you have broccoli?"

"A whole row."

"That's great!"

That's bad, Grace thought. If this keeps up, I won't be able to separate Marty from Uncle Travis with a stick of dynamite, and he hasn't even met him yet.

Phil looked up at the clouds gathering above the

lake. "We'd better take off. The weather's turning. If we don't, we'll be stuck on the mainland until the storm passes."

"The mainland?" Marty asked.

"Your uncle lives on an island off the Washington coast," Phil said.

"Wow!"

Two sticks of dynamite, Grace thought grimly.

With a lot of grunting and groaning, Phil managed to get the twins' suitcases into the storage compartment. Marty and Grace climbed into the tattered backseats, and Bertha heaved herself into the copilot seat next to Phil.

"Buckle up," Phil said.

They took off across the lake, heading west toward the Pacific Ocean.

Unbeknownst to the occupants of the noisy seaplane, they passed right over the top of a large mansion perched on a hill overlooking a beautiful zoological park. Inside the mansion was a man sitting at a desk in a dimly lit room without windows. Lying next to the man was a magnificent, fully grown Caspian tiger, thought to have gone extinct a half century earlier. The man's name was Noah Blackwood. The tiger's name was Natasha.

The only thing on the desk was a computer screen and a speakerphone. Blackwood had gray hair, blue eyes, and teeth as straight and as white as piano keys. His manicured hand lay on the tiger's back. He enjoyed the feeling of the soft black-and-gold fur and the taut muscles beneath the tiger's skin.

The phone rang. He punched a button and said, "I've been waiting for your call."

"Sorry," a man said over the speaker. "I was holding off until we had better news."

"And do you have better news?"

"No, sir. We haven't found her yet."

"I'm very disappointed."

"We didn't expect her to abandon her camper in Salt Lake City after we fouled the engine. She didn't take a bus, train, or airplane out of town. She didn't have enough cash to rent a car, and her credit cards were all canceled. I suspect she's still in town someplace."

"And I suspect you are wrong," Blackwood said coldly. The tiger tensed, feeling sparks of anger from his master's fingertips. "Did you search the camper?"

"Yes, sir. It was full of books and assorted junk, but we didn't find what you're looking for. If she has it, it's with her."

"She has it." Blackwood swept his blue eyes slowly around his study, taking in the huge hermetically sealed glass dioramas lining the walls. Each of them represented years of searching, a great deal of money, and no small amount of risk. "And Wolfe?" he asked.

"As far as we know he's still on the island. The Bishops took off this morning for the mainland, but Dr. Wolfe wasn't with them. According to our source, they're picking up his niece and nephew."

"Ah, yes . . . The tragedy in the jungle. So, the children are going to live with him?"

"That's our understanding."

He was pleased to hear this. Raising two youngsters would certainly complicate things for Travis Wolfe. "Anything else?"

"Are you sending Butch out here to give us a hand?"

"No. Butch is in the field on another assignment. He left yesterday and he'll be gone for some time."

"We could sure use some help here."

"Just find the woman!" Blackwood terminated the call and looked down at his magnificent tiger. "Soon, Natasha," he whispered. "Very soon."

wolfe 4

"Tighten your seat belts!"

Phil Bishop pushed the nose of the seaplane down through the thick clouds, and the twins found themselves above a large expanse of blue-gray water.

"There!" Marty pointed. In the distance was a fir-covered island shrouded in mist. "You don't suppose Uncle Travis has the island all to himself?"

Grace ignored the question. She leaned forward and tapped Bertha on the shoulder. "There's somebody in a small kayak down there."

"What are you talking about, dear?"

"A kayak. It's red."

Bertha looked over at Phil and they both scanned the surface of the water through the windshield.

"I don't see a thing," Bertha said.

"I don't see anything either," Phil added. "No one owns a kayak on the island, and it's more than a hundred miles from the nearest landfall. No kayaker in his right mind would be that far from shore."

"If Grace says there's a kayak," Marty said, "there's a kayak!" Grace had eyes like an eagle.

Bertha looked at Phil. "If she's right, the kayaker is in big trouble. It wouldn't hurt to look."

Phil sighed, dipped the left wing, and started circling.

A few minutes later Bertha pointed and said, "I see it! Grace was right."

Phil looked, then said something that would have gotten him expelled from the Omega Opportunity Preparatory School. He spoke into the microphone on his headset. The twins could not hear what he was saying, but they assumed he was calling for assistance.

Five minutes later they were skimming the relatively smooth water of the island's sheltered bay. As they taxied toward shore they passed a concrete dock with a large rusty ship moored to it. The ship was called the *Coelacanth*.

"Maybe they'll use the *Coelacanth* to rescue the kayaker," Marty said, pronouncing the name *koh-el-uh-kanth*.

Grace shook her head. "It's pronounced *see-la-kanth*."

"I knew that," Marty said (his usual response to something he did not know). "What's a coelacanth?"

"I think it's a fish," Grace answered. "But they

won't be using that ship to rescue anyone. It doesn't look seaworthy and it's too big."

"But they could use that." Marty pointed to the helicopter sitting on the forward deck.

"I suppose they could," Grace agreed, but the helicopter didn't look much better than the ship it was on.

Phil docked the seaplane, then climbed out and began tying it down. When it was secured, Bertha jumped out of the cockpit and the twins clambered out after her.

"What about the kayaker?" Marty asked.

"Don't worry, we'll get him," Phil answered, then turned to Bertha. "Why don't you run them up to the fort. We can bring the luggage and groceries up later."

"Fort?" Marty asked.

"You'll see." Bertha led them to a gravel lot above the dock where a lone vehicle was parked.

"Wow!" Marty said. "It's a Humvee." The blocky four-wheel drive was painted in desert camouflage and looked like it had been rolled a time or two. He ran ahead and gave it a quick going-over. When Bertha and Grace joined him, he pointed at a line of large holes across the driver's door. "What are these?"

"Bullet holes," Bertha said. "Fifty caliber."

"No kidding?"

"We have several Humvees on the island," Bertha explained. "Your uncle got them from the Army. They're not much to look at, but once you get them started, they'll go just about anywhere. A lot of our equipment is military surplus."

"Maybe Wolfe is one of those paramilitary paranoid wacko types," Grace whispered. "Have you ever thought of that?"

"You're the one that's paranoid," Marty answered.

"You think so?" She pointed to a huge sign at the front of the parking lot with three-foot-tall red letters.

NO TRESPASSING!

ELECTRONIC SURVEILLANCE!

TRESPASSERS WILL BE SHOT

"That does seem a bit extreme," Marty admitted.

"What's that, dear?" Bertha asked.

"I was just wondering about the sign," he said.

"We're very security conscious here."

"Why?"

"There are things on the island that . . ." Bertha hesitated. "Well, your uncle will explain everything when you see him."

"Is there a town on the island?" Marty asked.

"Heavens, no," Bertha said. "This is your uncle's island."

"The whole thing?"

"The whole shebang." Bertha got into the front seat of the Humvee.

Marty looked at Grace. "I guess your theory about him wanting our inheritance is down the tubes."

"Owning an island doesn't mean he's not hurting for money. And what about my paramilitary wacko theory? What about the fort?"

"You'll look great in camouflage fatigues," Marty said and climbed into the front seat next to Bertha. Grace got in the back. The veteran Humvee coughed and shook, but finally came to a roaring start. Before Bertha engaged the clutch, she reached into the glove box and pulled out two silver chains with square pieces of colored plastic hanging on them. She gave the blue one to Grace and the gray one to Marty.

"What are these?" Grace asked.

"Identification." Bertha pulled out a green tag from the neck of her dress. "We all wear them here."

The twins looked at the tags. They were blank on both sides.

"I don't understand," Marty said.

"Let me guess," Grace said. "Uncle Travis will explain it to us when we see him."

"That's right. Just put them on for now and don't take them off. That's one of the rules of the island."

"What are some of the other rules?" Marty asked.

"Don't wander around the island unless one of us

is with you—at least for the time being. If you think you shouldn't be doing something, ask before you do it. Never complain about my cooking. Have fun. And . . . well, I'm sure we'll come up with some more rules as time passes. We've never had children here before." She stepped on the gas, sending up a spray of gravel.

The twins weren't able to see much on the way up to their uncle's house because Bertha drove the Humvee as if she were trying to outrun a forest fire. The narrow winding road was a blur of green trees. They crossed a bridge and took a hard right onto another road, which led them up a steep hill. At the top, Bertha brought the Humvee to a skidding stop in front of a three-story house made out of moss-covered stone blocks. Parked in front of the house was another Humvee identical to the one they were in, without the bullet holes.

"Your uncle's inside," Bertha said. "I'm going back down to give Phil a hand."

The twins got out and Bertha drove away as fast as she had arrived.

Grace and Marty stood very quietly for a moment and took in their surroundings.

"It needs a good pressure washing," Marty said. "Or a stonemason. But it does look like a fort."

"More like a haunted castle," Grace said, knowing that about the only thing that spooked her brother was ghosts. "I have a very bad feeling about all this. I bet it's filled with zombies and ghouls."

Marty did his best to ignore her. He did not want to think about ghosts and haunted castles. The house sat on a high promontory. Strong winds and salt air had worn away the stonework. To the west was a sheer cliff and an endless span of water with drifting patches of fog above it. "Boy, would I love to hang glide off that!" he said. To the east was a thick forest of trees. On the far side of the island was a massive hill covered with several white spinning windmills. "What do you suppose those are for?" he asked.

"Wind turbines," Grace answered. "To generate electricity."

"I knew that," Marty said and turned his attention back to the house.

There were dozens of windows with stone balconies. The slate roof was covered with antennas and several satellite dishes of different sizes.

"He must get every TV station on earth," Marty said. At the boarding school they had not been allowed to watch much television, and when they did, they could only watch shows that Dr. Beasel had previewed and approved.

"The front door is wide open," Grace said. "But there's nobody here to greet us. Don't you think that's a little strange, Marty?"

Marty did think it was a bit odd, but before he

could respond, a very large raven flew through the front door and headed right toward them. "Watch out!" He tackled Grace and tried to cover her as best he could. The bird veered away from them at the last second. It circled the house twice, gaining altitude with each loop, then flapped out to sea, making a deep *quark*ing sound like a crow with a bad cold.

"Sorry about that." Marty helped Grace up, a little embarrassed at his overreaction. "I thought the bird was going to—"

"No, no, it's perfectly all right," Grace interrupted him. Her brother's gallantry and quick wits were two of his best traits and she wouldn't think of criticizing either, even though he had knocked her down and she had scraped her knee.

"Now that *was* strange," Marty said. "Why would Uncle Travis have a raven in his house?"

"Maybe it was feeding on a corpse," Grace said, brushing herself off.

Marty shuddered, then walked up onto the porch and knocked on the doorjamb. "Uncle Travis? It's Marty and Grace." There was no response.

"Now what?" Grace asked.

"I guess we go in."

Hesitantly, they walked through the doorway and found themselves in a large entry hall. To the right was a wide staircase, to the left a closed set of doors, and directly in front of them a long dark hallway.

"Whew!" Marty said. "Smells a little musty in here."

"Like a dungeon," Grace said. "Look." In the corner was a pile of duffel bags and backpacks. Off to the side was a roll of mosquito netting, coils of climbing rope, and soiled clothing.

"Looks like Uncle Travis just got back," Marty said.

Grace held up a vest. The bottom of it almost touched the floor. "And he's a giant."

Marty picked up a huge cotton glove with holes in it. "Fe, fi, fo, fum, I smell the blood of a Englishman."

"You're not funny."

"Come on." He walked down the hallway, which led to an enormous dining room with a table that was at least twenty feet long. "Looks like we're having newsprint for dinner," he said.

Stacked on top of the table were pile after pile of old, yellowed newspapers. Grace started going through them. "Most of these are trashy supermarket papers."

"I guess he likes to keep on top of current events," Marty said.

Grace picked one up and read the headline: "'Vampire Sucks Small Texas Town Dry.'"

"See what I mean?"

"I'm getting scared, Marty."

Marty was feeling a little nervous himself, but he wasn't about to admit it. He led Grace into the next room. "Whoa!" he said. "Now this is what I call a kitchen." There was an ancient oven, an enormous grill, a walk-in freezer, a commercial refrigerator, a huge butcher block that looked like a thousand cows had been carved up on it, and dozens of iron skillets and pans dangling from the ceiling. It was a far cry from the modern kitchen at school, but with a good cleaning and some organization, Marty thought it would do nicely.

They walked through a swinging door and found themselves in a living room that ran the entire length of the house. Floor-to-ceiling windows jutted out beyond the cliff edge. Grace looked out at the thick fog. "It feels as if you're floating above the ocean here," she said.

"Look, there's the kayak." Marty pointed to a red dot still some distance from shore. "And the helicopter!" It swooped in and hovered over the small boat. "That kayaker is lucky you saw him. He'd be shark bait by now."

They watched until a curtain of fog blocked their view. Marty wandered away from the window and started looking around the room. It was filled with mismatched but comfortable-looking chairs and sofas. The floor was covered with a threadbare Oriental carpet. Hanging on the walls were old oil paintings (which Marty found particularly interesting), assorted tribal masks, shields, spears, swords, and several stone gargoyles taken from old buildings. Standing next to the fireplace was a full suit of armor that looked as though it had been pushed off a cliff.

"I guess Uncle Travis is an antique collector," Marty said.

"Or he spends his weekends at garage sales."

"On an island?" Marty walked over to the plasma-screen television on the far side of the room. The screen was covered with thick dust.

"Do you really think Mom and Dad intended for us to live on an island in the middle of nowhere with a man we've never met before?" Grace asked.

Marty wrote his name in the dust on the screen. "It's not that bad, Grace. It just needs a good cleaning."

"You missed my point."

"What else is new? Come on."

Grace followed him back to the entry hall. "Upstairs or through the double doors?"

"The doors."

Marty pushed them open and they were hit with a blast of warm mildewed air. The warmth came from a blazing fireplace at the far end of an immense room. The mildew smell came from above. Circling the room was a balcony lined with books. A spiral staircase to the left of the door led up to it.

"I guess you didn't have to bring those books after all," Marty commented.

Running along the wall to the right of the room

was a laboratory bench covered with beakers, Bunsen burners, test tubes, a microscope, a magnifying light, and other paraphernalia.

"Perhaps Uncle Travis is a mad scientist." Marty did his best impression of Frankenstein's monster.

Grace was not amused. "You're as frightened as I am," she said. "You always joke around when you're scared."

"Oh, please," Marty said, but he knew she was right. He walked over to the stone fireplace, which was big enough to do jumping jacks in. On either side of it were large aquariums. In one were two of the ugliest fish he had ever seen. They were about four feet long and were covered with large, metallic blue scales that looked like armor plating. "What are they?"

Grace wandered over behind him. "I'm not sure."

"Well, that's a first!" Marty moved over to the second aquarium. "Even I know what these are."

Grace joined him and watched the ten-legged creatures darting around the artificial reef. "What kind of person would keep a school of squid in his library?"

Her question was answered by a high-pitched barking. A moment later, a tiny black dog dashed into the room. It tried to stop when it reached them, but slipped on the slick floor and slid ten feet past where they were standing. A pink identification tag hung from its tiny collar.

"What is it?" Marty asked.

"A dog, you dunce."

"It sounds like a dog, but it looks like a curly black squirrel without a tail."

"Welcome to Cryptos Island!" a deep voice boomed behind them.

Grace and Marty jumped, then looked in the direction of the voice, and saw a very large man framed in the doorway, leaning on a cane. He had long, black, unkempt hair and a bushy black beard.

Marty whispered to Grace, "That's the kind of man who keeps squid in his library."

He *is* a pirate! Grace thought. Just as Bertha said. The only thing missing is a black eye patch and a bloody cutlass. She felt herself go faint and put a hand on Marty's shoulder.

"You okay?" Marty asked.

"I'm not sure," she answered weakly. "Stay close."

The man walked over to them. His eyes were the same shade of brown as their mother's, but there was something wild and unsettling about them. He was dressed in baggy cargo pants, slippers, and a thick black sweater. Around his neck he wore a tag like the ones Bertha had given them, but his was turquoise.

"Uncle Travis?" Marty asked.

The man nodded. "But please call me Wolfe. Everyone does." The tiny dog started running circles around the group, yapping frantically. "Stop that nonsense, PD." The dog obediently sat down in front of him, panting with a tongue no bigger than a pinkie finger. "You'd better get used to these kids. They've come to live with us." He held his cargo pocket open and said, "Snake!"

To the twins' amazement, the dog jumped into his pocket, then poked its head out for one last defiant yap before disappearing.

"I'm sorry for all the confusion," Wolfe apologized. "Bertha and Phil probably already told you, but I just got back, and I wasn't able to get things ready the way I wanted. And now we have this kayaker problem."

"Did you get him?" Marty asked.

"Yes."

"Good." Marty pointed at his uncle's pocket. "What kind of dog is he?"

"It's a teacup poodle, and it's a *she*, not a he."

"PD is an odd name."

Hearing her name, the dog poked her head back out of the pocket and gave another yap. "Short for Pocket Dog," Wolfe explained. "We were in the desert, looking around one day, and she ran into a rattlesnake. There was no place to hide, so she hopped into my pocket. She's been doing it ever since."

"All you have to say is 'Snake'?"

"That's right. Let's get some more light in here." He turned on a lamp next to the sofa. When he turned back to them a look of astonishment crossed his rugged face.

"What is it?" Grace asked.

Wolfe closed his eyes for a moment, then opened them and stammered, "Nothing . . . I'm . . . I guess I'm more tired than I thought. We just flew in this morning and I've been—"

"There you are!" Bertha came into the library with her arms full of groceries. She set the bags down and walked over to Wolfe. "Sorry to interrupt, but Phil needs to talk to you right away."

"Of course. I'll see you both at dinner," Wolfe said hurriedly, obviously relieved at the interruption. "In the meantime, Bertha will show you to your rooms so you can get some rest. You must be tired after your long flight." He rushed out of the room with PD still in his pocket.

Bertha picked up the bags and said she would show them their rooms after she put the groceries in the kitchen. Marty started to follow her, but Grace held him back.

"What was that about?" she asked. "Did you see the way Uncle Trav . . . I mean, Wolfe looked at me?"

"I thought he was looking at me," Marty said.

"He wasn't. And he sure seemed to get over his exhaustion quickly. He didn't just leave the library. He fled from it."

Marty shrugged his shoulders. "It must have

been an emergency. Wasn't the Pocket Dog great?"

Grace was more interested in pursuing their uncle's peculiar behavior. "Don't change the subject."

"I'm not," Marty said. "By the way, what does cryptos mean?"

"I think it comes from the Greek word *kryptos* . . ."

Bertha came back in. "Are you ready?"

"Sure," Marty said.

Grace caught him by the sleeve. "The word means 'hidden,'" she whispered.

the gizmo 5

Marty was tired, but far too excited to rest.

His bedroom was much bigger than the one he had shared with Luther at the boarding school. It had a king-size bed, a television, and a private bathroom. No more running down the hallway trying to avoid painful towel snaps from the older boys. He wasn't happy about the circumstances that had brought him to Cryptos, but he was pleased with the island, the squid, the bedroom, and the house—even though it was a little spooky.

In the corner of the bedroom was a desk. On top of it was something about the size and shape of his Game Boy, which he had lost to Luther in a bet.

Marty,
The computer's yours. We call it a GIZMO.
Enjoy. . . .
Wolfe

It was the smallest computer Marty had ever seen. He carried it over to the bed, flipped open the cover, and pressed a button beneath the little screen. The computer booted up and eight icons appeared.

Marty found a stylus attached to the underside of the cover. He took it out and tapped the KEYBOARD icon and a small keyboard appeared on the screen.

"Cool."

He tried the TELECONFERENCE and CHAT icons, but nothing happened. He skipped the E-MAIL icon, figuring it wouldn't work without an e-mail account, and clicked the CYBERVAULT icon.

To establish vault
please insert your disk.

"Don't have a disk," Marty said.

He clicked the VIDEO icon. The screen went blank for a second, then filled with an aerial image of the *Coelacanth*. He saw Phil's seaplane still tied to the dock, then the camera swooped across open water. They must be using the helicopter to film this, Marty thought. But why? The camera circled back around and passed over the top of the red kayak. It was now resting safely on the beach, which he was glad to see.

The camera plunged downward over the parking lot, where Marty caught a glimpse of Phil and the back of another person getting into a Humvee. A moment later, the Humvee drove away and the camera followed it up the road for a while, then veered off into the trees and rose above them. The tops of fir trees flashed across the screen. In the distance he could just make out two small lakes with the last glimmer of orange sunlight reflecting off the surfaces.

Video Terminated

The seven icons reappeared. Marty whistled. "The

computer we built can't do that. Wait until I tell Luther!" He clicked the LOCATE icon.

Who do you want to locate?

Wolfe Grace Vid
Phil Sr. Marty PD
Phil Jr. Bertha Bo
Continue to next list

Marty clicked his own name. An instant later a floor plan appeared on the screen. In the southwest corner of *Bedroom #6* was a small gray square.

He carried the Gizmo from the bed over to the desk. The gray square moved across the little screen at the exact same pace he was walking. When he stopped the square stopped, when he moved the square moved. "Weird," he said, opening the bedroom door and stepping out into the hallway. The gray square was now in the hallway. He knocked on Grace's door. There was no answer. He walked in. The gray square moved into *Bedroom #5.*

"Very weird."

He glanced at Grace's desk and saw that she had a Gizmo identical to his. He sat on her bed and stared down at the gray square. "How does the Gizmo . . . ?" He noticed the identification tag dangling from his neck and suddenly realized how it knew where he was. He clicked Grace's name. A blue square appeared in the *Library*.

Grace had stayed in her bedroom less than a minute before heading back downstairs, clutching the one-armed monkey for security, which she was badly in need of after the day's events.

Mrs. Kouts, her English teacher, had told her that if she was curious about someone, all she had to do was look at their books. "You can read a person like a book by the books they read" was how Mrs. Kouts put it. And Grace was desperate to learn more about their guardian.

She hadn't noticed it when she was in the library earlier, but along the walls beneath the balcony was a glass display case. In it was an ancient illuminated manuscript, hand-lettered on parchment, beautifully illustrated, and written in a language Grace had never seen before. She stood in front of the case for a long time, staring at the two open pages, trying to decipher the words; but she could make nothing of them and finally turned away, walking up the spiral staircase to the library.

"Now, these books I understand," she said. Grace loved reading science books, and Wolfe had hundreds of them, carefully organized and labeled by subject.

Oceanography . . . Geology . . . Astronomy . . .

Meteorology . . . Chemistry . . . Mammals . . . Birds . . . Marty will love this section, she thought. Although I had better keep it to myself for the time being. He's already too excited about the island and Wolfe. *Reptiles . . . Fish . . . Insects . . . Dragons . . .* Grace stopped. Dragons? She looked at the next section. It contained books on *Sea Monsters*. Next to this was *Lake Monsters*, then a large section on *Bigfoot* and the *Yeti*, then *Mermaids and Mermen*, then *Little Humanoids*, which was divided into subsections: *Fairies, Leprechauns, Gnomes, Pixies, Ogres, Brownies, Trolls*, and finally, *Elves*. Oh no, Grace thought with a racing heart, Wolfe believes in Santa's helpers. If Mrs. Kouts was right about the books a person reads, then her uncle was a lunatic. Grace completed the circle, stopping at the last section labeled *General Cryptozoology*. She looked back at the shelves she had passed. Clearly, three quarters of the books were about monstrous impossibilities. Why had their parents made Wolfe their guardian? They couldn't have possibly known about all this.

She pulled out a book called *The Hidden Ones: A Compendium of Cryptids* and started to read.

INTRODUCTION

Cryptozoology is the study of animals that are believed to exist, but cannot be proven to exist scientifically. Cryptids are the rarest animals on earth, hidden by their isolation and low numbers. Perhaps the best known examples are the Yeti (Abominable Snowman) in Asia, or the Sasquatch (Bigfoot) in North America, but there are hundreds, if not thousands, of other cryptids of no lesser importance scattered around the globe waiting for scientific verification. These other cryptids include "Nessie" the Loch Ness monster of Scotland; the Giant Squid, or, Kraken, of which no *living* specimens have been found; the Chupacabra (Goat Sucker), found in the American Southwest, Mexico, and Central America; the . . .

Grace became so involved in the implausible subject that she didn't notice Marty walk into the library until he called her name. She thought about answering him, but instead she scooted farther into the shadows. On occasion Marty loved to scare the daylights out of her by jumping from concealed places when she least expected it. She swore that one day she would pay him back. This just might be the day, she thought.

Marty didn't see Grace anywhere and was disappointed that the Gizmo didn't work as he had thought. He slipped it into his pocket and walked over to the first aquarium for another look at the odd fish. "Come on, Carp Lips, show me some life."

51

He tapped on the glass. The fish didn't move.

Grace rather liked watching Marty talk to himself and decided not to give herself away. At least not yet.

Marty got bored with the passive fish and wandered over to the squid tank. "Hey, squids, it's Captain Nemo from *Twenty Thousand Leagues Under the Sea*, but this time I'm bigger than you." When he finished berating the squid he went over to the fireplace. He squatted down on the hearth and moved the embers around with the poker, then he picked his nose and flicked the harvest into the flames. Grace covered her mouth to stop herself from laughing. Marty and Luther were always calling people nose pickers. Who was the nose picker now?

Marty went back over to the aquarium for a final look at the fish. "Tell you what I'll do, Carp Breath. If you show me just a little bit of personality, I'll scoop a squid out and feed it to you." He waited a full minute. "Fine, then," he said. "No calamari for you." He headed for the door.

Grace took a deep breath and was about to let out a bloodcurdling yell, but changed her mind at the last second. She was comfortable sitting up on the balcony. It was the first time in nearly a week that she had felt reasonably content. She let him go, then slid out to the railing where the light was better, and returned to the cryptid book.

laurel lee 6

A woman came into the library, and once again, Grace was distracted from her uncle's book. She closed it and quietly scooted back into the shadows. The woman was short, slender, fit looking, and very tan, as if she'd been baked in an oven. She must be part of Uncle's Travis's merry band of pirates, Grace guessed. She had short red hair and wore running shorts and a tank top. Hanging on a chain around her neck was a yellow tag. Her feet were bare. She was carrying a black plastic bag, which she placed carefully on the table near the sofa. Although the woman was at least as old as her uncle, she moved like a much younger person. There was a lightness to her, something almost birdlike, that Grace found fascinating.

Like Grace, the woman spent a long time before the glass case, staring down at the book, then walked over to the aquariums and looked at the occupants. When she finished, she took a deep breath, lifted her arms straight out from her sides, and started walking in a straight line very slowly, one foot in front of the other, as if she were a gymnast performing on a balance beam. Grace thought it must be some kind of yoga exercise. She walked all the way across the library in this manner, and was halfway back to the fireplace, when she was interrupted by PD running in, ready to do battle.

"Aren't you adorable," the woman said, ignoring the poodle's high-pitched yapping. She held her hands out, and PD surrendered unconditionally by jumping into them without the slightest hesitation.

You little coward, Grace thought. Your bite is no bigger than you are.

The woman was cuddling and cooing over the tiny canine when Wolfe limped into the library without his cane—an angry scowl on his face.

"I'm Doctor Travis Wolfe," he said gruffly.

He acts as if he's going to make her walk the plank, Grace thought. If she's not one of his pirates, then who is she?

The woman put PD down, seemingly unperturbed by Wolfe's fierceness. "I'm pleased to meet you," she said. "My name is Dr. Laurel Lee."

"Snake!" Wolfe commanded, holding his pocket open. But the trick didn't work this time. PD gave a defiant bark, then jumped back into Laurel's arms. Wolfe's face turned crimson.

54

"She's fine. I love teacup poodles."

Grace was beginning to really like Dr. Laurel Lee. Wolfe towered over her, but she wasn't in the least intimidated by him.

"You're lucky you didn't die out there," Wolfe said.

Grace stifled a gasp of surprise. This was the person in the red kayak?

"I would have been fine," Dr. Lee said.

"You would have been crushed on the rocks," Wolfe said loudly. "My people risked their lives picking you up, and ruined our helicopter in the process."

"I spent the last of my cash renting the kayak," she responded easily. "So if you're suggesting I reimburse you for the rescue, you're out of luck."

"I'm suggesting no such thing! It's just . . . well, what were you doing out there?"

Dr. Lee did not answer his question. Instead, she walked over to the aquarium and looked at the fish again. PD barked at them. "These are very interesting specimens," she said. "Very primitive looking. Coelacanths, aren't they?"

Of course! Grace thought. Just like the name of the ship.

"The fish were discovered in South Africa by a woman named Marjorie Courtney-Latimer, in 1938," Dr. Lee continued. "She went down to the wharf to see if the fishermen had brought in anything she might be able to put in her small natural history museum. On the deck of one of the boats was a fish very much like these. That fish turned out to be the find of the century. A living fossil. A cryptid, if you will. A fish that was supposed to have died along with the dinosaurs."

Wolfe's eyes narrowed with suspicion. "Are you a reporter?"

Dr. Lee laughed. "Hardly. I'm a cultural anthropologist, and to answer your question about what I was doing out on the water in a kayak, I was coming to see you, Dr. Wolfe."

"Why?"

"I'll get to that soon enough, but first I have some questions for you."

"For me?" Wolfe sputtered. "Why—"

"Tell me about Noah Blackwood," she interrupted.

Wolfe stared at her in complete surprise.

Grace was surprised too. Noah Blackwood was a famous conservationist. He had his own television show, and several animal theme parks around the world called *Noah's Ark*. Marty and Luther were big fans and watched his show all the time. Even Dr. Beasel approved of Noah Blackwood. He had taken their class to the Noah's Ark in Paris on a school field trip.

"What does Noah Blackwood have to do with your coming here?" Wolfe asked.

"What's your relationship with him?"

Wolfe gave a harsh laugh. "We have no relationship, unless you consider being enemies a relationship."

"Rivals, perhaps?"

"Ridiculous."

"But you did work for him?"

"Briefly. A long time ago, and even then we weren't exactly fond of each other."

"Why?" Dr. Lee asked.

"You *are* a reporter," Wolfe said.

"I swear I'm not, but before I tell you why I'm here, I need to know more about you and Noah Blackwood. I've already made a terrible mistake with Dr. Blackwood and I'm not about to make another one."

Wolfe stared at her for a few moments, then squatted down in front of the hearth and put a log on the fire. When he stood up his attitude seemed to have softened a little. "Okay," he said. "What do you want to know?"

"Who is he?"

"What do you mean?"

"I know he's one of the world's foremost conservationists. I've talked to a lot of people about him, and to a person, they have nothing but praise for his work. I watched a couple of his television shows, and I have to say, he's an impressive man, but there seems something beneath the surface, something . . .

I don't know . . . something hidden, I guess."

Wolfe looked at her. "You're very perceptive. Have you met him?"

"No. I did manage to talk to him on the telephone a couple of times. He was pleasant enough, but there was something—"

"Noah Blackwood is a man absolutely void of love or compassion," Wolfe interrupted. "He lives totally for himself and his selfish needs."

"That's certainly not the personality he portrays on television."

"I didn't say he wasn't intelligent or charming," Wolfe said. "He's both. But he's not a conservationist. That image is nothing more than a clever mask he wears to get what he wants."

"A wolf in sheep's clothing?"

"Something like that. As a renowned conservationist, Blackwood can go into the woods and do anything he wants. If there's a question about his activities, he puts on his conservation mask and the doubts and questions vanish into thin air. Noah Blackwood would never do anything to harm an animal, the notion is outrageous—at least that's how the thinking goes."

"What kind of activities?"

"Noah Blackwood is a collector," Wolfe said. "His parks are nothing more than holding areas so he can make money off the animals before he harvests them."

"Harvest?"

Wolfe made a throat-slitting motion with his index finger.

"You're certain of this?"

"Absolutely certain. I've seen some of his so-called trophies. He has mounts that would turn the Smithsonian Natural History Museum green with envy. And I suspect that the stuffed animals are just the tip of the iceberg."

Dr. Lee shook her head in disgust. "Can we sit down? I'm feeling a little ill."

"Of course." Wolfe moved some of the pillows on the sofa and they sat down. PD seemed very content to stay in Dr. Lee's lap. "Now, what's this all about?"

"I'm not trying to be obstinate," Dr. Lee said. "But I still need a little more information about you and Noah before I can tell you."

Wolfe sighed and gave her a reluctant nod.

"What did you do for Noah?"

"I caught a great white shark for him," Wolfe said.

Grace wasn't certain she had heard correctly. She moved a little closer to the railing. PD looked up at the balcony and started barking. Grace froze and held her breath, hoping they wouldn't discover her.

Dr. Lee laughed. "I guess she doesn't like sharks."

"She doesn't, but I don't think that's what she's barking about." He looked toward the balcony.

Dr. Lee calmed PD down by scratching her head

and, to Grace's relief, the poodle stopped barking and Wolfe continued his story.

"After I graduated from veterinary school Noah hired me to catch a great white for his Seattle Ark. At that time, no one had ever been able to keep a great white alive long enough to put it on display."

"Or since, I understand," Dr. Lee said. "I read about this when I was looking into Blackwood's considerable accomplishments. But I don't recall seeing your name in connection with the shark."

"Blackwood was not into sharing the glory," Wolfe said. "Which was fine with me. He paid us half a million dollars for that great white."

"Us?"

"A friend of mine from college named Ted Bronson helped me. Ted knew virtually nothing about animals, but he knew everything there was to know about electronics and computers, which was a tremendous help."

"Ted is your partner in eWolfe now?"

"Yes." Wolfe got up and started pacing. "You see, the problem isn't catching great whites, it's transporting them. They either die on the way or within a few days after being put into the aquarium. Ted and I invented a shark transport box. The whole thing was computerized—water flow, temperature, oxygenation—the box was a thing of beauty. We managed to catch a fourteen-foot great white and brought it to Blackwood's Seattle Ark. It lived for five years, and people lined up for miles to see it. I bet Noah made ten million dollars off that fish."

"And you only got half a million dollars?"

"It was enough for me to get out of Blackwood's clutches," Wolfe said "And enough for Ted and me to start eWolfe. Blackwood wanted us to go out and catch more great whites for his other Arks. We refused. He wanted to buy our transport box, but we wouldn't sell it to him."

"Why not?" Laurel asked. "It's not as if great whites are endangered."

"If I'd stayed at Noah's Ark I would have been hooked just like that great white I caught for Blackwood," Wolfe answered. "Like everyone else who works for him. And if I'd sold him the box he would have used it to transport endangered animals for his private collection. He would have used me."

Mrs. Kouts is right, Grace thought. You *can* learn a lot by looking at the books a person reads, but you can learn even more by hiding among them. As Wolfe recounted his capture of the great white shark, he was transformed into a different person. His limp was less pronounced and a gleam came into his eyes that had not been there before.

"So, when you left the park what did you do?" Dr. Lee asked.

"Got eWolfe up and running with Ted. Then . . ." Wolfe hesitated.

"You went to Lake Télé," Dr. Lee finished the sentence for him.

There was a long silence. Grace could hear the snap of the logs burning in the fireplace. Finally, Wolfe said, "There are only a handful of people who know about the Lake Télé expedition." He locked his brown eyes on her. "And you didn't learn about it by checking my background, Dr. Lee. There is no record of that expedition anywhere."

"You're right." Dr. Lee opened her plastic bag and removed a cardboard box. She took several crumpled newspapers from the box, then very carefully pulled out a large, greenish egg.

Wolfe gently took the egg from her, which filled up both his giant hands, and carried it over to the laboratory bench, where he examined it for some time before whispering as if a loud voice might break the shell, "Where did you get this?"

"I stole it."

"From whom?"

"From Noah Blackwood."

"Where did he get it?"

"From me, I'm afraid."

Wolfe gave her a quizzical look. Grace didn't understand either. What was Dr. Lee talking about?

"Three months ago," she continued. "I was living with a group of Pygmies near Lake Télé in the Congo, and I met an old friend of yours."

"Masalito?" Wolfe asked in surprise.

Dr. Lee nodded. "I thought they were an uncontacted tribe, but I learned that you had gotten there fourteen years before me."

"He gave this to you?"

"A going-away present. As I said before, I've been out in the field for years. Lake Télé was to be my last field project for a while. I had decided to return to the States and teach at a small private university in Florida. I thought it was time to share what I'd learned from the indigenous people I'd met around the world." She stood and walked over to the fire, still cradling PD in her arms. "But the plan changed when Masalito gave me that egg."

"Did he tell you where he got it?"

"He said it came from the nest of Mokélé-mbembé."

Must be some kind of rare bird, Grace thought.

Wolfe shook his head. "There is no Mokélé-mbembé. Not anymore."

"Masalito said you might feel that way."

"Did he tell you why?"

"Yes. In fact, he told me quite a bit about his friend Wolfe."

"I bet he did," Wolfe said. "Look, I'm not saying the egg didn't come from Mokélé-mbembé. But it's obviously very old." He gave the egg a gentle shake. "It's brittle and there are some pieces missing. It could have been laid decades ago and preserved somehow."

"Masalito insists that Mokélé-mbembé is alive. After you left he found a nest with three eggs. Two of the eggs hatched. You're holding the third."

"Really." Wolf gently set the egg back in the box and joined Dr. Lee in front of the fire. "What happened to the two that hatched?"

"The male died last year before I arrived at Lake Télé. The female is still alive, but she's not well."

"Did you see her?"

Dr. Lee shook her head. "I begged Masalito to take me to her, but he refused. He said that he had promised you that he would never show Mokélé-mbembé to anyone."

Wolfe nodded. "Masalito has always been a man of his word." He squatted down and started poking at the fire again, then looked up at Dr. Lee. "Okay, it's your turn. And you can start by explaining how Blackwood fits into all of this."

"Fair enough," Dr. Lee said. "When I got back to the States I started looking into Mokélé-mbembé. I showed the egg to a few colleagues, and they suggested I send it to GeneArk Laboratories to have it analyzed."

Wolfe cursed and stood. "Blackwood's lab!"

"I had no funding," Dr. Lee said. "And they offered to analyze the egg for free."

"Of course they did!" Wolfe started pacing again. "Noah Blackwood lives for unusual samples. God knows what he's doing with the genetic material. My sister and brother-in-law were going to look into it, but they were . . ." He paused.

Grace was stunned. Her parents hadn't said a word about this. In fact, she couldn't remember them ever mentioning Noah Blackwood's name.

"I read about the crash," Dr. Lee said. "Is there any word?"

"No," Wolfe said quietly.

Wolfe walked back over to the sofa and sat down heavily. Dr. Lee joined him. "Believe me," she said. "I wouldn't have taken the egg to GeneArk if I had known what I know now about Blackwood."

"Tell me what happened," Wolfe said.

"Several weeks went by and I didn't hear a word from them, so I called. They told me they had lost the egg."

"In a pig's eye," Wolfe said.

"After several tries I finally got a hold of Blackwood, and he told me that it would turn up eventually, and that I shouldn't be concerned. The preliminary result was that it was nothing more than an old ostrich egg."

"That egg looks no more like an ostrich egg than I do," Wolfe said. "Did you tell him where you got the egg?"

"No."

"Did you tell him what you thought the egg was?"

"No."

"Well, at least you did that right."

"I'm afraid there's more to it," Dr. Lee said. She went on to explain that her apartment and office had been broken into. All of her field notes were stolen. "The day after the break-in I was fired from the university without explanation, my bank account was mysteriously emptied, and all my credit cards were canceled."

Wolfe closed his eyes and shook his head. "That has Blackwood written all over it," he said.

"Is he really that powerful?"

Wolfe nodded.

"Masalito is mentioned on nearly every page of my Lake Télé notebooks," Dr. Lee said miserably.

"Noah Blackwood had his henchmen break into your apartment and office," Wolfe said. "He had you fired with a simple phone call. He's one of the wealthiest men in the world and he doesn't hesitate to use his money and influence to get what he wants. You can't imagine the things he's tried to do to me over the years. He couldn't afford to have you running around telling people about Mokélé-mbembé, or pursuing the mystery on your own. He arranged for you to lose your job to cripple you. That's how he operates. You're lucky he didn't have you killed."

Grace found this difficult to believe. It was hard to picture the smiling, friendly television face of Noah Blackwood as that of a murderer. Why would anyone make such a fuss over an old bird egg?

"How did you get the egg back?" Wolfe asked.

"I broke into the lab and stole it back. Unfortunately, I didn't have time to find my field notes. A security guard interrupted my search. I told him I was the cleaning lady. I smuggled the egg out of the lab in a mop bucket."

Wolfe laughed. "You don't look like a cleaning lady, Dr. Lee."

Laurel smiled. "Thank you. And please, call me Laurel."

"Of course, and you can call me Wolfe. Your field notes were probably sent directly to Blackwood anyway. I'm certain he's combing the country for you and that egg right now."

"I think he might have caught up to me in Utah. Someone smashed my engine and ransacked my camper while I was in a store. I had to hitchhike the rest of the way out here."

Wolfe gave her a look of open admiration.

"I shouldn't have taken it to GeneArk," Laurel said.

Wolfe patted her hand. "Forget about it. The question now is, what do we do about it? Blackwood has no doubt already sent a team to Lake Télé. And the timing stinks. My . . ." He got up and started pacing again. "My niece and nephew just got here today. Twins. I was going to spend the next few weeks getting to know them and settling them in." He gave a bitter laugh. "The irony is that I was going to take them there eventually, but I sure can't take them on this trip."

"Take them where?" Laurel asked. "What are you talking about?"

Grace was asking the same questions herself.

Wolfe stopped. "It will take a few days to get ready, but you and I, Dr. Lee, are going to Lake Télé."

Why would Wolfe want to take us to the Congo? Grace thought with alarm.

"On more than one occasion, Masalito saved my life," Wolfe continued. "I'm not going to leave him out there for Blackwood's jackals to devour. We have to find him before they do."

"I'm not sure I'll be able to join you," Laurel said. "I need to start looking for a job."

"You have a job," Wolfe said. "I just hired you."

"As what?"

"You're my new chief anthropologist."

Dr. Lee gave him a grateful smile. "I guess I have no choice but to accept, under the circumstances. But what about your niece and nephew?"

Wolfe frowned. "I might have to send them back

to their boarding school. There's no time to arrange anything else."

Grace nearly let out a cheer.

"What if Blackwood's men get to Lake Télé before us?"

"They will," Wolfe answered. "But we still have an advantage."

"What's that?"

"I know Masalito's phone number and they don't."

"What are you talking about? Masalito doesn't have a phone."

"Is the *molimo* still there?"

"Yes," Laurel said. "It's on the roof."

What roof? What kind of animal were they talking about now? Grace thought.

"Good," Wolfe said. "Let's go find Phil and start figuring out what we'll need for the expedition."

After they had gone, Grace pulled out *The Hidden Ones* and looked up Mokélé-mbembé. It was not a bird.

In the kitchen, Bertha verified that the tags were tracking devices and insisted that if the Gizmo said Grace was in the library, she was in the library, unless she had taken her tag off and left it there.

Marty slipped his soufflé into the oven, then wandered down to the library again. The Gizmo said Grace was there, but there was still no sign of her. Why did she take her tag off?

"Boooooooooooooo!"

Something hit Marty in the back. He screamed, collapsed on the floor, and covered his head, expecting a flying banshee to tear him to shreds . . . until he heard someone laughing. He looked up. "That's not funny!" he shouted. "Not funny at all." When he stood, the Frankenstein monkey (which Grace had hurled from the balcony) fell to the floor.

"I wish you could have seen your face," Grace managed to gasp.

"You'll pay for this!" He sprinted up the spiral staircase. Grace was small, but quick. He couldn't get within twenty feet of her. "Okay, okay," he said breathlessly, after four laps around the balcony. "Truce. I have something really cool to show you."

Grace wasn't sure if she should trust him or not. "Do you promise not to grab me or do any other horrible thing?"

"Yeah, I promise."

Monkey lay below, so he could not seal the deal, but Grace allowed Marty to approach her anyway, keeping a sharp eye out for any sign of treachery.

"You're in a pretty good mood," Marty observed, pleased to see the change in her. She almost seemed like the old Grace. He showed her the little computer. "It's called a Gizmo."

"What is it?"

"Watch." He clicked her name, and blue and gray squares appeared next to each other on the screen. "That's us. The tags Bertha gave us are tracking devices." He gave her a suspicious look. "Were you up here the first time I came through?"

Grace grinned.

"Why didn't you say something?"

"Nose picker," Grace answered.

"I don't know what you're talking about," he said innocently and continued his Gizmo demonstration. "I turned this video thing on and saw Phil and the guy they rescued from the kayak get into the Humvee."

"The guy is a woman."

"No way!"

"Her name is Dr. Laurel Lee."

Grace recounted most of the conversation she had overheard, omitting the reason she was in such a good mood. By the time she finished, Marty had all but forgotten about the Gizmo. He started browsing the cryptid sections. Grace followed along. "So, Wolfe believes in Bigfoot?"

"I think so," she answered.

He continued down the shelves. "And mermaids?"

"Maybe."

He reached the Little Humanoid section. "Elves, fairies, and leprechauns?"

"He might."

"And this crypto—whatever you call it is—"

"Cryptozoology," Grace said. "The study of hidden animals."

"How do you study something that's hidden?"

"By finding the hiding places, I suppose. I was just reading that some people call the place where cryptids live the Goblin Universe."

Marty laughed. "Sounds like Halloween."

"Wolfe is dead serious about it. I told you there was something the matter with him. You should have seen the look in his eyes when he saw that egg.

72

It was scary, like he was possessed or something."

"So, what's this Monkey Bembee thing?"

"It's pronounced Mo-Kee-Lee-Em-Bem-Bee," Grace answered. "It's a dinosaur."

"You're joking."

Grace opened up *The Hidden Ones* and read the description.

> Mokélé-mbembé is a small sauropod dinosaur slightly larger than an elephant. Its overall length has been reported to be between 16 to 32 feet. The length of the neck is 5 to 10 feet. The length of the tail is 5 to 10 feet as well. Its footprints are rounded in shape and 1 to 3 feet in diameter, with three claws. The distance between tracks is about 7 to 8 feet. The last specimens are thought to live near Lake Télé in the Republic of Congo in central Africa.

"Wow! A real dinosaur." He looked at the drawing in the book, which wasn't very good, in his opinion. "Let me get this straight," he said. "Wolfe is going to the Congo to save a friend of his from Noah Blackwood, who isn't who he appears to be?"

Grace nodded.

"And Mom and Dad were going to investigate Noah Blackwood before they disappeared?"

"Apparently," Grace said.

Marty leaned over the balcony. "And in that box down there is a real dinosaur egg?"

"Alleged dinosaur egg."

"What's Wolfe going to do about us?" Marty asked.

Grace had been waiting for this question but wasn't prepared to answer it. She thought it best if their uncle told him that he was sending them back to boarding school. "I guess we'll have to ask him."

Marty flipped open the Gizmo and clicked their uncle's name. The third-story floor plan appeared. Unlike the first and second floors, which had several rooms, there were only two rooms on the third floor. The small room was labeled *Bedroom #1*. The remaining room was called the *Wolfe Den*. And that's where the turquoise square appeared. "Let's go talk to him," Marty said. "Wouldn't it be great to go to the Congo?"

No, Grace thought, it would be horrible. And she had no doubt that, given enough time, Marty could talk Wolfe into taking them with him. At one time he had talked Dr. Beasel into taking their entire class to Spain for two weeks in the middle of the school year despite the headmaster's intense dislike and distrust of Marty. The trip went well until Marty was arrested for setting free the bulls from a Madrid bullfighting ring. She needed something to distract her adventurous brother and saw her chance on the Gizmo's small screen. "That's the kayaker," she said, pointing to Laurel's name.

"Oh, yeah?" Marty clicked the button and a yellow square appeared in the *Living Room*.

"And where are these other people?" Grace asked.

Marty happily started clicking through the names. Phil Sr. and Phil Jr. were in their houses in the *Staff Compound* along with a half dozen other people. It looked as if each staff member had a separate residence within the compound because they were labeled *House #1, House #2*—all the way up to twelve.

Bertha was still in the *Kitchen*. "I was just in there helping her make dinner," Marty explained. "She has a lot to learn about cooking, but I think I can bring her along. I whipped up a simple soufflé, and she was pretty interested in the process." He looked at his watch. "In fact, I have to take it out of the oven in a few minutes." He continued clicking names. Someone named Bo was on the north side of the island. Vid was on the south side of the island near a place called Lost Lake.

"Who do you suppose Bo and Vid are?" Marty asked.

"More importantly," Grace said. "What do you think Bo and Vid are doing out in the middle of the woods at this time of night? And why are they and the others out here on an island in the middle of nowhere?"

"They obviously work for Wolfe."

"Doing what?"

"Who knows?" Marty turned the Gizmo off. "Let's take a look at that dinosaur egg."

Before Grace could stop him, Marty was halfway down the spiral staircase. She caught up to him just as he was opening the cardboard box. "I don't think you should touch it."

"There's no harm in looking." He took it out of the box and held it under the light. "Wow, a genuine dinosaur egg!"

It looked more like a semideflated soccer ball to Grace.

"Wouldn't it be great to see a dinosaur?" Marty asked.

"There are no more dinosaurs," Grace said. "And there is no such place as the Goblin Universe." She knew where Marty was heading, at least in his imagination, which had no boundaries. She had to stop him before he passed the point of no return. "The last dinosaur died sixty-five million years ago. If there were any dinosaurs left we would know about them. Every inch of the earth has been mapped."

"Mapped by satellite, not necessarily explored," Marty said, proud that he actually remembered something from his geography class. "If Mokélé-mbembé doesn't exist, why is it described in that book? And why would a Pygmy lie about it?"

"That's an excellent question," Dr. Lee asked from behind them.

The twins jumped and Marty nearly dropped the egg.

"You must be Grace and Marty," she continued. "My name's Laurel." She looked up at the balcony then smiled at them. "But you already knew that. The conversation you overheard must have been very enlightening."

Grace flushed with embarrassment. "You knew I was up there?"

Laurel laughed. "Not you specifically, but now I know it was you. I sensed *someone* up there. PD nearly gave you away."

"Why didn't *you* give me away?"

"It wasn't my place. I'm sure you had your reasons for staying hidden."

"Did my uncle know?"

"If he did, he didn't mention it." Laurel looked at Marty. "Perhaps we should put that egg away." Marty handed it to her and she placed it back in the box. "Now, let's get back to Marty's question about a Pygmy's telling lies. I've never known a Pygmy to tell an outright lie."

"Well, they are certainly capable of exaggeration," Grace said. She liked Laurel, but she was a little annoyed at the intrusion. She wanted Marty to herself so she could convince him how crazy all of this was.

"Mokélé-mbembé probably started out as an animal in some story concocted by a Pygmy to impress his friends. The story was passed from one Pygmy to the next and over the years they started to believe that the animal was real. This is how most legends begin. I wrote a paper on the origin of legends at school."

"That's an interesting theory," Laurel said. "But you're forgetting a very important point. How would that first Pygmy know what a sauropod looks like? They don't have televisions, movies, or books. They have no idea that the earth was once dominated by dinosaurs, and yet they can give you a perfect description of a sauropod."

It was a good point, but Grace was not about to give up. "Maybe some explorer came through the area years before and told the Pygmies he was looking for dinosaurs. Perhaps he drew them a picture of a sauropod and that's where the idea came from."

"That's possible, but not very likely," Laurel said. "Lake Télé hasn't really been explored—not by the scientific community, anyway. It's not on the way to anywhere and there are no major rivers near it."

"What do rivers have to do with it?" Grace asked.

"Everything. They're the superhighways of tropical exploration—the only way in and out of some of these remote areas. Explorers have been using them for centuries. But the problem with rivers is that you only see what's on the fringe of the environment. It's like driving on an interstate freeway. You really don't see much. The earth's last mysteries will be found in the deep interiors. In places where no one goes except for a few tough indigenous people. And believe it or not, there are still a lot of these places left. If you saw the Lake Télé region you'd understand how a dinosaur could hide out for several million years."

"We'd love to go!" Marty exclaimed.

Laurel laughed. "That was not an invitation, Marty. And it's not up to me, I'm afraid."

"What about that soufflé, Marty?" Grace asked. She had to put a stop to this.

"Huh?"

"The soufflé," she repeated. "Didn't you say—"

"You're right!" He looked at Laurel. "Are you having dinner with us?"

"Yes."

"Great! We can talk about our trip then." He ran out of the library.

Laurel watched him leave, then turned to Grace and said, "Your brother's very self-assured."

Grace nodded. "He's also very impressionable."

"You mean open-minded?"

"I mean easily taken in."

"I see." Laurel raised her eyebrow. "But not you."

"Just because I don't believe in living dinosaurs

or the Goblin Universe doesn't mean I'm not open-minded."

"I suppose you're right," Laurel said with a gentle smile. "Tell me about yourself."

Grace gave her a brief outline of her and Marty's history.

"So, you hadn't met your uncle until this morning?" Laurel asked, surprised.

"We didn't even know we had an uncle until a few days ago."

"That is rather odd," Laurel said. "What do you think of him?"

"I'm not sure," Grace hedged. "We haven't really had much of a chance to talk."

"How old are you?"

"Thirteen."

"Really."

Grace saw a glimmer of disbelief cross Laurel's face. "I'm small for my age."

"So was I," Laurel said. "In fact, I'm still pretty small."

Grace smiled. She liked Laurel even better close up than she did from the balcony. "What were you doing when you came into the library?"

"You mean this?" She held her arms out and closed her eyes.

"Yes."

"I was walking an imaginary high wire."

"Why?"

Laurel put her arms down and opened her eyes. "Because I was afraid."

"You didn't look frightened when you came into the library."

"Looks can be very deceiving," Laurel said. "My unorthodox arrival caused your uncle a good deal of trouble, and I knew he would be upset. I was nervous. Before I spoke to him I had to deal with my fear."

"And you do that by pretending you're walking a high wire?"

Laurel nodded. "Before I became an anthropologist I was an aerialist in a circus. It's been a long time since I've been up on a real wire, but I still practice in my imagination. It helps me focus and control my fears."

Grace would have given just about anything to learn how to control her fears. "It must have worked," she said. "You didn't seem intimidated by Wolfe in the least."

"Your uncle is a formidable man, but when I'm on the wire I'm taller than everyone."

"I could never do that," Grace said.

"Walk on the high wire? Of course you could. The only way to overcome fears is to get over them a little at a time."

Grace shook her head. "I'm afraid of heights."

"You don't start out very high," Laurel said.

"When I was your age I was afraid of heights too. My father was a circus clown. The ringmaster made it clear that if my father wanted to stay with the circus his little girl was going to have to get up on that thin wire and thrill the audience."

"They made you?"

"They sure did."

"What about you mother? What did she—"

"She passed away when I was very young," Laurel said. "It was just me and my dad."

"I still don't think I could get up on a high wire," Grace said.

"If you had to, you could."

PD ran into the room barking, and jumped into Laurel's arms. She cuddled the poodle for a moment, then looked at Grace. "Do you know why PD barks?"

"Because she's aggressive," Grace answered.

Laurel shook her head. "She barks because she's afraid, and she's afraid because she's little. If she were the size of a normal dog, I don't think she would bark nearly as much."

Grace was certain that her own fears were caused by more than her size, but there was some truth to what Laurel was saying.

"My biggest problem in learning the high wire," Laurel continued, "was my tendency to faint whenever I got scared."

"That happens to me too!" Grace said.

"Like a light switching off?"

"Yes," Grace said. "Everything goes completely black. How did you get over it?"

"By practicing. Eventually, I learned to use my fear instead of letting it use me. When I focused on the thin wire, time seemed to slow down. I saw the world more crisply. Balancing my body seemed to balance my heart. I found that it worked on my other fears as well. They're still with me, but I've learned how to control them."

"How did your mother die?" Grace asked.

"She fell from—"

Marty walked into the library wearing an apron that was way too big for him. "Dinner is served," he said.

dinner 8

Marty knew better than to jump right into the subject of going to the Congo with his uncle. Things like this had to be handled with great delicacy.

At the dinner table were the Bishops, their daughter, Phyllis (also known as Phil Jr.), Laurel Lee, Grace (who looked a little pensive after her conversation with Laurel), and Wolfe (who was tapping away on his Gizmo with furious speed, virtually ignoring the plate in front of him).

"Bertha, this food is delicious," Phil said. "I mean it."

"I can't take much credit," Bertha said. "Marty had a hand in every dish. It turns out that he's quite a chef."

Marty saw his opening. "I'm an even better cook in the field," he boasted. "I'd take a campfire under the open sky over an oven any day."

Wolfe continue tapping as if he hadn't heard. Grace gave her brother the stink-eye. Here we go, she thought.

"Where did you learn to cook?" Phyllis asked. She looked more like her father than her mother. Marty guessed her to be in her early thirties.

"Oh, here and there," Marty said. "School mostly. But I learned field cooking during one of my wilderness-survival courses."

"You've taken survival courses?"

"Dozens of them."

More like half a dozen, Grace thought.

Marty continued. "A few of my instructors said I knew more about wilderness survival than they did. And cooking . . . I don't want to brag, but I can make boa constrictor taste like chicken cordon bleu."

Wolfe still did not look up, but there was a definite pause in his tapping.

Now, Marty thought. "I should be able to cook up some pretty good grub when we're in the Congo," he said.

The tapping stopped. Wolfe looked up from his Gizmo. "Did you say the Congo?"

"Yes, sir, I did. The rumor is we're going there to find a dinosaur and help a friend of yours out of a jam with Noah Blackwood."

"And where did you hear this?" He glared at Bertha, who shook her head.

Marty did not answer. He didn't want to get Grace into trouble for spying.

"I—" Grace started.

"I'm afraid I let the cat out of the bag," Laurel interrupted.

Wolfe shot her an angry look.

"Laurel didn't do it!" Marty said, jumping into the deceit with both feet. "I found the dinosaur egg in the library. I asked Laurel what it was and one thing led to another."

"I see," Wolfe said.

"That's not what—" Grace began, but Marty cut her off by asking Wolfe if he was a cryptozoologist.

"Yes, I am."

"Incredible," Marty said. "I've been interested in cryptids for ages."

Grace rolled her eyes.

"What a coincidence," Wolfe said without much enthusiasm.

"So, when are we leaving?" Marty asked.

"The Congo is no place for kids," Wolfe said. "It's one of the most hostile environments on earth. The rivers and swamps are filled with crocodiles, venomous snakes, and biting insects. It's a hotbed of malaria, Ebola virus, and other deadly diseases. I'm afraid—"

"So, how big is this dinosaur?" Marty interrupted, even though he already knew. He had learned from experience that the longer he could avoid the word *no*, the better chance he had in getting a *yes*.

"Not big as far as dinosaurs go," Wolfe said. "A

little bigger than an elephant, which is one of the reasons Mokélé-mbembé survived for such a long time."

"So, you've seen this Mokélé-mbembé?" Marty asked.

Wolfe got a far-off look in his eyes. "Yes," he finally said. "I saw the very last two. I saw them just before they died."

"Maybe there are others," Marty offered.

Wolfe shook his head sadly. "Doubtful."

"Well," Bertha said cheerfully. "How about some ice cream for everyone?"

"Sounds good to me," Phil said.

Marty was not about to be bought off with a bowl of ice cream. "Is there such a thing as Bigfoot?" He would get back to the Congo in due time.

"Of course," Wolfe said. "And I believe there's an Asian version as well."

"The Abominable Snowman, or Yeti," Marty said.

"That's right, although I haven't seen one of those yet. But we were very close when we were last in China."

"But you've seen Bigfoot?" Marty asked.

Wolfe nodded.

"Where?"

"Right here in Washington."

"Wow! What's it like?"

"Intelligent, shy, and somewhat aggressive when cornered."

"You've cornered one?"

"It's a long story," Wolfe answered. "I'll tell it to you sometime, but right now I'd better get back to my e-mail."

Grace let out an exaggerated yawn. "I'm tired," she said. "Maybe we should go to bed and let Wolfe get his work done."

"Go ahead," Marty said.

And leave you alone with Wolfe? Grace thought. Not in sixty-five million years.

"I was wondering how you send e-mail with the Gizmo," Marty said.

"Don't be rude, Marty," Grace protested. "He just said he had work to do."

"That's okay," Wolfe said, obviously relieved to talk about something other than the Congo and cryptids. "Come over here and I'll show you. It will only take a minute."

Marty walked around the table and stood behind Wolfe. "Let me see your Gizmo." Marty handed it to him. "You might as well get in on this too, Grace. It will save me from going through it twice. I don't have time to show you everything the Gizmo does tonight, but I can take you through some of the basic functions."

Grace was not interested in electronic gizmos, but it was better than talking about going to the Congo.

Wolfe asked to see Marty's identification tag. He

slid it into a slot on the top of the Gizmo and the screen came to life.

WELCOME, MARTY!

"You mean the tags aren't just tracking devices?" Marty asked.

"They're a lot more than that. Your tag will activate any Gizmo and make it your own. You can also activate unassigned tracking tags by putting them into the slot."

"So you have to insert the tag every time?"

"No, just once." Wolfe pointed at the icons on the screen. "You can now access your private Cybervault, e-mail—"

"But I don't have an e-mail account here," Marty said.

"Yes you do, and you don't need a phone line. The Gizmos are directly linked to our Hunter Satellite, which beams your e-mail right to the unit."

"You have your own satellite?"

"Yes, and we're hoping to launch a second one next year if we can get the funding. You can send and receive e-mail from nearly anywhere in the world, providing you have a clear shot at our satellite."

"Wow!" Marty pointed at the screen. "What's a Cybervault?"

"That's one of the Gizmo's best features." Wolfe

pointed to a small lens above the screen. "This is a built-in camera. You can use it for live teleconferencing, meaning you can talk to anyone face-to-face if they have a camera connected to their computer. If you want to save something, say a sketch or a document, all you have to do is hold it up to the lens and take a photo of it. The image is automatically downloaded into your personal Cybervault. That way your work will be virtually safe forever."

"Unless you lose the Gizmo," Grace said. Marty was always losing things.

Wolfe shook his head. "If you dropped your Gizmo into the crater of an active volcano and it turned to ash, what you've saved would still be perfectly safe. Your Cybervault is not in the unit. When you store or save something with the Gizmo, it's uploaded to a satellite, then beamed down to your Cybervault back here on Cryptos. And only you have the combination to get into it. I wouldn't want the Gizmo to fall into the wrong hands. There are only six in existence. But lost or not, your data is perfectly safe in the Cybervault. All you have to do is insert your identification tag into another Gizmo and you'll be ready to go again."

"I'll be careful," Marty said. The first thing he was going to do was to download every drawing and comic book idea in his sketchbook. He always worried about losing them. "How does this video thing work?" he asked. "I saw a little clip this afternoon after Laurel was rescued. Did you shoot it from the helicopter?"

"Not exactly." Wolfe glanced at his watch. "Look, Marty, I really need to get my work done. We should have some time tomorrow to talk about the Gizmo's other features. Can we continue this later?"

"I guess so."

Wolfe gave him back the Gizmo and stood up. "I'll see you two tomorrow morning. Please don't get the wrong impression. I'm delighted you're here with me and I'm sorry for the rough beginning we've had, but there are some things I absolutely have to take care of tonight. We'll start again in the morning and see if we can't smooth things out."

"Can we talk about the Congo tomorrow as well?" Marty asked.

Wolfe gave him a weary nod. He started out of the room, then stopped and turned. "Bertha probably already told you, but I don't want either one of you wandering around the island until I have a chance to explain how it works around here. There are things on the island . . ." He hesitated. "What I mean to say is that I don't want you getting lost, so please stay close to the house for the time being."

"We will," Grace assured him.

Marty was already checking his e-mail on the Gizmo.

lost lake 9

Quark . . . quark . . . quark . . .

"Run!" Bigfoot was chasing Marty through a dream. He snapped his eyes open, relieved to find himself safe in bed in his new room, and not in the soiled hands of a giant primate. "Grace and her stories," he grumbled. After dinner they had gone back to the library, where Grace had read him cryptid horror stories until after midnight in an attempt to get him to give up on the Congo idea. It hadn't worked. "Today I will get Wolfe to agree to take us to the Congo," he declared, swinging his feet out of bed.

Quark . . . quark . . . quark.

"What is that?" He looked across the room through the sliding glass door and saw a raven perched on the balcony wall. He walked over for a closer look, tripping over his suitcase on the way and bumping his head on the glass. "Ouch!" The raven flew off.

After a quick shower he opened his bag and found

his favorite pair of faded jeans—the ones with the left knee blown out by a nasty fall he had taken while climbing in the Alps. He pulled on the pants along with a T-shirt and sneakers, and topped the ensemble off with a baseball cap that looked as though it had been kicked halfway around the world—which it nearly had if you counted the various outdoor camps he had attended during his summer breaks. He stepped out onto the balcony and took in a deep breath of crisp Pacific Ocean air. His room was on the east side of the house, and there was an excellent view of the island. It was much clearer than it had been when they arrived, and he could see the two lakes he had seen on the Gizmo the day before. Just past the second lake were two huge metal Quonset huts big enough to house several blimps. "What could Wolfe be storing in those?" Marty wondered aloud.

He carried the Gizmo downstairs and found Grace asleep on the sofa in the library. Her Moleskine and Frankenstein monkey lay across her stomach, and on the floor were dozens of books. He shook her awake.

Grace squinted irritably up at him. "What time is it?"

"After dawn," Marty said.

"Too early," Grace complained. She had only been asleep a couple of hours, having spent the night reading about cryptids and thinking about what Laurel had told her about overcoming fear. To top everything off, when she finally fell asleep she'd had the nightmare again, which was her biggest fear. How do you overcome something you can't even remember?

"Let's do some exploring," Marty said.

"We need to wait for Wolfe."

"I checked him on the Gizmo," Marty said. "He's up in the Wolfe Den, probably working. I don't want to bother him."

"Since when has bothering someone bothered you?"

"Let's go," Marty said.

"He told us to stay in the house," Grace said sleepily. "I'm not going anywhere."

"His exact words," Marty pointed out, "were, 'I don't want you getting lost.' I'm not going to get lost. We won't go very far. The island's not that big."

"Marty, we don't know what he has on this island."

"You mean Bigfoot?" Marty made a monster face.

"Idiot."

"Have you thought more about going to the Congo?"

"Yes."

"And?"

"And I'm going back to sleep." Grace rolled over and closed her eyes.

Marty ran down the long hill, escorted by the quarking raven. He was annoyed with Grace. How could she pass up an opportunity to search for a living dinosaur, for crying out loud? How could she take the opportunity away from him? Why does she have to be afraid of everything?

But by the time he reached the bottom of the hill, with the warm air tickling his skin through the tear on his pant leg and the wonderful sensation of dampness beginning to build in the sweat band of his favorite cap, his bad feelings were gone. He had never been mad at anyone for more than five minutes in his life. This beats school any day, he thought. An island all to myself. I wonder if there are fish in the lake. I wonder if Phil will teach me how to fly. I wonder . . .

He heard a rustling noise in the trees off the side of the road. He stopped and listened. The sound stopped. It must have been a squirrel or a deer, he thought, and continued running down the road. But a hundred yards later he heard the rustling again, and slowed down. Maybe I should go back up to the house, he thought. Don't be ridiculous! I've seen polar bears in the arctic, rattlesnakes in the desert, and giant moray eels in the Red Sea. He continued on, thinking about the Congo and cryptids and . . .

The rustling sound came again. This time it was in front of him. A few seconds later he heard the sound behind him. He whipped around, but saw nothing. It was a loud skittering noise, as if the animal making it were quick and extremely agile. He began to regret not waiting for Wolfe, as Grace had suggested, and was still nervous when he reached the lake.

Quark . . . quark . . . quark.

The raven circled above the water.

The first thing that struck Marty about the lake was its size. It seemed much bigger than it had from the balcony. The other thing that surprised him was that it appeared to be man-made. There was a concrete retaining wall all the way around the perimeter. He leaned over the edge to see how the water was, thinking he might go for a swim.

"Whoa! Not without a wet suit." He shook the cold water off his hand, and a few drops hit his lip. "Salt?" He leaned down again and dipped his finger into the water and tasted it. "What's a saltwater lake doing in the middle of an island?"

He didn't have time to answer his own question because a horrendous howl erupted behind him. He twisted around and saw a very large, hairy creature charging out of the forest.

"Bigfoot!" Marty dove into the icy water of the lake and swam for his life. With each terrified stroke he berated himself for not listening to his sister, and prayed that Bigfoot could not swim. He didn't stop until he got to the center of the lake. Breathing hard, he looked back through salt-stung eyes, relieved beyond belief to see that the creature was still on shore, hooting and howling, tearing up bushes and tossing them into the lake.

He treaded water and tried to catch his breath. His teeth chattered with fear and cold. He knew that if he didn't get out of the cold water soon, hypothermia would set in and Bigfoot would be the least of his problems. But he was wrong about this.

Out of the corner of his eye he caught a swift movement to his right and another movement to his left. A moment later, three large fins broke the surface and sliced toward him with deadly speed.

"Sharks!" he yelled. "Sharks!"

But the only things that seemed to hear him were the creature raging along the shore and the raven circling above his head.

Grace felt something cold and clammy nuzzle her face. Reluctantly, she opened her eyes and found PD climbing on Monkey. "No," she moaned. She picked the little dog up, put her on the floor, and saw Wolfe sitting in the chair opposite the sofa. His head was turned away and he was wiping his eyes as if he had been crying. When he turned back toward her she saw that he had trimmed his beard and combed his hair and looked a lot more presentable than he had the day before.

Grace put Monkey behind her. She knew she was

too old to be sleeping with a stuffed animal, but she couldn't help herself.

"Good morning," he said. "I see you've been doing some reading."

Grace nodded, still wondering if he had actually been crying, and if so, why?

He picked up one of the books. "You've made some interesting selections."

"Yes I—" Grace glanced over to the side of his chair and saw a pair of well-used aluminum crutches. She wondered who they belonged to, then gasped in surprise. The right leg of Wolfe's pants was pinned up just below the left knee.

He followed her gaze. "I'm sorry," he said quickly. "I should have warned you. I guess I'm just so used to it being gone I don't think about it anymore. I usually wear a prosthesis . . . an artificial leg. I didn't mean to make you uncomfortable."

Grace knew what a prosthesis was. And she was not uncomfortable about his missing leg, just surprised and deeply embarrassed by her reaction to it. Some doctor I'll make, she thought.

"I was going to put it on before I came down," her uncle continued, becoming more flustered with every word. "But the . . . uh . . . uh . . ."

Grace sat up. "Stump," she said, trying to redeem herself.

"Yes." Wolfe looked relieved. "The stump was

sore from my trip and I thought I should give it a rest."

"Of course," Grace said. "How did you lose it?"

Wolfe stared at her for a long time, as if he were debating with himself. "It's a long story," he finally replied. "And if it's all right with you, I'd like to tell it to you another time."

Grace nodded, though she was dying of curiosity.

Wolfe pointed at the books. "I know this is all a little hard to grasp," he said. "And believe me, I would have preferred to ease into the subject of cryptozoology with you and Marty instead of leaving you to discover it the way you did. You probably think I'm a lunatic."

"Marty doesn't," Grace said.

Wolfe gave her a gentle smile. "And what's you're opinion?"

"I . . ." Grace did not really want to give him her opinion, so she took a page out of Marty's book. She changed the subject. "I'd like to clear something up that happened yesterday."

"Yes?"

"I was hiding on the balcony when you had your conversation with Laurel. That's how I heard about Mokélé-mbembé, Noah Blackwood, Masalito, the Congo—all of it. I told Marty what I overheard. Laurel had nothing to do with it. I'm sorry I eavesdropped on you."

"I admire your honesty," Wolfe said. "I also admire Marty and Laurel's covering for you. And just so you know, at your age I would have hidden on the balcony, too. It's fun to listen to grown-ups when they don't know you're there."

Grace smiled. Her uncle might be a lunatic, but he was a nice lunatic.

"I have a lot to explain," he said. "Where's Marty?"

"He went for a walk."

A look of concern crossed Wolfe's face. He took his Gizmo out and flipped it open.

"Is there something the matter?"

"Probably not. But he should have waited for me to show him around." He booted up the program and clicked Marty's name. "Oh my God! We've got to get down to the lake." He grabbed his crutches and pulled himself up.

"What going on?"

"Marty's drowning!"

Grace was amazed at his dexterity and speed. She and PD could barely keep up with him as he rushed through the front door and down the steps to the Humvee.

Marty was on the verge of blacking out. The sharks had attacked him several times, but surprisingly, he felt no pain. He thought the cold water had numbed his mangled legs and he was grateful for that. This did not explain the lack of frothing blood in the churning water, but his hypothermic mind was not clear enough to grasp this. He closed his eyes and simply waited for the end, feeling sad about all the people and things he would miss.

Something wrapped itself around his neck and begin to pull him. He thought it was probably the tentacle of a giant squid. It must have outgrown the aquarium in the library. He did not struggle. No point in that now, he thought hazily.

Grace and Wolfe arrived just as Laurel was hauling Marty out of the water. Grace leaped from the Humvee before it came to a complete stop and ran over to him. His eyes were closed and his skin was a sickly pale blue. First Mom and Dad, and now Marty, she thought. What will happen to me?

Laurel flipped him over on his stomach and began pushing on his back to expel the water from his lungs.

"Is he . . . dead?"

"Far from it," Laurel answered breathlessly. "Just a little waterlogged. I was on my way to meet Phil at the hangar, and I heard someone shouting something about sharks."

Wolfe joined them. "Did you say sharks?"

"That's what I thought I heard." Laurel started massaging his limbs. "We need to get him warmed up."

Wolfe looked at Grace. "There's a blanket and first-aid kit in the Humvee."

Grace ran back to the Humvee with PD behind her. She opened the back end and found the blanket and kit. As she grabbed them and turned to leave, she found herself face-to-face with the most hideous creature she had ever seen. Before she could scream, the creature scooped PD off the ground and ran back into the forest, shrieking in victory. Don't faint, she told herself. Marty needs you. Don't faint! But it was too much for her. Her knees buckled and she collapsed onto the ground.

She came to a few minutes later with Laurel bent over her. "Are you all right?"

Grace didn't answer. She grabbed the blanket and ran back over to Marty, who had his head in Wolfe's lap. He grinned when he saw her. Grace had never been more happy in her life. She got down on her knees and started tucking the blanket around him. Laurel came up behind her with the first-aid kit.

"Di-di-did y-you s-s-see th-th-the Bi-bi-big f-f-foot?" he asked Grace through chattering teeth. "It a-ta-ta-attacked m-m-me."

Wolfe and Laurel looked at him as if he were delirious.

"I saw it!" Grace glared at Wolfe accusingly. "It just snatched up PD and carried her off into the woods. It was awful."

"And th-th-the sh-sh-sharks?" Marty tried to sit up, but Wolfe wouldn't let him. "Are b-b-both m-m-my l-l-legs g-g-gone?"

"You're legs are just fine," Wolfe answered. "There are no sharks in the lake." He looked at Grace. "And there is no Bigfoot—at least not on Cryptos. And PD is safe."

"Then where is she?" Grace demanded.

"I'll show you." Wolfe took a silent dog whistle from his pocket and blew it. A moment later the hideous creature burst out of the forest and ran down to them.

"It's a ch-ch-chimp!" Marty said, although with all the twigs and leaves clinging to its fur it was difficult to tell exactly what kind of primate it was.

Grace was too stunned to speak. The chimpanzee was holding PD in the crook of its arm and the little dog seemed as content as she had the day before when Laurel was holding her.

"Her name's Bo." Wolfe pulled a handful of peanuts out of his pocket. Bo gently set PD on the ground and took them from him. "And it looks like she's wearing more of her nest this morning than she left up in the tree." He started picking the debris out of her fur. "She's a bonobo chimpanzee from the Congo."

During his near-death experience Marty had completely forgotten about the Congo. Wolfe tried to stop him, but Marty brushed his hand away and sat up. In an attempt to repair some of the damage he had done to his cause, he cleared his throat and said, "The bonobo was discovered in the Congo in 1929. Before that time, scientists thought there was only one species of chimpanzee. The bonobo can be distinguished from the common chimpanzee by its longer limbs and the black pigment on its face."

Wolfe stared at him, clearly impressed. Grace had seen this carnival act before. Marty had a photographic memory. The problem was, there were only a few things that interested him enough to take a picture of with his mind. Recipes, animal trivia, survival tips, and whole comic book plots were the things he most commonly memorized.

"Where did you learn that?" Wolfe asked.

"Oh, I don't know," Marty said. Actually, he knew exactly where he had gotten the information: he had lifted the bonobo quote directly from a Noah Blackwood animal video. He and Luther had watched the video half a dozen times. "I've always been fascinated with the animals of the Congo. I've made quite a study of them over the years."

Wolfe looked a little skeptical, and Marty thought it wise to change the subject for the moment. Shakily, he got to his feet. "If those weren't sharks in the lake, what were they?"

Wolfe handed him one of his crutches.

"I don't need a crutch," Marty said, then noticed Wolfe's empty pant leg.

"The crutch isn't for you to walk with," Wolfe said. "I want you to take it down to the water and slap it on the surface twice."

Marty continued to stare at the pant leg.

"It wasn't sharks," Wolfe assured him, pulling himself up with the other crutch. "Go ahead and slap the water. You have my word that nothing will come out and bite *your* leg off."

Marty slapped the crutch on the water. At first nothing happened. The water was as smooth as glass. Then suddenly, three large animals broke the surface in unison, rising at least twenty feet in the air before splashing back down into the depths.

"Jeez, they're bottlenose dolphins!" Marty said with a mixture of wonder and embarrassment. Bo threw her remaining peanuts away and began running up and down the shore, hooting at them. "I can't believe I mistook them for sharks." He gave the crutch back to his uncle.

"Bo isn't fond of the dolphins," Wolfe explained. "They're constantly teasing her. I suspect that she saw you near shore, thought you were a dolphin lover, and decided to have a little fun. Your brain probably short-circuited when you saw her. And the stuff sticking to her didn't help. You aren't the first person to mistake a great ape for Bigfoot."

"That must be what happened," Marty eagerly agreed. "I didn't get a very good look at her before I jumped in the water. Even Grace thought Bo was Bigfoot, and she doesn't even believe in cryptids. So why do you have these animals?"

"We use them as scouts." Wolfe took his Gizmo out and was about to turn it on, then hesitated. "Maybe we should do this some other time."

"I'm fine," Marty said. "Tell us about the scouts."

"All right," Wolfe said. "But then you're going up to the house to get into some dry clothes." He clicked the video icon and an aerial scene of Lost Lake appeared on the tiny screen. Standing on the shore were four humans, a tiny dog, and an angry bonobo.

"This is live?" Marty looked up, trying to figure out where the camera was.

"Compliments of Vid," Wolfe said. "Our eye in the sky."

"Your satellite?"

"No," Wolfe said, pointing at the black bird circling above them. "Vid is a raven. Short for Video. He wears a lightweight harness with a built-in miniature camera."

"We saw him fly out of the house when we got there," Grace said.

"I replaced the camera battery yesterday afternoon just before you arrived," Wolfe explained. "He must have given you a scare."

"Nah," Marty said. "It takes a lot more than that to scare us. The raven is in the corvid, or crow family. If I'm not mistaken, its scientific name is *Corvus corax*."

Grace rolled her eyes.

"You're not mistaken," Wolfe said. "Vid was flying over the lake when you were having your little problem. I saw Laurel jump in the water and swim out to you."

"A bird's-eye view," Marty said.

"With Vid that's exactly right. And with the dolphins we're able to see underwater. Bo climbs trees and helps us see what's going on in the canopy. So we have Vid cam, Bo cam, Dolphin cam, and others. We even have a camera for PD, although we rarely use it because she sticks so close to us."

"Poodle cam," Marty said, glancing at Bo, who was still lambasting the dolphins. "Bo's not wearing a tracking tag," he said. "But we saw her marker on the Gizmo yesterday."

"She would just tear a tag off. We use subcutaneous implant transmitters just beneath the skin of all the animal scouts except for PD. Hers is on her collar."

"How do you control where they go?"

"Other than calling them to me with the whistle, I can't. And I don't want to control them. Every animal species has its own way of looking at things. You can learn a lot by seeing the world from their perspective. We'll be taking Vid and Bo to the Congo to help us keep an eye on things."

"What about Grace and me?" Marty asked.

Wolfe looked terribly uncomfortable. "We'll talk about that up at the house after you get into some dry clothes." He turned to Laurel. "Did you know those were dolphins when you jumped in after Marty?"

"No," she said. "But to be honest, I didn't think there were sharks in there, either."

"I see. Well, I'm indebted to you for pulling Marty out of the water."

"Me too," Marty said, giving her a wet hug.

the backpack 10

Marty had taken a long, hot shower and was sitting on the floor of his bedroom tying on a pair of dry sneakers. Grace was sitting on his bed.

"Did you really think the dolphins were sharks?" she asked.

"I sure did! I'm happy to have feet to put into these shoes. For a while there I thought they were at the bottom of the lake going for a run without me."

"I take it that you still want to go to the Congo?"

"Duh *du jour*," Marty answered (meaning "duh of the day," one of his and Luther's favorite sayings). He stood and looked out the window. "I have to admit that when I was in the middle of the lake being torn apart by sharks, there were a few seconds when even Omega Prep was looking pretty good. But now that I'm whole again . . ." He walked over to the suitcase and found a T-shirt. "I doubt Wolfe is going to take us to the Congo now. I really blew it!"

Grace was just thinking how *she* had blown it by fainting when Marty needed her most. And she also felt terrible for not trying harder to stop him from leaving. But what she felt even more guilty about was her first thought upon believing he had drowned.

"How did Wolfe lose his leg?" Marty asked.

"He wouldn't say," Grace answered.

Wolfe was waiting for them in the library. He had a fire burning in the fireplace and a thermos of hot chocolate on the table in front of the sofa. Sitting next to the thermos was a small backpack and a miniature camp stove with a bottle of fuel. The twins stared at the objects in numbed silence. The backpack and camp stove had belonged to their father.

"Where did you get them?" Grace whispered.

"In the Amazon," Wolfe said. "At the crash site. I flew there as soon as I heard about it. I just got back yesterday."

"You've been looking for them for six months?" Marty asked.

Wolfe nodded. "I know it may not seem like it, but my sister and I were very close. And Timothy was a good friend." He took a deep breath. "I'm afraid the pack is as close as I've come to finding them."

Marty had intended to march into the library and start right in on his Congo campaign, but he hadn't expected this. He brushed his fingers across the faded blue fabric of the backpack. His father had carried his notebooks and tape recorder in it, as well as the little camp stove, which he used to brew coffee. He couldn't remember a time his father didn't have it with him.

"The pack was empty except for the camp stove, and your father's journal, which was all but ruined. And this . . ." He reached into the pack and pulled out the Mother's Day card they had sent. Paper-clipped to it was a sketch Marty had drawn of himself and Grace walking along a beach holding their mother's hands.

The twins stared at the card and were nearly overcome with sadness.

"I haven't given up on finding your parents," Wolfe said. "I have people down there looking right now, and they'll continue the search until every lead, however small, has been exhausted. I'm in constant touch with them. If your parents are alive, we'll find them."

"Do you think they're alive?" Grace asked.

"To be honest," Wolfe answered quietly, "I don't know. Six months is a long time. But they must have survived the crash or we would have found their bodies at the site. They either wandered off on their own, or else they were injured and someone came along and moved them. There's a number of uncontacted tribes in the area. They might be in one of their camps recuperating. I've spent most of my life

111

looking for things people don't believe exist, and I've had a pretty good success rate. The only reason I came back was because of you and to take care of some pressing business." He looked them both in the eye. "I haven't given up on finding them, and I don't want you to give up either."

"We won't," they said in unison, feeling better about their parents' disappearance than they had in months.

"Good." Wolfe took a deep breath. "I know you both have a lot of questions for me, but let's clear up this Congo thing first."

"I think you should take us with you," Grace said.

Marty stared at his sister in amazement. He had never liked her more than at that moment.

Grace was equally surprised. Until she blurted this out she had wanted to return to school. Perhaps nearly losing Marty had changed her. Perhaps she was finally ready to confront some of her fears.

"I'm with Grace," Marty added quickly. "I know my stunt at the lake this morning might have scared you a little, but I promise to follow your rules to the letter from now on."

"It scared me a lot," Wolfe said. "But your swim has nothing to do with my decision. I made up my mind last night. I can't take you to the Congo."

"Why not?" Grace asked with a mixture of disappointment and relief.

"First, you have more than a month of school left. My plan was to hire a tutor and have you finish up the year right here. Unfortunately, Laurel and I have to get to the Congo right away, so there's no time for me to find a tutor. If I'd known about the egg I would have waited and had you come after school was out. I'm afraid I'm going to have to send you back to Switzerland."

Marty was dumbfounded. He had just about given up on Wolfe taking them to the Congo, but he didn't think they would be sent back to the school.

Grace was not at all surprised by Wolfe's decision. He had said as much the day before in the library. But now that she had changed her mind, she wasn't going to give up without a fight. "We'd learn a lot more in the Congo than we would at any school," she said.

"That's probably true," Wolfe admitted.

"And you told Laurel that you were planning on taking us to Lake Télé eventually anyway," Grace argued. "Why not get it over with?"

"You were going to take us to Lake Télé?" Marty asked, wondering what else Grace had neglected to tell him.

"Yes, I was," Wolfe said. "And I promise I'll take you there one day, but not this trip. It's too dangerous."

Marty was still confused. "Why do you want to take us to Lake Télé?"

"I'm afraid the answer is going to have to wait until I get back. It's complicated."

"Why can't we just stay on Cryptos?" Marty asked.

"Everyone here has at least two full-time jobs, and there will be no one to watch after you."

"We don't need babysitters," Marty protested.

"I'm sure you don't, but I'll feel a lot better knowing you're at the school where it's safe. I've already contacted Dr. Beasel and he's looking forward to your return."

"I bet he is," Marty said.

"I know this is disappointing, but I promise I'll make it up to you. When I get back we'll start all over again." Wolfe stood up. "Here's my new plan. We have a jet, of sorts. Phyllis will fly Laurel and me to the Congo, then fly up to Switzerland and drop you and Grace off. When we finish at Lake Télé we'll pick you up and take you back to Cryptos."

"What if school isn't out yet?" he asked.

"I'll take you back to Cryptos anyway, and that will be the last you'll ever see of that or any other boarding school again."

preparations 11

Grace and Marty saw very little of each other over the next few days.

Marty spent his time exploring the island and doing his best to wear down every member of Wolfe's merry band of pirates. He left the house at dawn and returned well after dark, determined to see every nook and cranny on Cryptos, and to learn everything he could about Wolfe's operation before he was sent back to school.

One of the things he learned was that his uncle operated on a shoestring budget. Almost all the money eWolfe made was put back into the company for research and development. This left little ready cash for cryptid research, or to fix things—like the engine on the jet Wolfe was to take to the Congo. Marty was in the hangar when Phil, Wolfe, and his two mechanics were discussing what to do about it.

"The engine's shot," one of the mechanics said.

"There has to be some way to fix it," Wolfe insisted. "You've never let me down before."

"There's always a first time," the other mechanic said. "She needs a new engine."

"I can't afford a new engine," Wolfe said.

The mechanics shrugged and walked off. There were plenty of other broken things in the hangar for them to fix.

"What are you going to do?" Phil asked.

"I have no idea."

"What about Ted? I bet he could come up with something."

Wolfe shook his head. "I haven't even seen him since I got back to the island. He's sealed in his lab working on something. You know how he is."

"Yeah," Phil said. "He's weird."

"I have an idea," Marty offered, ignoring Wolfe and Phil's skeptical expressions. "I'm sure Mom and Dad left Grace and me plenty of money. You're welcome to use my portion to buy an engine."

"That's the best offer I've had in a year," Wolfe said, smiling for the first time in two days. "They did leave you a good sum of money, but I put it into a trust fund until we find them or until you're twenty-one. I'm afraid it won't help us today."

"Even if we had the cash," Phil said, "I doubt we'd be able to find an engine for her. She's a pretty old bird."

Wolfe explained to Marty that their expedition money came from contract work. They hired themselves out to conduct scientific surveys for universities and governments. "And our next contract isn't until this summer. Until then, we have a slight cash-flow problem."

"What else is new?" Phil said.

"Where's the contract?" Marty asked.

"New Zealand. Look, Phil and I have to make some phone—"

"Will Grace and I be going with you?"

"Yes. We've been hired to help a research team to get a good look at a Kraken."

"What's that?"

"Giant squid, also known as *Architeuthis*." Wolfe and Phil started to walk away.

Marty followed. "Like the ones in the aquarium?"

"No, those are a very common species. Over the years a few giant squid have washed up on shore, but no one's ever been able to study a live specimen."

"Wow! New Zealand."

"Now, if you don't mind, I—"

"Sure," Marty said. "I'll just go poke around the island some more."

The rule about not exploring the island alone had been forgotten almost immediately—as Marty hoped it would be. Everyone was too busy getting things ready for the Congo trip to pay much attention to what Marty was doing (although Wolfe did periodically check in with him on the Gizmo to make sure he was okay). In fact, Marty had pestered everyone so much that, one morning, Phil gave him a helmet and a dented, but serviceable, four-wheeler.

"Here's the deal," Phil said before handing over the keys. "You have to spend at least six hours a day riding this thing, and I don't want you anywhere near the hangar when you're on it. You're a great kid, but we have a lot of work to do and you're driving everyone crazy. Do I make myself clear?"

"Yes, sir!" Marty gave him a salute.

"Then get outta here."

"Did you figure out what to do about the jet?"

"No. Now—"

"I'm outta here," Marty said.

The only place Marty had not gained access to was the second Quonset hut, known as QAQ—the Question and Answer Quonset—which is where all the R&D, research and development, was done for eWolfe. No one was allowed inside except Wolfe, his partner, Ted Bronson, and the half dozen scientists that worked on Ted's research team. Marty had waylaid each member of the team on their way into the building in an attempt to talk his way inside, or at least find out what they were doing in there. But they were a tight-lipped bunch with a very different look from the mechanics who worked in the jet Quonset with grease under their nails and whisker stubble on their faces. The QAQ gang carried heavy briefcases, wore thick glasses, and were uniformly pale, as if they didn't get much sun. Ted Bronson actually lived inside the QAQ and the rumor was that he had not stepped outside its doors in more than three years. When Marty asked Phil about the rumor, he said, "It's been longer than that."

Grace spent her time in the library, but she was not reading books. Laurel was teaching her to walk the high wire. The library floor was covered with mattresses to soften her many falls. She had managed to make it across the thin wire at six inches, a foot, and a foot and a half, but at two feet high she had yet to make it halfway across. She fell, over and over again, but she didn't mind. Laurel was teaching her a great deal more than how to balance on the thin wire.

"My mother was born under the big top and loved every aspect of the circus life," Laurel told her one day. "She tried her hand at acrobatics, the high wire, training bears—she was even shot out of a cannon a time or two—but her true love was the trapeze. I wish you could have seen her! When I was little I thought she could actually fly and wondered where she hid her wings when she was on the ground. But I learned that she didn't have wings." Laurel paused. "Her last performance went flawlessly until the finale—a quadruple somersault—a very difficult feat, but one she had completed a thousand times before. This time though, the catcher was a fraction of a second late. When she came out of the fourth rotation, his hands weren't there. She fell."

"Wasn't there a net?" Grace asked.

"Yes, but she only caught the very edge of it. It wasn't enough to stop her from hitting the ground."

"I'm so sorry."

Laurel gave her a wistful smile. "She died doing what she loved and what she was born to do. My father never got over it. He changed his clown makeup from a smile to a sad frown. And when the greasepaint was off, the sadness still remained. She was his life. It took me a long time to get over it, too. Before the fall, my parents had to watch me every second of the day. If they took their eyes off me, I would be out the trailer door, toddling beneath the elephants or trying to pet the kitties, which were actually lions and tigers."

Grace laughed.

"After the fall I stayed in our trailer most of the time, refusing to leave," Laurel continued. "It was the only place I felt truly safe. If the ringmaster hadn't forced my father to put me on the wire I don't know what would have happened to me."

"I think you would have been okay," Grace said. "You started out bold, then changed, and became bold again. I would never have crawled under an elephant or tried to pet a lion. I've always been afraid of things."

"Even when you were little?"

"Always."

Laurel gave her a thoughtful look. "What's your earliest memory?"

"That's easy. Marty climbing to the very top of my parents' floor-to-ceiling bookcase to get his bag of Halloween candy. It must have been twelve feet high."

"You were afraid he would fall."

"No," Grace said. "I was afraid he would fall on *me*."

Laurel laughed. "There's nothing wrong with a little fear. Being fearful can save your life—it's saved mine on more than one occasion—but too much fear can stop you from living." She stepped onto the wire and began walking forward and backward. "Just remember, it's all a matter of balance. One thing that helped me was to make a list of all my fears. I took them on one at a time. There are still a number of fears on that list, but it's gotten shorter over the years."

"How did you take them on?"

"I simply visualized myself overcoming the fear. The great thing about the technique is that you can practice whenever you want and wherever you are."

Laurel closed her eyes as she walked the wire. "Take deep breaths, relax, then confront the fear in the safety of your imagination. Remember what I taught you about gaze anchoring. Look at the wire in front of you, whether in your imagination as I'm doing now, or for real. Don't look down at your feet. Look beyond your fear at the goal. Try not to think about the steps."

In the evenings, Grace worked on her fear list in her Moleskine under the title *Fears du Jour*. The list was depressingly long, with her nightmare holding the number-one spot. But how do you confront a fear you can't remember? She wanted to talk to Laurel about this, but didn't know how to broach the subject without looking foolish.

Wolfe was considering taking a commercial flight to the Congo and putting Marty and Grace on another flight back to Switzerland. "We won't be able to bring much in the way of equipment," he told Laurel. "And of course, Bo and Vid will have to stay behind, but I don't know what else to do. We have to get to Lake Télé!"

If I don't tell her about the nightmare now, I might not get another chance, Grace thought. What if something happens to Laurel in the Congo? What if she decides to stay in the Congo? Her university job is gone. There's really nothing for her to come back to here. And what if Wolfe breaks his word and leaves us at the boarding school? Grace didn't think he would, but she wasn't certain. She hardly knew the man, and every time she had seen him the past few days he was off in another world. The few times they had spoken it had been painfully awkward for him. He either glanced at his watch and said he had something important to attend to, or he passed her off to someone else, like Bertha or Phil, and quickly disappeared.

"Laurel," Grace began. "I've been meaning to ask you about—"

The library door burst open. It was Wolfe. "Ted Bronson came through for us," he said breathlessly. "He and his crew spent the night fixing the engine."

"I thought you said it couldn't be fixed," Laurel said, still balancing on the wire.

"Ted's a genius. They manufactured new parts from old junk we had laying around the hangar."

"Will it be safe?"

"We just tested it. It works better than the other engines."

"When are we leaving?"

"Right now." He turned and left them, without a word about the mattresses on the floor or his new anthropologist on the wire.

Noah Blackwood stood in front of the newly opened giant panda exhibit at his Seattle Ark. He was surrounded by a group of reporters, city officials, and wealthy patrons.

"I have a little surprise for you," he announced, then nodded at his curator. The curator spoke into his two-way radio, and a hydraulic door began to slowly open in the back of the exhibit. At first nothing happened, then a small black-and-white head appeared in the open doorway. There was a gasp from the crowd.

"A baby panda!" someone shouted.

The reporter's cameras started clicking and whirring. A moment later a second head appeared, then a third.

"Three little surprises," Blackwood said with a smile as bright as the camera's strobes. "They were born at my Paris Ark six months ago."

"I thought the two pandas you had there were too old to reproduce," a reporter said.

"We thought so too," Blackwood agreed. "But I guess the special diet I developed revitalized them."

"Aren't triplets rare?"

"Unheard of . . . until now."

None of this was true. The three cubs had been flown in directly from China two weeks earlier. Blackwood had sent Butch McCall (his right-hand man) over there with enough cash to hire a poacher, and together they stole the three cubs from three different mothers. The money Blackwood had paid was nothing compared to the money he would make from the lines of people flocking to the Ark to see the black-and-white miracles.

"Why didn't you tell anyone about the birth before this?"

"The mother refused to raise her cubs, so I hand-raised them myself," Blackwood answered smoothly. "I kept it quiet to reduce the cubs' stress level. I felt their survival far outweighed any need for publicity." His cell phone rang. "Excuse me." He stepped away from the crowd to answer it.

"Wolfe has left the island," a man said.

"How?"

"In his jet."

"You told me the engine was beyond repair."

"Yeah," the man said. "But not beyond Ted Bronson's brain."

Blackwood shook his head in disgust. "Who's on the airplane?"

"His crew, the kids, and . . ." The man hesitated. "Dr. Laurel Lee."

Blackwood swore, a little too loudly, and several heads turned in his direction. He smiled them away and hissed into the phone, "When did she get to the island?"

"A few days ago. I didn't even know she was here. She's been up in the house most of the time."

"Where are they going?"

"According to their flight plan, the Congo, then up

to Switzerland. Wolfe and Dr. Lee are going to the Congo and the kids are being taken back to their school."

Blackwood swore again, then hung up, and made another phone call. When he finished he walked back over to the reporters. "I can take a small group of you into the exhibit for some close-ups if you like."

the flight 12

Subject: Give me a break!
From: luther_smyth@xlink.com
To: marty@ewolfe.com

Marty,

First of all you're a liar! Cryptos island, my butt! You had me going there for a minute, but when I read about the chimp you thought was Bigfoot, I knew you were putting me on. I printed your e-mail and handed it around to the other guys. Unfortunately, it fell into the hands of the head nose picker himself (aka Dr. Weasel). He called me into his office and told me to quit circulating this "ridiculous fiction" or he would take my e-mail privileges away. He still hasn't discovered our secret computer (the comic money is piling up and we should have enough to go to press soon). I think he's afraid we'll steal a boat and sail off to Cryptos, leaving a lot of empty dorm rooms and no tuition to pay for the upkeep of the school, and more important, the Weasel's salary.

It really bugs him that his number-one hooligan (aka you) is still disrupting things from thousands of miles away. (Speaking of bugs, they fumigated the school a couple of days ago for termites and we got a whole day off—just as you predicted.)

You should have seen the Weasel's face when he heard you were coming back! Which reminds me . . . I have some good news: the annual field trip to Teter's Dairy Farm is in a few days. The NP nearly canceled it in your honor, but the faculty talked him out of it. They assured him that there would be no "bull" this year.

Luther

P.S. Is your uncle serious about flying your friends to Cryptos whenever you want?

Marty answered Luther's e-mail from a seat aboard his uncle's private jet.

Subject: Re: Give me a break!
From: marty@ewolfe.com
To: luther_smyth@xlink.com

Luther,

I'll be careful what I say here just in case this falls into the boogered hands of the head NP himself.

As far as I know, Wolfe (my uncle) was very serious about flying our friends out to Cryptos. He has his own jet. It's a surplus Air Force bomber he's refitted as a transport. He keeps the jet in a gigantic hangar on Cryptos. And there's a runway long enough for a space shuttle to land on. The island was a secret military base during World War II. Wolfe got it in exchange for some work he did for the government. (I'd tell you what it was, but then I'd have to kill you. Just kidding. Everyone here is very tight-lipped about what the work was.)

I was telling you about Bertha and Phil Bishop . . . Well, I found out today that they're both ex-military. Phil was a Colonel in the Air Force and Bertha was an Army general. I'M NOT KIDDING! According to Phil, she was in the Rangers and knows 106 ways to kill a man with her bare hands. One thing for sure, I won't be complaining about her cooking when we get back to the island this summer. She stayed on Cryptos, but Phil is along with us, helping his daughter, Phyllis (aka Phil Jr.) fly the airplane. Phyllis is Wolfe's chief pilot and she was in the Air Force, too.

In addition to us humans, we have with us the chimp you thought I was lying about, a raven named Vid, and the pocket dog, who is just along for the ride. Grace and I have been put in charge of taking care of them.

Wolfe has enough supplies onboard to last him for years, including a Humvee, which he's using to get to Lake Télé. The jet isn't exactly first class. In fact, it's more like a flying school bus with bunk beds, but it seems to fly okay. Up by the cockpit is the communication room. It's manned by a half dozen geeks. They sit in this dark room with their eyes glued to color monitors. I'm not sure what they're monitoring. I've popped in a couple times and asked them what they're doing, but so far they've given me the boot. Speaking of which, there's a second Quonset on the island that is so top secret they won't even let me inside.

I know you're laughing right now, thinking I'm lying, so I've attached a digital photo of me in the cockpit with Phyllis and her dad. Also, I've attached a rough map of Cryptos (what I've seen of it anyway). I climbed up to the top of the inactive volcano on the west side of the island and discovered that you can get down into the crater. I didn't have time to go very deep, but when I get back to Cryptos I'm going to see where it leads. Check out the map.

And wait until you see the Gizmo. I thought I wrecked it when I went for my swim, but it's completely waterproof. How cool is that?

I'm going to head up to the cockpit and see if they need a hand flying this monster. I'll see you back at the cell after I land.

Marty

P.S. Looking forward to renewing old acquaintances at Teter's Dairy.

P.P.S. Wanna go deep-sea fishing in New Zealand this summer?

Marty closed the Gizmo and buttoned it in his shirt pocket. When he got to the cockpit he was surprised to see Wolfe in the pilot seat instead of Phyllis.

"I didn't know you were a pilot."

"I'm not nearly as good as Phyllis," Wolfe said. "Or her dad."

"Don't believe him," Phil said from the copilot's seat. "Your uncle's an ace."

Marty laughed and turned to Phyllis, who was sitting behind them typing commands into the navigation computer.

"We're going to make a supply drop at Lake Télé before we land at the airport," she explained. "It'll save Wolfe and Laurel from having to haul everything in on their backs."

"Supply drops aren't like they used to be when I was in command," Phil said.

Phyllis rolled her eyes. "Oh please, Dad, not again."

"I'm serious," Phil insisted. "It's all automatic now. The computer calculates the airspeed, the size of the chute, altitude, wind speed and direction, target—all of it. You don't even get to push the button anymore."

Phyllis grinned, then tapped Wolfe on the shoulder. "Everything's set. It's nap time for me. Think you can handle the controls for a while?"

"No problem," Wolfe said.

"If Dad starts getting on your nerves just hit the eject button."

"I heard that," Phil said.

"How are the animals?" Wolfe asked Marty.

"The last time I checked they were okay, but Bo is a little jumpy."

"She doesn't like being in a cage," Wolfe said. "And I don't blame her. We'll make it up to her when we get to Lake Télé."

Marty stayed for a while, then wandered down to the galley to make something to eat.

* * *

This airplane feels as if it's going to shake itself apart. My cursive looks like it was written with a palsied hand. And every time I try to talk to Laurel, she's with someone. We'll be to the Congo soon and I'll have missed my opportunity. . . . I should have talked to her back on Cryptos when I had a chance. . . . Back to fear du jour . . .

#99 Spiders with their eight spindly legs. Their webs sticking to your face and hair. Fangs that desiccate insects—bundling the dead in cocoons for lean days.

#100 Broken bones. Especially in my left hand . . . the one I write with, the one I'll do surgery with when I become a doctor.

#101 Escalators. Being pushed down one from behind. Or somehow being sucked down with the bottom step as it disappears into the floor.

I'm not sure what good this is doing me. . . .

#102 Smothering. I might want to move this one a little higher on the list. Maybe as high as . . .

Marty found Grace sitting at the conference table, scribbling in her Moleskine, with PD on her lap. She was wearing her school uniform. Marty was wearing a pair of cargo pants Wolfe had found for him, an old baggy shirt, and his baseball cap. He didn't want to disappoint Dr. Weasel when he arrived in Switzerland.

"You writing a novel?" he asked.

"Just trying to work some things out," Grace answered vaguely without looking up.

This meant she might be working on a quantum physics problem or venting her frustration at something annoying someone had said to her. Probably me, Marty thought. "What volume are you working on?"

"This is number forty-six."

The other forty-five completed diaries were under lock and key in the school's basement (or "dungeon" as Marty and Luther called it) awaiting a permanent shipping address. Grace's writing style had changed dramatically over the years. Her first few Moleskines were filled with carefully recorded events in perfect detail, with dates, times, people, and places. Now the words flowed from her mind onto the paper like a roaring stream, with little regard for punctuation or content.

"You should use your Gizmo to keep your diary," Marty suggested. "Save a few trees."

"I didn't even bring the Gizmo with me," Grace said as she continued to write. "I prefer using a real pen."

"Suit yourself." Marty pulled up a chair. "You and PD seem pretty tight."

"Not by choice," Grace said. "At least not my choice. She won't leave me alone."

"Maybe you can work your way up to a real animal someday."

"Very funny," Grace said, but that was precisely

why she was allowing PD to sit in her lap. Many of the fears on her list revolved around animals. She was not afraid of tiny poodles, but she thought that spending time with PD might be a tiny step in the right direction.

"This is the only way to fly, isn't it?" Marty continued. "Phyllis is a hoot. Did you know that she flew a bomber in the Gulf War? And Phil flew bombers in Vietnam. You should hear some of their stories. And did you know Wolfe is a pilot? He's flying the jet right this minute while Phyllis gets some sleep."

Grace sighed. When Marty wanted to have a conversation there was virtually no way to avoid it. She put her pen and Moleskine in her father's backpack. Using the backpack made her feel a little closer to her parents. "Have you seen Laurel?" she asked.

"Yeah. She's playing chess with one of the geeks, and I think she's winning."

Grace sighed again.

"Is everything okay?" Marty asked.

Grace shrugged. "I guess."

"You've been awfully quiet the last few days."

"What's unusual about that?"

"Nothing. It's just . . . well, you know, Mom and Dad and—"

"Everything's fine," Grace assured him. "As good as can be expected."

"I haven't had a chance to thank you for trying to

convince Wolfe to take us with him," Marty said.

"It was nothing. Besides, it didn't do any good."

"It's the thought that counts. And that's what surprised me. I thought you were dead set against going to Lake Télé."

"I was."

"What changed your mind?"

That was one of the questions Grace had been mulling over for the past few days. She still didn't have an answer. "Would you believe I just wanted to do something you wanted to do for a change?"

Marty laughed. "No."

"Well, it's true," Grace insisted. "At least, that's part of it. When I saw you lying on the shore, presumably dead, my first thought was, 'What's going to happen to me?' It was such an ugly, selfish thought. I was ashamed of myself. I realized that when it comes to you and me it's always *me*. Poor, little, frail Grace afraid of everything. You're always trying to protect me. It's time I did something about that. You're not my knight in shining armor, you're my brother."

Most of the time Marty enjoyed being Grace's knight. "More like tarnished armor," he said. "What's the other part of it?"

"The nightmare," Grace answered. "And the feeling, almost a premonition, that the mystery of the nightmare lies somewhere in the Congo."

"We could tell Wolfe about your premonition.

Maybe that would be enough to make him change his mind."

Grace shook her head. "I think it's best to leave everything the way it is. Back at school I'll have a chance to think things through a little more and maybe figure out what's going on."

Marty doubted it. Grace had been alternately fleeing from the nightmare and trying to remember what it was about her entire life. But he decided not to pursue the subject any further. He had adjusted to Wolfe's plan. After seven years at Omega Prep he could certainly stand a few more weeks. He looked at his watch. "We'd better check on the animals."

Grace and PD followed him through several bulkhead doors to the cargo hold at the rear of the airplane. As soon as they got there PD started running in circles and barking.

"I know how to stop that," Marty said confidently. He held his cargo pocket open and commanded in his best Travis Wolfe voice, "Snake!" PD continued running in circles barking. "Snake!" She slowed and eyed him suspiciously. Marty grabbed the tiny canine and stuffed her into his pocket. "That's more like it."

"The trick looked a little more impressive when Wolfe did it," Grace commented.

"The results are the same."

"Barely. Let's get this over with. I was in the

middle of something important when you interrupted me." She walked over to Vid's cage and picked up an overturned food tray from the floor.

Marty joined her. "That's weird."

"What?"

"The last time I was here I left a pile of chopped fruit on that tray. Now it's all gone." He looked past Vid's cage to Bo's. The chimp's door was wide open and she was nowhere in sight. "I didn't do it!"

"Then who did?" Grace asked, staring in horror at the open cage.

"Well . . ." Marty looked at the padlock. "I could have sworn I locked it last time I was in here."

"You let her out of her cage?"

"Just for a few minutes. She was going crazy."

"How could you—"

"It doesn't matter!" Marty said. "She's loose and we've got to get her back in the cage or Wolfe will never let me come back to Cryptos." PD jumped out of his pocket and started sniffing along the floor. "She's on to something! Follow her. I'll close the cargo door. We don't want Bo running amuck in the main cabin."

"Maybe we should get help," Grace said.

"Don't worry. I can handle this."

Grace wasn't so sure, but she didn't want to get Marty into trouble with their uncle. Reluctantly, she followed the mini bloodhound deeper into the cargo hold and watched in surprise as PD disappeared through an open hatch in the floor.

Marty came up behind his sister very, very quietly. "Boo!"

Grace nearly jumped out of her school uniform.

Marty laughed. "Payback for the library."

"That's not funny!"

"Yes, it is. What are you doing?"

"PD jumped down this hatch."

The opening was just big enough for a human to fit through, or a chimp. Marty got down on his knees and listened. He heard a faint hooting. "Unless PD can imitate a chimpanzee, I'd say our fugitive is somewhere below. I'll get some fruit and see if I can't tempt her out." He headed to the galley, leaving Grace to guard the hatch.

Grace did not like dark, confined spaces; in fact they were number thirty-nine on her list, which was why she was considering climbing down the hatch. *I took them on one at a time*, Laurel had said. Chimpanzees were not on the list, but Bo was. Grace was convinced that Bo did not like her.

Perhaps I can take on two fears at a time, she thought. Imitating Laurel, she closed her eyes and started taking deep, even breaths, while she imagined herself climbing down through the narrow opening into the darkness. Her skin became clammy with perspiration, her mouth turned to parchment, she felt her legs tremble. *Go!* she told herself. If you wait any longer, Marty will return and pop down the hole like a rabbit, and you'll have missed your chance to conquer number thirty-nine. She descended a short aluminum ladder and found herself in a compartment the size of a long closet, with very little headroom. Remarkably, it wasn't nearly as terrifying as her imagination had led her to believe. The warm air was thick with the oily smell of fuel and machinery, which was far from pleasant, but if she concentrated on her breathing she found she could endure the confinement.

Bo was at the far end of the compartment, straddling a round cylinder, eight or nine feet long and at least six feet around, that appeared to be covered with some kind of mesh. She was holding PD in the crook of her arm.

"What are you doing, Bo?"

Bo glanced up, gave Grace a quiet hoot, then went back to work. It looked like she was trying to unravel the mesh around the cylinder.

"Are you there?" Marty called down the hole. He was wearing his father's backpack, which he had grabbed from the conference table to carry the bananas, apples, and pears. The camp stove and Moleskine were in it, as well as the Frankenstein monkey.

"Yes," Grace yelled. "And Bo's here too. Bring a flashlight." She scooted closer to the busy chimpanzee.

Marty knew all about number thirty-nine, and he was shocked that his sister had gathered enough courage to climb through the hatch with a chimp below. He awkwardly made his way down the ladder with a small flashlight and crawled up behind her. "Did you fall down the hole?"

"Very funny," Grace said.

"Just asking." He shined the light past her and caught Bo in the beam. "What's she doing?"

"I think she's trying to disassemble the airplane."

"Perfect."

"Hand me the bananas," Grace said. She pulled one off and started to peel it very slowly. "Mmmm, mmmm, boy, do I love ripe bananas."

So did Bo. She grabbed the whole bunch out of Grace's hands.

"Hey! Give those back!" Grace made a lunge for the bananas, but Bo was too quick. She jumped backward out of reach. PD barked.

"Now what?" Marty asked, shining the flashlight on the munching chimpanzee.

"I guess we'll just have to wait her out. She'll get hungry."

"Not with six pounds of bananas in her hands."

"Good point. Maybe we can get them away from her."

Grace crawled slowly toward her with Marty right behind. Bo clutched the bananas to her chest. "I don't think this is going to . . ." A green light came on, followed by a loud alarm. "What is that?"

"Uh-oh," Marty said. *It's all automatic now. The computer calculates the airspeed, the size of the chute, altitude . . .* "I didn't do it!"

The floor beneath them disappeared.

free fall 13

Falling 18,000 feet was not on Grace's list, but she fainted anyway.

It wasn't on Marty's fear list either, but he would have put it on the list if he'd had one. As they dropped from the belly of the jet he managed to hook one arm through the mesh and grab his limp sister with the other. Out of the corner of his wind-blurred vision he saw something small and dark falling next to him. PD's ears were standing straight up and her little brown eyes were bulging out of her skull. The only way he could snag her was to free one of his hands. He looked up. The canister was dropping perpendicular, like a bomb, and Bo was perched on the very top, baring her teeth in a frozen-fear grimace. The mesh extended beyond the end of the canister where Bo was sitting, forming a shallow basket. If he could get Grace up there she would be relatively safe for the time being. He managed to get her over his shoulder and climbed to the top. Once there, he found several straps securing the canister. He quickly loosened one of them and cinched it around her waist. He wasn't worried about Bo. She was holding the mesh so tightly it would take a jackhammer to loosen her fingers and toes. PD was another story.

The little poodle was still hurtling toward earth— an activity Marty was no stranger to. The summer before, his father had secretly taken him skydiving. *If you tell your mother about this she will kill me,* he had said. Marty told no one about their secret outing, including Luther and Grace. He had done well on the course he had taken prior to his jumps. He looked at the rapidly approaching ground, estimating they had fallen about eight or nine thousand feet. In a few seconds a parachute would deploy. At least he *hoped* it would deploy.

He scrambled back down the side of the canister. PD had drifted out of easy reach. He hooked his feet into the mesh and leaned back with both arms outstretched, and to his delight, the canister inched toward the falling canine. It took him three tries, but he finally managed to grab PD's leg and pull her in. He stuffed her into his cargo pocket. As he was climbing back up he heard a loud *pop!* He braced himself. The parachute snapped open, jarring every bone in his body. He stared at the bright yellow canopy billowing above Grace and Bo, thinking it was about the most beautiful thing he had ever seen, but he didn't have time to appreciate his good luck.

Beneath them was a lush carpet of green trees that Marty knew would not feel like a carpet when they crashed through them. *Pick your landing spot with the utmost care,* his instructor had said. *The ground is the only part of the fall that can kill you.* There were several small lakes to the right. Marty didn't want to land in the water, but he figured it would be better than braking through tree limbs. He leaned out from the canister, and the parachute began to drift toward the largest of the lakes. Now all he had to do was wake Grace so she wouldn't drown when the canister hit the water and sank. He started back up to the top to do just that, when a terrifying word popped into his mind. That word was *crocodiles*. A few months earlier, he and Luther had watched a documentary on the fourteen-foot-long carnivorous reptiles with one hundred and sixty sharp teeth. *They store their victims under water until the meat is soft enough for them to tear off and gulp down in chunks,* the gnarly television host had commented. *Tenderize 'em in the sun till they're like butter. And the Congo is crawlin' with big crocs.* At the time, Marty would have given just about anything to see a living, breathing crocodile. Not anymore. The lake below looked like a pot of soup stock awaiting its main ingredients: two humans with a dash of chimp and a pinch of poodle dropped in for flavor.

Marty undid Grace's strap and shook her. "Wake up!" She didn't move. Grace could swim like a fish. Without her, he wouldn't be able to help Bo and PD to shore. And if there were hungry crocodiles in the lake . . . "You gotta wake up!" He slapped her. Her eyelids didn't even flicker. They were within seconds of splashing down. He grabbed her by the arm and was on the verge of jumping off, when a gust of hot humid air came out of nowhere, catching the chute and pushing the canister across the surface like a Jet Ski. "All the way to shore!" Marty shouted, punching the air with both fists in encouragement. "Go, baby, go!" He probably should have been holding on, because twenty feet from shore the canister slammed into a submerged log. Marty was catapulted into the air and did two complete somersaults before doing a belly flop in the waist-deep, brackish water. He got to his feet, coughing and spitting and scooping the mud out of his eyes, just in time to see the parachute drag the canister ashore. He was relieved to see Grace still attached. The canister lingered for a moment just above the ground, giving Bo a chance to jump off and disappear into the trees.

"Wake up, Grace!" Marty sputtered, watching in horror as a gust of wind started lifting the canister straight up into the air. "No!" He struggled forward, hindered by the ooze sucking at his sneakers. "Wake up! Jump!" Grace did not wake up, but a very large crocodile did. It slithered into the water fifty yards to his right. As he stared in dismay at the flesh-gulping reptile, he felt something nibbling on his thigh, and nearly fainted himself, until he remembered that crocodiles don't nibble. "PD!" He reached into his cargo pocket and pulled the gasping poodle out. "Jeez, I'm really sorry. I . . ." He looked back at the crocodile, which had, alarmingly, cut the distance between them and its resting place in half. "We're outta here!"

They reached shore just ahead of the crocodile, but well behind the canister. It had disappeared above the tree canopy and headed east. Marty ran several dozen yards, stopped to catch his breath, then threw up.

the parrot 14

Grace thought she was having a dream. She was lying on soggy ground beneath the branches of an incredibly tall tree. Perched on the lowest branch, looking down at her with great curiosity, was a gray parrot with a red tail. She stood and brushed the dead leaves and mud off her uniform skirt.

Of all my dreams, she thought, this is by far the most vivid.

The air was thick and hot and smelled like rotting fruits and vegetables. Long eerie fingers of fog drifted just above the ground as if hunting for something. Insects swarmed and the trees were alive with the songs and calls of concealed animals. Despite all this, Grace was not overly concerned. After all, it was just another dream.

Or was it? Perhaps she was having some kind of premonition. It wouldn't be the first time she'd had one.

Maybe her parents were calling to her from the Amazon—it certainly looked like the Amazon—and she had found a window or portal to find them. She tried to remember what had happened just before she woke under the tree.

Yes, she remembered. Marty and I were searching for Bo down a hatch in Wolfe's cargo hold. Bo snatched the bananas from me. I must have bumped my head, because the back of it is a little sore and so is my left arm. Marty will shake me awake in a moment, but I hope he waits until I have a chance to look around a little.

The parrot fluttered to the ground and started picking through the leaves, then lunged for her shoelace with its black beak and began tugging on it. "That worm is attached to my foot, little bird," Grace said. The parrot stopped the hopeless tug-of-war, fixed its beady eyes on her, and let out a piercing shriek. Grace covered her ears. "That is very annoying." The parrot yanked on her shoelace again, and Grace took a step forward to stop it from tearing the lace off. The parrot continued pulling, until Grace had taken several steps from where she had fallen. "All right, I give up," Grace said. "I'll follow you, but I hope you're leading me to my parents."

Wolfe relinquished the pilot's seat to the rested Phyllis Bishop. "We've made pretty good time."

"The tailwind helped." Phyllis said. "Unfortunately, Dad and I will be fighting a headwind all the way up to Switzerland." She started the procedure for their initial descent into the Congo.

"I'll go back and make sure Grace and Marty are buckled in." Wolfe turned to leave the cockpit and nearly bumped into a panicked Laurel Lee.

"They're gone," she shouted.

"Who's gone?"

"Marty and Grace."

"Impossible!" Wolfe said. "They must be hiding."

Laurel shook her head. "I don't think so. Bo and PD are gone too."

Marty staggered, tripped, and fell through the thick green tangle in an easterly direction, hoping to find his sister in one piece and to put as much distance between himself and the crocodile as he possibly could. After fighting his way for a quarter of a mile, the word STOP floated to the surface of his addled brain. He sat down to catch his breath. PD jumped out of his pocket and started sniffing around.

"Watch out for snakes," he warned her. "*Real* snakes."

PD ignored him.

"Fine." He turned his attention back to STOP, which was an acronym for: Stop, Think, Observe, Plan—a concept taught to him in every survival course he had ever taken. *Stop*. He was already stopped except for his flailing arms swatting at the insects trying to eat him alive. *Think*. I have just fallen out of a jet at 18,000 feet and I *think* I'm lucky to be alive. *Observe*. I'm in the middle of a treacherous jungle filled with vicious insects, hungry crocodiles, and a teacup poodle. He felt his head. And I've lost my favorite baseball cap. *Plan*. I've got to find Grace. If she wakes up suddenly, she'll probably fall off the canister. If the fall doesn't kill her, something in the jungle will. He started trudging forward again and was nearly beheaded when the chain around his neck caught on a branch. The Gizmo! It was buttoned in his shirt pocket. He turned it on and touched Grace's name with the stylus. The blue square was moving. She was either riding the canister, walking, or a large carnivore was dragging her to its dank, smelly lair.

He touched the *Show All* button. A world map appeared, peppered with dozens of colored squares—most of which Marty didn't recognize. Wolfe seemed to have people, or at least tracking tags, all over the world, and he was happy to see that a number of them were flashing in Brazil—presumably people searching for his parents. Below the map was a *Zoom* button. He touched it.

Please select geographic location. . . .

He chose the Congo, then zoomed in on his gray square. In his immediate vicinity were Grace's blue square, Bo's purple square, PD's pink square, and a stationary yellow square the same shade as the parachute, which he guessed was the canister. Grace was now moving away from him *and* the canister. He zoomed in a bit closer and a detailed map appeared. He estimated that he was no more than two miles away from her, but in between them were swamps, streams (acres of quicksand, no doubt), and nothing that remotely resembled a road or trail. He wished he had a machete, or better yet, a chain saw. He also wished his sister would stay put until he reached her. Where was she going?

Grace didn't know where she was going, but the parrot was obviously leading her someplace. It had given up on her shoelace and was flying from branch to branch, waiting for her to catch up, screeching loudly when she dawdled. She had stepped over two very large snakes (fear number twelve) without the slightest trepidation. She had walked under a flock of roosting bats as big as house cats (fear number forty-three) and actually paused to observe them for a moment without any anxiety. The humid air filled her with a comfortable warmth. Moving along the soft mist-covered ground was like walking on clouds. She wondered if this was how Marty felt all the time.

Two hours later, Marty drew to within shouting distance of his wandering sister. As he stopped to check the map on the Gizmo, it beeped, and the map was replaced by his uncle's anxious face.

"Marty!"

"I didn't do it!" Marty said.

Wolfe was too overcome with emotion to respond to Marty's denial. He broke down sobbing. And he was not the only one. They were offscreen, but it sounded like Laurel, Phyllis, and even tough old Phil, were shedding a few tears. It went on for over a minute, then Wolfe wiped his eyes and got down to business. "What happened? How did you and Grace get separated? Is she all right?"

Marty quickly related the story of their fall, omitting Grace's fainting, the crocodile, and his puking—no need to upset his uncle more than he already was.

"You'll have to find her before dark," Wolfe said.

Duh *du jour*, Marty thought. "No problem. How soon will you be here to pick us up?"

Wolfe frowned. "I'm afraid it's not as simple as that."

"What do you mean?"

Wolfe explained.

The gray parrot led Grace down a narrow winding path carved through thick green foliage. The tangled branches blotted out the sun, grabbed her blouse, and snagged her skirt. Despite her belief that she was still having a dream or premonition of some sort, doubt began to take hold of her. She stopped. Is it really leading me to my parents?

The parrot let out an angry shriek and hopped farther down the animal trail, disappearing into the darkness ahead. "I'm not going with you," she called after it. "I'm tired of this dream."

"Yeah . . . well, you'd better get used to it."

Grace turned and was astounded to see Marty standing behind her, looking rumpled and exhausted.

"How did you get here?"

"I fell out of the jet with you and Bo and . . ." He pulled an exhausted poodle out of his pocket.

Grace's mouth dropped open. "Did you just say we *fell* out of the jet?"

Marty nodded.

"Where are we?"

"The Congo," Marty answered and stepped forward, fully expecting Grace to faint again, but she didn't. And this was not his only surprise. Aside from a few little tears in her uniform blouse, his sister looked remarkably well. She was barely sweating and she didn't appear to have a single insect bite on her. Marty was covered in scrapes and itchy welts, and the insects were still trying to devour him, one nip at a time.

"So it's not a dream," Grace whispered.

"I wish it was." Marty adjusted the straps of his father's backpack, which were digging into his shoulders.

Grace was disappointed that she was not on the track of her parents, but she was also elated that she had just taken a walk through the jungle with virtually no apprehension. In fact, she was still feeling relatively calm, in spite of Marty's news of how they had gotten here. She was beginning to wonder if her walk had really happened.

"You're taking this a lot better than I thought you would," Marty said.

"I guess I am. The last thing I remember is you and me going down the hatch to retrieve Bo."

Marty thought back to the fall and gave an involuntary shiver despite the heat. "It's just as well," he said, then went on to explain what had happened, emphasizing how he had saved her and PD, and ending with the croc trying to eat him and the poodle for lunch.

"Thanks for saving me," she said.

"Just another day in the life of a knight in tarnished armor."

Grace actually smiled at his joke, which made Marty a little nervous. There was something different about her, and it wasn't just the absence of insect bites.

"Where's Bo?" she asked.

"I haven't seen her since she jumped. Wolfe says there's a spare dog whistle in the canister. We're supposed to call her and put on the video harness."

"You've talked to Wolfe?"

Marty held up the Gizmo. "Face-to-face, more or less."

"What did he say?"

"He wasn't mad, if that's what you mean."

"That's not what I mean. When's he going to pick us up?"

"We'd better get moving." He turned around and started back down the path.

"Marty?"

"A week," he said casually. "No big deal."

Grace ran to catch up with him. "Like, in seven days?"

"They can only take the Humvee as far as the Ubangi River," Marty answered. "After that they have to walk to Lake Télé. He's pretty sure they'll get here faster than a week, but he wants us to prepare for the worst."

"Can't they send someone in to pick us up sooner?" Grace asked. "A rescue team?"

Marty sighed. "I asked Wolfe about that, and there's a little problem. He and Laurel are here illegally. We are too. He didn't have time to get a visa or a permit to go to Lake Télé. That would have taken

156

weeks, and he doesn't think he would have gotten one anyway. If the government finds us here we'll be arrested and put in jail. I guess they're having some kind of a revolution."

"Revolution?"

"Don't worry, it won't affect us out here."

Grace was still having difficulty sorting out what was real and what wasn't. "When you found me, did you see a parrot?"

Marty shook his head.

"It's about the size of a crow, but light gray with a red tail."

"I didn't see it. Why?"

I must be losing my mind, she thought. "It's not important. What are we supposed to do for a week? How are we going to live out here?"

"The canister's full of supplies." Marty slapped a rather large insect that landed on his arm. "And bug juice. Tomorrow morning we're going for a little hike through the jungle. Wolfe wants us to go to a place called the Skyhouse."

Grace looked around in bewilderment. "And where's that?"

Marty shrugged. "Somewhere in the Goblin Universe."

Wolfe and Laurel drove for more than twelve hours straight before getting stuck in the middle of a river. Laurel stood on the Humvee's roof, keeping an eye out for crocodiles, while Wolfe waded to the other side with the winch cable over his shoulder. He hooked it around a stout tree and gave Laurel a thumbs-up. She engaged the winch, and the Humvee inched its way to the opposite bank.

"That wasn't so bad." Wolfe wiped the mud from his face and began feeding the cable back onto the winch spool. "If I recall, we have three more rivers to cross before we get to the Liboko village. We should be there by tomorrow afternoon."

"Four more rivers," Laurel corrected. "And you'd better let me drive. You haven't slept all night."

"All right," Wolfe said, climbing into the passenger seat. "But I'm not sure I'll be able to sleep."

"Marty has things under control."

"He's only thirteen."

Laurel eased the Humvee up the steep bank and managed to find the road, which was little more than a rutted, slippery scar cut through the dense green. "A very resourceful and resilient thirteen," she said. "I've never seen anyone recover from hypothermia and a near drowning faster than Marty did at the lake. He shook it off like a cold shower."

"He's tough," Wolfe said. "But Little Grace isn't made the same."

"She doesn't like to be called *Little* Grace," Laurel corrected gently. "And I wouldn't be so sure about what she's made of. She's every bit as tough as Marty, but in a different way."

"You might be right," Wolfe admitted. "She did seem to be in pretty good spirits when we talked to her last night."

A few bumpy miles passed in silence, then Laurel said, "If you're determined to stay awake, you might as well talk to me so that I don't fall asleep. Tell me how Dr. Travis Wolfe became a cryptid hunter."

Wolfe continued staring through the windshield. "In a roundabout way my father was responsible. He was a big-game hunter."

"You mean as in lions, tigers, and—"

"Bears, oh my." Wolfe laughed mirthlessly. "And many other animals as well. I spent most of my childhood in the field, helping him pursue his trophies."

"He sounds uncomfortably like Noah Blackwood."

"He should. Blackwood and my father knew each other. In fact, they were members of the same club."

Laurel glanced at him in surprise. "What club?"

"A very exclusive club. So secret it doesn't have a name, and I couldn't tell you for sure how many people are in it, or who they are."

"The club still exists?"

Wolfe nodded. "My father took me to one of the meetings when I was seventeen years old, and that's where I met Noah Blackwood for the first time. It was at the Seattle Ark. Back then the club was made up mostly of trophy hunters, like my father. They got together once a year to talk about their hunts and complain about how the environmentalists were ruining things for them. In my father's defense, just before he died, he had a change of heart about all this. He could see what was happening to the animals and places he loved, and he didn't like it."

"How far back did Noah and your father's friendship go?"

"Years. But they had a falling out after Blackwood showed up at one of the meetings with a Thylacine."

"A Tasmanian Wolf?" Laurel was shocked. "Alive?"

"Barely," Wolfe said.

"But I thought the last Tasmanian Wolf was killed sixty years ago."

"So did everybody else. I wasn't there, but apparently it caused quite a stir. The animal didn't live long enough for Blackwood to put it on public display, but it sure whetted the club members' appetites. There was a shift in their attitudes. They lost interest in big trophy animals and began hunting endangered animals instead. Size no longer mattered. They liked their meat rare. My father and some of the other old-timers dropped out. After this, the club became even more secretive because some of the animals they were hunting were protected."

"Not all of them?" Laurel asked.

Wolf shook his head. "You can't protect something that isn't supposed to exist. People might get upset if you shot a Bigfoot, but in most places it isn't against the law. This is one of the reasons I'm searching for cryptids. Proving that a cryptid exists is the first step toward getting legal protection for it.

"But Blackwood took it a step further. He realized that the trophies were worth more alive than dead. He started sending out bounty hunters with tranquilizer darts instead of bullets. When the animal dies, Blackwood gets the skin anyway, so why not make money while it's still breathing? People will stand in line for hours and pay just about anything to get a glimpse of something strange or rare. He's made millions on the animals he's collected before putting them in his private dioramas."

Laurel shook her head in dismay. "So the public pays for his collecting."

"They pay for a lot more than that. I can't prove it, but I think he's trying to clone animals. He might even be trying to make new animal species."

"Is that possible?" Laurel asked.

"Most people don't think so," Wolfe admitted. "But I'm not so sure. Have you ever heard of *El Chupacabra*?"

"The so-called goat sucker of Puerto Rico and Mexico? I thought that was a hoax."

"I've looked at the evidence and some of it's pretty convincing," Wolfe said. "But if the Chupacabra exists, it's not like any animal that's ever preceded it, which makes me suspect that it was manufactured in a laboratory."

"But why?"

"The answer is simple. Money. People would line up for miles to see something like that. I wouldn't put it past him to make a Chupacabra in his lab, then let it go for a while to build the myth, then recapture it and put it on display in one of his arks.

"I'm all for scientific advances, but I'm afraid that the breakthroughs are coming so fast, we haven't had time to consider the moral and environmental consequences of our cleverness.

"The egg you sent to them wouldn't have enough DNA to work with, but if Blackwood could get his hands on a fresh egg—or fresh sauropod tissue—who knows what he could do with it? With the DNA, he might be able to clone a sauropod for each of his six parks. And Mokélé-mbembé doesn't have to be alive for him to use its DNA. A bit of flesh might do the job."

"I don't understand how you could have worked for him," Laurel said. "It couldn't have been for money alone. You don't seem the type."

"There was another reason," Wolfe said. "A very important reason." He stared out the windshield in silence for another half mile before turning back to Laurel. "At seventeen I wasn't that interested in the club. A bunch of old guys sitting around smoking cigars, talking about their hunting conquests wasn't my idea of a stimulating vacation. I loved my father and the chase, but for me, getting close to the animal was enough, which was a big disappointment to my father. Anyway, I spent the three days we were at Noah's Ark wandering around the exhibits talking to the keepers. During one of my rounds I met a beautiful girl. And my life has never been the same."

jungle breakfast   16

Subject: Where are you?
From: luther_smyth@xlink.com
To: marty@ewolfe.com

Marty,

The whole dorm stayed up waiting for your arrival last night. About 2 A.M. the head nose picker pulled up in front of the school, slammed the door to the van, stomped inside, then slammed the door to his living quarters. There was something very important missing from the van, namely—THE O'HARA TWINS! What happened?

Looks like you're going to miss the annual . . . that's right, you guessed it. DAIRY DAY! Stop crying.

Luther

Marty answered Luther's e-mail while he waited for the freeze-dried eggs and vegetables to cook.

Subject: Re: Where are you?
From: marty@ewolfe.com
To: luther_smyth@xlink.com

Luther,

I don't have time for a long explanation here, because Grace and I are about to head off into an unexplored and hideously dangerous jungle.

The short of it is that we fell out of Wolfe's jet. Stop laughing. I'm serious. As we were trying to catch the chimp in the cargo hold, we got dropped into the Congo along with Wolfe's supply canister. Luckily, it had a parachute and we're okay.

I mean it, Luther, stop laughing. It's not funny. I just spent a miserable night with about 6 billion insects drilling for my blood despite the mosquito netting and the insecticide bath I took before climbing into my hammock.

When I reached for my socks this morning, I found them covered with butterflies. I'M NOT KIDDING! Have you ever tried to get a hundred clinging butterflies off your socks without hurting them? It's not easy. Grace said they were attracted to the odor, but I think she's wrong.

She didn't have any butterflies on her socks, and we all know how her feet smell.

To top this off, as I was pulling on my socks I discovered a school of bloodsucking leeches on my legs (and a couple other places I don't want to mention in case this e-mail is intercepted by the head NP himself). Grace, on the other hand, seems to have insecticide for blood. Bugs hate her. Go figure.

Anyway, we're heading to a place called the Skyhouse to wait for Wolfe and Laurel. They expect to meet us there in about a week or so. I guess they didn't want to take the same shortcut Grace and I took to the Congo. I don't blame them. Wolfe says that Phil is looking into a way of getting us out of here sooner, but he's doubtful it will work out. So, it doesn't look like we'll be returning to school anytime soon, if at all.

In a while crocodile . . . (Actually, I saw six of the brutes yesterday while I was looking for Grace. They were all puny . . . around 12 feet long.) You should have seen the one that tried to eat me. I'M NOT KIDDING!

Bwana Marty

Marty folded the eggs over (wishing he had some Tabasco and extra-sharp cheddar), then touched the last leech with a hot stick from the fire and watched it drop from his ankle and sizzle in the coals. He looked over at Grace lying in her hammock, writing in her Moleskine, which was a little soggy from his splashdown and sticky with smashed bananas and pears. PD was curled up next to her. They looked as if they were resting in someone's backyard instead of a steaming jungle. Marty shook his head in wonder. The girl in the hammock looked like his sister and sounded like his sister, but she sure wasn't acting like his sister. For instance, when he confessed that he knew about the supply drop before they fell, Grace did not get angry. She merely smiled and said it made no difference, she would have ended up in the Goblin Universe eventually anyway. When he told her the Skyhouse was a tree house, Grace actually laughed and said, "You Tarzan, me Jane." He was beginning to wonder if the bump on the head she got when she slipped off the canister had caused brain damage. "Eggs are ready," he called over to her.

Grace barely heard him.

Something very strange is happening to me. Yesterday I stepped over snakes and under bats without the slightest fear. Of course, I thought I was having a dream, but still. . . .

After the fall, Marty followed my trail and confirmed everything I saw except for the curious gray parrot, who I believe now was a figment of my imagination. Wild parrots do not lead people through the jungle.

And this morning I still feel good, a little nervous, perhaps, but not frightened. I slept through the entire night without waking, no nightmare, no . . .

Marty blew the silent dog whistle loud enough for Grace to hear it. Reluctantly, she closed her Moleskine and told him she was coming.

"Good," Marty said. "Because your eggs are getting cold. But that's not why I blew the whistle." He blew it again and looked up in the trees.

Grace then remembered the fourth member of their marooned party. She got out of her hammock, put PD on the ground, and joined Marty at the smoldering fire. "Do you think she heard?"

"Everything within five miles heard," Marty answered. He showed Grace the purple square on the Gizmo. "As you can see, she's not moving, which means she's probably still sleeping. Wolfe told me that Bo always sleeps in. Speaking of which, how did you sleep last night?"

"Good."

"What about the bugs?"

"There weren't any under my netting."

"Well, your netting wasn't soundproof. What about the noise?" Marty had found the jungle incredibly loud with buzzing insects, calling birds,

screaming monkeys, and an assortment of uniden-
tified skitterings, rustlings, and mysterious grunts.
He spent the entire night clutching the handle of
the machete he had found in the canister.

"I don't know why," Grace said, "but the sounds
were somehow soothing. Isn't that strange?"

Marty felt ants dancing on his neck again, but
this time they were real. He brushed them off.
"What I think is strange is that you don't have a
single insect bite."

"I have a couple," Grace said. "But you're right,
the insects don't seem to bother me as much as they
do you." She glanced at Marty's legs and was alarmed
to see rivulets of blood running down them. "What
happened?"

"Leeches," Marty said. "No big deal."

"It will be a huge deal if the wounds ulcerate and
turn septic, which is very likely in the tropics. You
could die, Marty."

"Okay, doctor."

Wolfe had included a well-equipped medical kit in
the canister, with bandages, scalpels, sutures, pain-
killers, antibiotics, tranquilizers, sleeping pills,
malaria pills, sunscreen . . . everything a real doctor
would need. Marty periodically blew the whistle
while Dr. Grace tended his wounds, but there was still
no sign of Bo. He checked the Gizmo. "She's in the
same spot. I guess we'll just have to take her harness

and put it on her when she decides to join us."

Grace finished disinfecting the wounds on his legs. "Are there any more?"

"A couple," Marty admitted. "But I'll take care of them myself." He disappeared into the brush with the antiseptic.

While he tended his private wounds, Grace ate her eggs and thought about their situation. She had talked to Wolfe briefly on the Gizmo the night before. He'd told her he didn't know exactly how long it would take Marty and her to reach Lake Télé and the Skyhouse. "It depends on how many swamps you have to go around to get there," he had said. "But don't worry, you won't get lost. The Gizmo will lead you right to it, and of course, we'll be monitoring your position. If you get confused, I'll get you back on track."

Grace didn't think it was possible to become more confused then she already was. "When's the last time you were at the Skyhouse?" she had asked.

"It's been nearly eleven years," Wolfe answered quietly.

"That seems like an awfully long time. Are you sure the house is still there?"

"Yes . . . uh . . . well . . . hang on, Laurel can tell you."

At least he's consistent, Grace thought. She was growing accustomed to her uncle's awkward manner.

"Hi, Grace," Laurel said. "Masalito showed me to the Skyhouse just before I left Lake Télé. He's been keeping an eye on it over the years. It's not exactly a luxury hotel suite, but it will do in a pinch. How are you holding up?"

Grace was happy to see Laurel, even if it was only on a two-inch screen. "I feel . . . it's difficult to describe, but if we were back in the library I think I could walk the wire backward with my eyes closed."

"Goodness," Laurel said. "That's a change."

"I know," Grace said. "And it has me a little worried."

"Don't forget that the wire is thin," Laurel said. "You still have to be very careful when you're on it."

Grace would have liked to pursue the subject further, but Laurel's image began bouncing violently.

"Rough road?"

"You've got that right," Laurel said. "I'd better shut this down and find something to hang on to."

As Grace finished her last bite of eggs and vegetables, Marty emerged from the bushes. He put the first-aid kit in the small backpack, next to the camp stove and Monkey.

"Let's check and see where Wolfe and Laurel are," Grace suggested.

Marty clicked their names. "They're about a hundred and fifty miles from the Ubangi River and they're . . . Hey! The Vid cam's on."

The twins' birds-eye view of the Humvee bumping along a muddy road was interrupted by Bo wandering into their makeshift camp wearing Marty's baseball cap. Marty was delighted to see both the chimp and the cap. "It looks better on me," he said, snatching it off her head and putting it on his own. Bo picked up PD, then scooted over to the fire and started rummaging through the ashes for breakfast scraps. "If you had come the first time I called, I would have made you your own plate."

"She doesn't look as if she's starving," Grace observed. "Her stomach's as tight as a drum."

It did have a satisfied bulge to it. Marty looked through the canister and found the video harness along with some spare Gizmo batteries. He stuffed the batteries into a large backpack he had been loading all morning for their trip to the Skyhouse. In it he had freeze-dried food, energy bars, a water purifier, rope, canteens, rain tarps, matches, a flashlight, mosquito netting, extra pants, shirts, socks, underwear (Grace had changed into a set of Laurel's spare clothes, which were too big for her), a knife, binoculars, fishing line, hooks, and various other essential items. The pack was getting so heavy, Marty was beginning to wonder if he should have just tied ropes to the canister and dragged it through the jungle to the Skyhouse. He was also wondering how easy it was going to be to get Bo strapped into her harness.

Wolfe said Bo sometimes was not in the mood for the camera. He looked at Grace's disheveled black hair and remembered something he had seen on a chimpanzee documentary. "We need something to distract Bo while I get this thing on."

"Such as?" Grace asked.

"Your hair," Marty answered.

"I beg your pardon?"

"If you were to sit down next to her I bet she'd start grooming your head."

Grace wasn't thrilled with the idea. The last time she had gotten within arm's length of Bo, she had fallen from a jet. "I don't think my head needs grooming."

"Actually, it does," Marty corrected. "Have you looked in a mirror lately? Your head looks like a dust mop."

"Yours doesn't look much better," Grace said indignantly, but she walked over to the foraging chimp. Bo stopped what she was doing and gave Grace the stink-eye. "Now what?"

"Sit down with your back to her," Marty said.

"You're kidding."

Marty shook his head.

"She doesn't like me."

"I've noticed," Marty said. "But we have to get the harness on her so Wolfe can keep an eye on us."

Grace took a deep breath and sat down next to

her. "If she attacks me, use your machete on her."

"I promise," Marty assured her.

"What makes you think this will work?"

"It's kind of a social thing chimps do," Marty said.

"Like, you scratch my back, I'll scratch yours?"

"Yeah, something like that. Actually, they pick lice and ticks out of one another's fur and eat them, which is beneficial to the groomer and the groomee, I suppose."

"She's not going to find any lice or ticks on me."

"That's okay. By the look of her belly she doesn't have room for a tick."

Bo put PD down on the ground and peered intently at the back of Grace's head.

"What's she doing?"

"Just sit still." Marty quietly moved up behind Bo with the harness and sat down. He started to gently groom Bo's neck and back, and after a while, Bo started to groom Grace.

"Ouch! That hurts," Grace complained. "She's pulling hard intentionally."

"Don't be such a baby." Marty found a few crawling things dashing through Bo's thick fur, but he wasn't sure if they were lice or not. He waited for the chimp to relax a little, then eased the harness over her shoulders. Bo gave him a sharp look, but she seemed content to dig through Grace's mane and didn't resist. He buckled the straps and turned the tiny camera on, then stood and touched the video icon on the Gizmo. A perfect picture of thick black fingers flitting through Grace's hair appeared on the screen.

"Can I get up now?"

"Sure."

Grace got to her feet. "Is my scalp bleeding?"

Marty laughed. "Not too badly." He started taking down her hammock, wondering how he was going to get it into his backpack. Grace was having the same problem getting her Moleskine into their father's pack. "Maybe you should leave it behind," Marty suggested.

"I noticed that you managed to get your sketch-book and pencils into your pack." Grace wedged her Moleskine into the little pack and put her fountain pen into the pocket of Laurel's pants. Marty handed her a hat from the canister. "What's this for?"

"Your head," Marty answered. "I know the insects seem to be terrified of you, but all it takes is one bite from an infected mosquito and you'll get malaria." He took a piece of netting he had cut out, draped it over his head, and scrunched his baseball cap on top of it.

"That reminds me." Grace dug the first-aid kit back out and found the vial with the malaria pills. She shook one out into Marty's palm. "We have to take one a week."

After he choked the pill down, Grace followed her brother into the shadowy jungle.

the liboko village 17

Marty and Grace watched with envy as Bo swung through the branches overhead, sporadically swooping down to grab PD and take her for a joyride through the lush green canopy. Below, where the twins were, was not nearly as pleasant—with thorns stabbing their skin, vines tripping their feet, and the boggy ground trying to swallow them. For the first few hours, Marty was able to keep up a running monologue about the hippos, elephants, monkeys, and the other animals they came across from his vast store of memorized wildlife documentaries. After a while though, he fell silent. It was all he could do to swing the machete and keep the sweat bees from crawling under his netting and up his nose. Every half hour or so they stopped to catch their breath, drink water, and check their location on the Gizmo. By early evening they were less than halfway to the Skyhouse.

Marty sat down in an exhausted heap and pulled his second bottle of insect repellent from the pack. "You know," he said, slathering the smelly juice on his face beneath the netting, "if I were to jump in that swamp I bet the amount of poison on my skin would kill every fish in there . . . crocs, too." He was certain that under her netting, Grace was the same sweaty mess as he was. She lifted the veil to take a drink a water. She was barely sweating. "What's the matter with you?"

"I'm carrying the little pack, and I haven't been swinging a machete all day."

Marty thought that by this time he would be carrying her as well as the big pack. "That doesn't quite explain it, does it?" He wiped his face with a dry shirt and wrung it out. "If I were stark naked, carrying nothing, I'd still be sweating like Victoria Falls. Maybe you haven't noticed, but it's a little hot in the jungle."

"I've noticed," Grace admitted with a worried expression. "Ever since we got here something strange has been happening to me."

"Like what?"

"I can't explain it. I just feel . . ." She tried to think of the right word. "Comfortable, I guess."

"In that case, you can use the machete when we . . ." A branch cracked to their right. Marty put his finger to his lips and the binoculars to his eyes. "Unbelievable," he whispered. "It's an okapi with a calf." He handed the binoculars to Grace.

About fifty yards away was the most unusual animal Grace had ever seen. It had a long muscular neck, big ears, a beautiful sable brown body, and striped legs. "It looks like a short giraffe."

"That's because it's related to the giraffe," Marty said. "The Pygmies hunt them for their meat and skin. It didn't become known to science until the nineteen hundreds. The first live okapi reached Europe in 1918. Before that nobody believed they existed. Sound familiar?"

"Sounds like another one of your wildlife documentaries," Grace answered.

"It is, but that's not what I was getting at. The okapi was a cryptid until somebody discovered it."

Grace handed the binoculars back to him. "There's a big difference between a giraffe and a dinosaur."

"Laurel said if we saw this area we'd understand how a dinosaur could hide out for millions of years."

Grace looked at their surroundings—the giant trees draped with thick lianas filled with chattering monkeys and birds, the soft sunlight-dappled ground covered with ferns and palms—she didn't think that the area concealed dinosaurs, but she was growing certain there were other secrets hidden among the deep shadows—secrets she wasn't sure she wanted revealed. "We're not going to reach the Skyhouse tonight, are we?"

"Duh *du jour*," Marty said. "In fact, I was just thinking this might be a good place to spend the night. The Skyhouse isn't far as the crow flies, but we're not crows and I'm pooped. Speaking of *corvids* . . ." He took the Gizmo out of the pack and turned it on. The Vid cam showed the Humvee pulling into a village next to a river. Marty checked the map. "They're at a place called Liboko, on the Ubangi River."

As Wolfe and Laurel stepped from the Humvee, they were surrounded by a large group of laughing, smiling people. The men and boys wore threadbare shorts and T-shirts with more holes than cloth. The women and girls wore sun-faded shifts that had lost their form and color long ago. Several of the older Liboko recognized Wolfe. They crowded around him, shouting and pointing at his right leg.

"They want to know how your leg grew back," Laurel translated.

Wolfe exposed the miracle by lifting his trouser cuff and showing them his prosthesis. This seemed to excite the Liboko more than if he had grown a real leg back. They all wanted to touch it, which Wolfe invited them to do. The last time he had been in the village, he had arrived lying on his back in a crude litter pulled by Masalito. He didn't remember much about that visit because he had been in shock from blood loss, fever, and grief. The Liboko had taken care of him for more than a week until he was strong enough to be moved to a clinic run by missionaries, two hundred miles away. Despite his worry and weariness, he was very happy to see these kind people again.

They were escorted to an empty hut to rest, before a dinner in their honor with the village elder. Wolfe called the twins. He was disappointed at their slow progress, but pleased with how they were holding up. Especially Grace. Laurel had been right, Grace was much tougher than she looked. Grace told him that as soon as Marty finished cooking dinner they were going to sleep so they could get an early start in the morning. She suggested that Wolfe do the same. He took her advice, which was much easier after seeing how well they were doing, and he awoke a couple hours later feeling somewhat revitalized.

He found Laurel sitting with the village elder outside his hut above the river. After their simple meal, Laurel explained to the elder in fluent Liboko that they had come to find Masalito.

He told her that he hadn't seen him in several months, which was not unusual. "Masalito only comes out of the forest three or four times a year to work as a guide. In fact, a little over a week ago a group of men were here looking to hire him for that very purpose."

Wolfe did not understand Liboko, but the look of concern on Laurel's face was clear. "What did he say?"

"Just a second." She asked the elder how many men were in the group.

"Four," the elder answered. "Three men from the Congo and an American. I told them that they wouldn't find Masalito unless he wanted to be found. But they crossed the river anyway in the direction of Lake Télé." The elder laughed. "Masalito will watch and listen to them unseen. If he doesn't like what he sees, they will have wasted their time. Masalito is like the wind coming up off the river. He cannot be caught or seen."

Laurel translated.

Wolfe cursed. "What did the American look like?"

Laurel asked the elder.

"He was a big man with brown hair on his lip and no hair on his head. The men with him were not friendly. I hope they do not return."

After Laurel translated, Wolfe said, "Butch McCall."

"You know him?"

Wolfe nodded. "Butch is Blackwood's number-one guy. He's ruthless and very good in the woods. I got to know him pretty well when I was working at the Ark. We didn't get along. He's dangerous and he's had plenty of time to reach Lake Télé. We need to get across the river!"

"We can't cross at night," Laurel said. "We're no good to the children if we drown, or die from exhaustion halfway there. You know as well as I do that we have to pace ourselves. The hardest part of our trek is on the other side of the Ubangi."

"But if Butch finds—"

Laurel put her hand on his. "The only people in the world who know the location of the Skyhouse are you and Masalito."

"And you," Wolfe added.

"Butch McCall is looking for Masalito and dinosaurs, not children and tree houses," Laurel continued. "Grace and Marty should reach Lake Télé tomorrow."

"I hope you're right."

When he got back to his hut, Wolfe called them on the Gizmo.

"Hello," Marty answered groggily.

"Were you asleep?"

"Yeah, I guess so."

"Something's come up," Wolfe said, and told him about Butch McCall.

"Butch McCall," Marty repeated. "We'll keep our eyes open for him."

"When you get to the Skyhouse call Masalito with the *molimo*." Wolfe explained where it was and how to use it. "There's a ladder a couple trees over from the Skyhouse. You can use it to get up into the tree.

Taped to the bottom rung is a box with a key in it. You'll need it to open the trapdoor."

"Got it," Marty said.

"We'll be crossing the Ubangi early tomorrow morning," Wolfe continued. "It's pretty rough going on the other side, and we won't be able to stay in touch as much as we have from the Humvee."

"Fine," Marty said.

"Is everything all right, Marty?"

"Sure, what could be wrong?"

Wolfe could have given him a dozen answers to this question, but it looked like Marty had dozed off.

Marty woke the following morning with only the vaguest recollection of Wolfe's call the previous night and the sorest muscles he had ever experienced. I hurt in places I didn't know were places, he thought, looking over at Grace, who was asleep in her hammock with PD snuggled up next to her. Now, what was it Wolfe told me last night? He dug the Gizmo out of his backpack. There was no word from his uncle, but there were a couple e-mails from Luther.

Subject: The Big Cow Expedition
From: luther_smyth@xlink.com
To: marty@ewolfe.com

Hey, O'Hara,
    You and your sister may think that you're having the adventure of your lives, but I've got news for you. You missed THE BIG ONE. That's

right, Teter's Dairy Farm. I know you're going to find this hard to believe, but we were actually able to see cows being milked by a machine. And . . . hang on to your seat . . . we actually touched real dairy cows. I swear it's true. Aren't you sorry you got dumped into the Congo now?

The only negative on the trip was that all the guys (including me) were frisked for cows before we left. Guess who started this tradition?

Attached is a photo of our old roommate, Bill.

Your co-rustler,

Luther

Marty opened the image and laughed. The digital photo was of a good-sized Jersey bull. He was surprised at how much Bill had grown during the past year, but there was no mistaking him. There was a small notch in his right ear, which he had gotten when Luther mistakenly slammed it in their dormitory door. The boys had stolen Bill from Teter's Dairy the previous year (when they learned he was destined for the slaughterhouse) and they managed to keep him hidden in their tiny room for nearly two months.

For the first time since they had left, Marty actually felt himself missing school . . . or at least Luther, anyway. He opened his friend's second e-mail.

Subject: Where are you?
From: luther_smyth@xlink.com
To: marty@ewolfe.com

Marty,
 I thought you said the Gizmo thing worked anywhere in the world. Where are you? Mars? Did your battery go dead?
 Luther

Marty tapped out a sweaty response with the stylus.

Subject: I'm here
From: marty@ewolfe.com
To: luther_smyth@xlink.com

Luther,
 The Gizmo battery did not go dead. (We have plenty of spares.) It was MY battery that went dead. I've been so tired I haven't had the energy to even read my e-mail. In fact, I was so sore this morning, it took me about an hour to get the Gizmo out of my backpack, which weighs about 600 pounds.
 I spent all day yesterday hacking down spider-infested brush with a dull machete in melting heat and a tornado of biting insects following me.

In the evening I found a place where there weren't too many venomous snakes, set up camp, blew out the bugs that had lodged in my nose, picked off my leeches (27 of them), ate, slept (barely), and now we're about to go through it all over again. Don't you wish you were here?

But enough of my whining. On the bright side, we've seen hundreds of animals. (Nothing as exotic as dairy cows, of course.) Here's a partial list. . . . Elephants, chimpanzees (the wild variety), leopard (just one sleeping in a tree with a dead duiker still dripping blood), gorilla (I think . . . it ran off and we only got a glimpse of its back), bats, birds, rock python . . . Well, you get the picture. Speaking of which, I've attached a couple of digital photos I snapped with the Gizmo. The images are a little blurry, but you'll be able to make out what they are if you squint your eyes and use your imagination.

Anyway . . . I'd better send this off and get moving. The oven is already starting to heat up and it's just after dawn.

Marty

After he sent the e-mail he tried to reach Wolfe on the Gizmo, but there was no answer. Marty wished he could remember what Wolfe had told him the night before.

"Any word from Wolfe or Laurel?" Grace asked from her hammock.

"Not really," Marty answered.

"What do you mean by that?"

"He called last night, but I didn't catch everything he said. Something about a *molimo* and a guy named Butch McCall."

"Did he say what the *molimo* was?"

"I can't remember."

"Who's Butch McCall?"

"I don't know."

Butch McCall was not in a good mood. Their first night at Lake Télé a silverback gorilla had taken a shortcut through his camp. Normally, this would not have been a problem, but at the same moment the gorilla was ambling through, one of his men got up to relieve himself. The gorilla and the man collided, which caused the gorilla to go berserk. He slammed the man against a tree, then began to systematically take their camp apart. Order was restored with the blast of a shotgun, but not before the gorilla had destroyed most of their food and a good deal of the equipment Butch and his three men had hauled into Lake Télé on their backs.

The man who had collided with the gorilla had been moaning for three days, and was still moaning as Butch watched from what was left of his shelter.

He was tempted to put the man out of his misery—not because he was sympathetic to the man's pain—Butch was simply tired of listening to him. The two remaining men were standing at the fire cooking a couple of roasts from the gorilla's thighs, jabbering away in French. Butch had supervised the skinning. The silverback would be a nice addition to Blackwood's gorilla diorama, and perhaps make up for the fact that, after three days at Lake Télé, Butch had made absolutely no progress contacting the Pygmy named Masalito.

The satellite phone rang. Butch swore. There was only one person in the world who had the number. "Good morning, Dr. Blackwood," Butch answered.

"Morning, Butch. How goes the hunt?"

"We haven't found him yet." Butch's answer was met with a chilling silence. "He's around, though," he continued. "We've seen plenty of signs. I'm sure he'll show himself soon. It's just a matter of time."

"That's one thing we don't have, Butch. Wolfe and that woman landed in the Congo two days ago and are headed your way."

"I can handle Wolfe," Butch assured him.

"I don't want you to *handle* Wolfe! I want you to get me an egg or the beast itself. And I want you long gone before they arrive. We've been over this a dozen times. I realize you have a vendetta against Wolfe. So do I. But he knows more about the animals we need than anyone on earth. If we lose him, we lose the trail. I won't allow that to happen."

"I understand." There was only one thing in the world that Butch was afraid of, and that was the man on the other end of the line. "We did manage to bag a silverback a few days ago."

"You're out hunting gorillas?" Blackwood shouted. "I can breed as many gorillas as I need. I want you—"

"We weren't exactly hunting," Butch interrupted, then explained the circumstances.

"I'm sorry, Butch," Blackwood said, regaining his composure. "I didn't mean to be so short with you. It's just that this is critical. If Wolfe gets there he'll block our chances of bagging Mokélé-mbembé. I feel bad sending you out in the field so quickly after you brought back our three black-and-white friends, which are thriving, by the way. I'll tell you what I'll do. If you bring me a viable egg, I'll give you a bonus of ten thousand shares of Ark stock. If you capture the beast, I'll give you thirty thousand shares."

The morning had just taken a turn for the better. Butch smiled for the first time in two weeks. Ark stock was as good as money in the bank. "You'll get your egg. And if there's an egg, there's an animal."

"Find it for me, Butch."

After Blackwood cut the connection, he mulled over his stormy history with the Wolfe family.

Travis was very much like his father—smart,

proud, stubborn, competitive, with incredible drive and fortitude. But there was one thing he had not inherited from his father—Travis could not pull the trigger at the end of a hunt. A pity, Noah thought. Because he had never seen a man more dedicated to the chase than Travis Wolfe. When he was just a teenager, Travis had found an ivory-billed woodpecker in a Louisiana swamp—a bird last seen in 1944. During his sophomore break from veterinary school he discovered a pink-headed duck in the jungles of Burma. During his junior break he found a pride of atlas lions in northern Africa. Since graduating from veterinary school, Travis had personally discovered five primate species previously unknown to science. In all these cases he refused to take any credit, going so far as to insist to governing authorities that his name be kept out of announcements of the discoveries.

But Travis has not reported all of his discoveries, Noah thought. The important ones he keeps all to himself, like his most recent: the active den of a Yeren (or Sasquatch) at the Shennongjia National Park in central China. Blackwood was about to mount an expedition to the same area himself, but Wolfe had beaten him to it—again. Fortunately, Travis's expedition had been interrupted by the helicopter crash in Brazil. If that hadn't happened, Travis might have found the beast itself. Noah's contact on Cryptos said that Travis was resuming the Yeren search as soon as he had the funding. When this happened, Noah planned to be close behind . . . or perhaps a few steps ahead.

After the great white shark, Blackwood had tried everything he could to get Travis to join his team. But Travis refused all of his offers. Noah thought he had finally met a man who could not be bought, but this turned out not to be true. Travis refused because he was after a much bigger prize. A prize Travis ultimately lost, for which Noah would never forgive him.

After another long, grueling morning of stumbling, sloshing, and hacking, the twins finally reached the shore of Lake Télé.

"Are you sure this is the lake?" Grace asked.

Marty nodded. "Unfortunately, the Skyhouse is way over on the other side." He gazed along the brushy shoreline, wondering how many more leeches, bugs, snakes, and thorns he was in for. "Why is it that everything in this country either bites or jabs you?"

"I don't know." Grace looked across the large lake while she massaged her aching shoulder. Throughout the morning she had spelled Marty on the machete, discovering that her willingness was much stronger than her arm. "It's so—"

"Boring," Marty said. The famous Lake Télé was

nothing more than a shallow, smelly lake with clouds of bugs hovering over it. He hadn't expected to see dinosaurs munching grass along shore, but he had expected something a little more dramatic than what he was looking at. He picked up a rock and skimmed it across the glassy surface. "Five skips."

"Three," Grace corrected, but Marty didn't seem to hear her. He was staring wide-eyed at something across the lake. He grabbed Grace's arm and pulled her to the ground. "What are you doing?"

"Can't you see it?" He pointed to the far shore with a shaking finger.

"No."

"Mokélé-mbembé!" Marty hissed. "Get the binoculars."

Grace dug them out of his pack and focused on the place he was pointing. All she saw was a tree that had fallen into the lake with a single moss-covered branch sticking out of the water, which might be mistaken for a sauropod if you had a wild imagination like her brother's.

"Do you see it?" Marty whispered excitedly.

"Yes," Grace said. "Amazing."

"I told you there were living dinosaurs."

"You sure did. A real Log Ness monster."

"It's called the *Loch* Ness monster, you dunce." Marty grabbed the binoculars. "And the Loch Ness monster . . ." he continued as he put them to his eyes, "is thought to be a plesiosaur, not a sauropod like Mokélé-mbem. . . . Oh, jeez!"

"I knew that," Grace said and began laughing harder than she had when she scared Marty in the library back on Cryptos.

"That's not funny!" Marty said.

Butch McCall was squatting behind a tree not a hundred feet from where the twins were. After breakfast he had sent his two remaining men out individually, thinking that Masalito would be more likely to approach a single man than a group. The day before, they had found the warm ashes of a fire and a pile of bird bones left over from a meal, which Butch was convinced belonged to Masalito—no one else lived near Lake Télé. "He's watching us," Butch told the men. "We've got to draw him out. I want you to walk in a straight line for three hours, then come back along a different route. If he makes contact, invite him back to camp. If he resists, hog-tie him and drag him back to camp."

After the men left, Butch headed toward Lake Télé with the intention of walking all the way around it, but his stomach put an end to the circumnavigation. The silverback was taking his final revenge inside Butch's small intestine, which was why he was squatting behind the tree. At first he thought Grace's laughter was the call of a bird he wasn't familiar with. A rare bird perhaps—a bird Noah Blackwood might pay good money for. He quickly pulled his pants up and crawled forward. It wasn't a bird. It was a boy. He was standing next to the shore pointing at a large snag sticking out of the water on the other side of the lake, and next to him was another kid, rolling on the ground laughing. Butch was flabbergasted. He couldn't see the face of the youngster on the ground because of the mosquito hat, but by the sound of the laugh it was a girl. What were they doing out in the middle of the Congo? He was about to find out, when he heard the boy say, "Well, it could have been Mokélé-mbembé."

Watch and wait, Butch thought. They can't possibly be out here on their own.

He followed the two children, expecting them to lead him to their camp or their parents, but there was no camp and no adults. Just a boy and a girl slicing their way along the soggy shoreline, hour after hour, until they arrived at the opposite side of the lake.

the clearing 19

Marty pointed at the thick wall of impenetrable vines in front of them. "The Skyhouse is through here," he said with a sigh.

"Maybe there's another way," Grace suggested, pulling her mosquito hat off.

"There might be, but there's no time to look for it," Marty said. "It'll be dark soon." He started chopping at the vines, but he gave up after a few weak swings and sat down in a weary heap. "I guess we're sleeping outside again. I'm done for." He fell back with the pack still attached to his shoulders and closed his eyes.

Butch McCall's hands trembled as he held the binoculars on the girl with coal-black hair and startling blue eyes. "Unbelievable," he said under his breath. "How in the . . ."

He caught a sudden movement to the girl's right

and swung the binoculars. A full-grown chimp dropped out of a tree near where the boy was slumped. It ambled over to the girl. Butch sharpened the focus and his mouth dropped open in surprise. The chimp was carrying a tiny poodle, and perched on its shoulder was an African gray parrot. He thought perhaps the meat he had eaten had affected more than his stomach. I must have some kind of brain fever. This can't be real. The poodle barked and the girl said something, but Butch was too far away to hear what it was.

Grace stared at the parrot in wonder. "You're real."

The parrot jumped off Bo's shoulder and started walking toward her. Grace glanced at her sleeping brother and was tempted to wake him to prove that the parrot was not a figment of her imagination, but she didn't have the heart. The past two days had been difficult, especially for Marty, and he deserved a rest.

As the parrot continued its slow deliberate walk in her direction, PD struggled to free herself from Bo's clutches and, finally succeeding, she made a rush for the little gray bird. The parrot stopped, turned, and very calmly bit the poodle on the nose. PD yipped, then ran over and jumped into Marty's lap. Marty didn't budge. The parrot hopped the rest of the way over to Grace and began pulling on her shoelaces.

"Not this again." Grace pushed the parrot away with her foot. The parrot fixed its beady eyes on her and let out one of its terrible shrieks. Bo covered her ears, then grabbed Marty's cap and disappeared up a tree.

"Quiet! You'll wake Marty." Her brother was still asleep, but even he couldn't remain so under such a loud assault. "All right, all right," Grace shouted. "What do you want me to do?"

The parrot fluttered about fifty feet away and started pacing back and forth in front of a large boulder partially covered in thick vines. It let out another ear-splitting screech, then disappeared behind the vines.

"I'm not following you," Grace said.

PD had no such qualms. She shot out of Marty's lap and dashed in behind the parrot. There was another shriek, a yip, then total silence.

"This is ridiculous!" Grace ran over to the boulder and squatted down to see if she could see any sign of the two combatants. She couldn't, but she did discover that behind the vines was an opening large enough for a human to crawl through.

Or a leopard.

Being mauled by a big cat was well down on Grace's list (somewhere in the mid-sixties), but combining it with her fear of confined spaces significantly increased her dread of crawling through the crack in the rock.

If they've already been killed by a leopard, Grace thought, there's no point in me crawling in after them. This rationalization was shattered by a muffled shriek and a yap some distance away, which led to another rationalization. They're fine, she thought. They'll come back when they're ready.

A large drop of rain splattered on her back. She looked up at the sky. It was going to pour. Perhaps I should wake Marty so he can . . . She stopped in mid-thought. Isn't that what I always do when there's a problem? Get Marty? He can't set up camp or find us shelter. It's up to me now, and this leopard's cave might just be the shelter we need. She ran back and retrieved the machete from the sleeping knight's hand. With a few deft swings she was able to clear away enough of the vines for her to crawl through the narrow opening on her hands and knees. Halfway down the tunnel it became clear that it would not work as a shelter. It was barely big enough for her to squeeze through. But in front of her was a sliver of daylight. She quickly crawled toward it and discovered another opening blocked by vines. Slicing through them, she crawled out onto a muddy game trail. As she got to her feet something big grabbed her thighs from behind. She screamed, thinking a leopard was pulling her into its snarling maw, but when she looked down for the spotted paws she saw instead two black hairy hands with opposable thumbs.

"Bo!"

The chimp jumped backward and began rolling on the ground, hooting with glee.

"That's really hilarious. Are you sure you aren't related to Marty?"

PD and the parrot were nowhere in sight, but the soft ground was peppered with dainty little dog prints. Grace looked at Bo, still in the throws of her chimpanzee belly laugh. "When you're finished," she said. "Perhaps you can help me find your little friends."

Bo did not seem very interested in helping. Grace left her there and began pursuing PD and the parrot on her own.

Butch McCall stood above the sleeping boy, watching a line of drool leak from the corner of his mouth onto his wrinkled shirt. Which was not nearly as interesting as the gray plastic tag lying next to the stain. The girl had been wearing a similar tag around her neck. The boy wasn't much older than twelve or thirteen, and the girl was even younger than that, judging by her size. Who were these kids? He was tempted to shake the boy awake to find out, but one of the things a life in the wilderness had taught him was patience.

He had tried to follow the girl after she and her menagerie slipped through the opening, but it was too narrow for him to squeeze through. He wasn't worried, though. Those who knew him said he could track a mosquito through a swamp—an exaggeration Butch didn't try to discourage. If need be, he would find another way around and pick up her trail on the other side. Tracking the kids would be as easy as tracking a herd of elephants across a mudflat.

He gently went through the boy's pockets. The boy shifted, but didn't wake. Sound sleeper, Butch thought. And strong, judging by the size of the pack strapped to his back. Both good things to know.

The sky rumbled. He stood and looked at the dark clouds. Have to head back to camp soon. See if the men found Masalito. But I may have found something more important than the Pygmy, he thought with satisfaction. Maybe even more important than Mokélé-mbembé.

He slipped back into the undergrowth. Watch and wait.

Something very strange was happening to Grace. Her legs were somehow operating independently from her brain. She no longer had to stare at the ground to follow PD's paw prints—her feet seemed to know where to go, which was both exhilarating and terrifying at the same time.

"Enough!" she shouted.

Thunder boomed above the canopy.

"Stop!"

She dropped the machete.

"That's it!"

Wind roared through the trees.

"Please, please stop!"

She tried to turn around, but the more she tried, the faster her legs pulled her forward until she was sprinting through the pelting rain. Just as she thought her lungs would explode and her heart would burst, she came to a sudden stop at the edge of a clearing. In the center was a pond with a small mound of rocks next to it. PD and the parrot were sitting on the mound as if they had been friends since they were a pup and a chick.

Grace stood where she was, gasping for breath, dizzy, her legs shaking. But none of these symptoms were due to her run through the wet jungle.

She walked across the clearing toward the pond as if she were in a dream.

A loud crack of thunder and a bright flash of lightning lit up the shore of Lake Télé. The boy's eyes snapped open and he tried to sit up.

"What the—"

Such language, Butch thought with a smirk, reading the boy's lips through his binoculars. He's like a turtle flipped over on its back.

The boy struggled against the weight of the heavy

pack. "Grace!" he shouted. "Grace! Help me out of this thing."

So, the girl's name is Grace.

The boy managed to free his arms and got to his feet. "Grace?" He looked up and down the lake shore, then cupped his hands over his mouth. "Grace?"

A flock of birds exploded from a tree. A crocodile splashed into the water. A lizard scurried under a rock. Butch missed nothing.

It'll be dark in an hour. Time to check on the men.

The boy gave up calling and started looking at the ground.

So, he knows something about tracking.

The chimp came through the opening in the rock, hooting.

Bo ambled over to the perplexed Marty, still sporting the baseball cap.

"That's my cap!" Marty made a grab for it, but Bo dodged and ran away. "Where are you going? Where's Grace?"

Without looking back, Bo disappeared into the foliage. Marty followed and found Grace's footprints, the freshly cut vines, and the opening.

"Grace?"

No answer.

"PD?"

No yap.

He jogged back to the pack, found one of Wolfe's headlamps, and slipped the elastic band over his forehead. Halfway through the opening he got stuck, but managed to wiggle free. On the other side there was no sign of Grace or the poodle. Something grabbed his legs from behind.

Bo's joke didn't have nearly the impact on Marty as it'd had on Grace.

"You moron!" Marty made another lunge for the cap, but missed again.

Bo retreated up a tree.

"If you lose my hat," he threatened, "you won't have a head to wear it on."

Bo hooted and Marty started following the tracks, wishing his sister had not wandered off, and wondering what had gotten into her lately. She had picked a very bad time to become independent. Walking without the heavy pack was a pleasure in spite of the rain, which was filtering down through the canopy by the warm bucketful. He wished he had his cap. Within half an hour the tracks were all washed away and he began to wonder if he was still on the right trail. He stopped to look at the Gizmo, but found it wasn't in his shirt pocket. A search of his other pockets came up empty as well. He had a vague recollection of it being slipped out of his pocket while he was sleeping. Grace, he thought, shaking his head. She doesn't even know how to use it.

He trudged into the gloom for another half hour and was about to turn around, when his headlamp caught the glint of the machete blade. He picked it up with a worried expression. For Grace to have gotten this far she would have had to have been running. Running from what? And why had she dropped the machete? He started to jog, arriving at the clearing fifteen minutes later in a wind-driven downpour. A bright flash of lightning revealed his sister sitting out in the open next to a pond. He walked over to her. PD was sitting in her lap, shivering, looking a great deal like a drenched rat. Grace didn't look much better. "Are you okay, Grace?"

"Yes, of course," she answered calmly.

Marty wasn't sure if he should be relieved or irritated. "Did you forget something?"

"Like what?"

"Like me!" He chose irritated. "I'm fine, by the way. A hungry croc didn't come out of the lake and drag me into the water while I was sleeping, or anything, which I'm sure you were worried about."

"I'm sorry," Grace said without taking her eyes off the pond.

Who is this girl and what has she done with my sister? Marty thought, then said, "This is no place to be wandering around with a teacup poodle. There are things out here that can kill you, Grace. A lot of things—" His lecture was punctuated by a lightning strike that was close enough for them to hear the tree it hit crack and fall. "See what I mean?"

"The parrot led me here," Grace said.

"What?" Marty ears were ringing from the strike and he couldn't quite hear what she said.

"The parrot showed me the opening in the rock."

"Not the parrot again."

"It's true," Grace insisted.

"Where's this magic parrot of yours now?" Marty asked.

"It left when the lightning started."

"Which is exactly what you should have done."

"I thought about it, but I was afraid I might get lost in the dark."

Marty glanced around the clearing. "You don't call this being lost?"

Grace shook her head. "I know this place."

"Now what are you talking about?"

"I think this is one of the places in my nightmare."

"Well, it's like a nightmare," Marty commented. "Have you noticed the rain, wind, thunder, and lightning?"

"Duh *du jour*."

Marty managed to smile. Perhaps this girl was his sister after all. "We're going to be dead *du jour* if we don't get out of the rain and lightning," he said. "The only good thing about this weather is that all the insects have drowned."

Grace turned and pointed to a very large tree directly behind them.

"Good idea," Marty said. "It will be a lot drier next to the trunk than it is out in the open."

Grace shook her head. "That's the tree the Skyhouse is in."

Marty looked up at the swaying branches and saw no sign of a tree house. "How do you know that?"

"I just do," Grace said. "Check the Gizmo. It'll tell us if we're in the right place."

"Okay, hand it over."

"I don't have it."

"Didn't you take it from my pocket when I was asleep?"

Grace shook her head.

"I could have sworn . . ." Marty checked his pockets again, then grabbed their father's pack and rummaged through it.

"Maybe it's in the big pack," Grace suggested.

"It might be," Marty said. "Unfortunately, I didn't bring the big pack."

"Why not?"

"Because I didn't expect to be spending the night out here. Besides, it wouldn't have fit through the opening you found. I barely fit through myself."

"Oh well," Grace said and walked over to the tree. It was drier, but not by much. Bo dropped out of another tree and joined her.

Marty brought the small pack over and snatched his cap off Bo's head. "Thanks." He wrung the cap out and put it on his head, then pulled a small flashlight out of the pack and shined it up through the thick branches as he walked around the tree. When he got back to where Grace was standing he said, "I'll need a rope to reach the lowest branch. The rope is in the other pack. Here are our choices. We spend the night like a couple of salamanders, or we hike back to the lake, crawl under one of the tarps and come back in the morning when it's light, and hopefully, a little drier."

"There's a third choice," Grace said.

"I'm not getting the other pack tonight and hiking back here," Marty protested.

"That isn't what I had in mind."

"Good. Then I'm all ears. What's the third choice?"

"The ladder," Grace said.

"What ladder?"

Grace took the flashlight from him and walked a couple trees over. "This ladder."

Marty and PD joined her. In the beam of the flashlight was an old aluminum ladder with years of undergrowth clinging to it as if it might try to escape.

"I think Wolfe might have said something about the ladder," Marty admitted.

"He didn't say anything to me about it," Grace said. "I just knew it was here."

"Whatever." Marty freed the ladder with his machete, then dragged it over and started pushing the extension up along the trunk. Before he had it set, Bo scrambled up the rungs, grabbing Marty's hat on the way. "Show-off!" Marty shouted as she disappeared through the lower branches.

"What do you think about climbing a metal ladder in the middle of a lightning storm?" Grace asked.

"It's bad idea," Marty said. He stuffed the drenched poodle into the pack and started to climb. "Last one to the top is a rotten sauropod egg!"

Climbing an aluminum ladder in the middle of an electrical storm was not on Grace's list, but she was certainly going to add it if she lived through the experience. She climbed up after him.

Marty balanced on the top rung of the ladder, groping the wet trunk for a handhold, hoping he didn't grab a snake, or worse, a hairy spider the size of his head.

Grace clung to the shaking ladder, wishing she had waited until the following morning to tell Marty about the tree, which she was certain was going to be uprooted any second.

"Hey!" Marty called down. "There are metal handholds bolted to the tree. They're a little hard to see though, and they're slippery." He clambered up, stopping every few feet to make sure Grace was still behind him. The higher he climbed the more the tree swayed. He waited for Grace to catch up to him. "Are you sure this is the right tree?" he shouted above the roaring wind and thunderclaps.

"It has to be," Grace shouted back. "Why else would it have metal handholds?"

"I knew that." Marty continued his ascent and, sixteen handholds later, he reached a small platform. But he was not the first to arrive. Bo was sitting in the corner, triumphantly holding Marty's cap above her head like a victory trophy. Marty ignored her and pulled Grace up to the platform.

"Well, that was horrible," she said.

"We must be at least a hundred feet off the ground."

"That's not very comforting."

Marty shined the headlamp above them and saw a trapdoor with a large padlock dangling from it. He shook his head in weary disgust. "Lockbox," he said.

"What?"

"I just remembered another thing Wolfe said. There's a key taped to the bottom rung of the ladder."

"What else did he say?"

"It'll come to me," Marty answered.

Grace looked down below into the wet darkness.

Marty sighed. "I guess I'll have to go back down and get it, unless you can spring that lock."

She took a close look at the padlock with the flashlight. She hadn't picked a lock in years, despite her brother's constant pleas for her to do so. It was a simple lock. She rubbed off the moss covering the key cylinder. "Let me have your pocketknife." Marty fished it out and handed it to her. The knife had several tools, but she would still need a separate piece of wire to pick the tumbler. She asked Marty to look in the pack for something that would work.

At the very bottom of the pack beneath PD (who Marty had set on the platform), the Frankenstein monkey, the camp stove, three packets of freeze-dried eggs, and the Moleskine, he found the Mother's Day card. Attached to it with a paper clip was the drawing he had sketched for her. He hesitated to use the clip because it was one of the last things his mother had touched. Reluctantly, he removed it. "Will this work?"

Grace nodded. She straightened the clip and slid it into the opening, then used one of the knife's several screwdrivers to turn the cylinder. The padlock opened with a satisfying pop.

"You're going to have to show me how to do that sometime," Marty said.

"Fat chance," Grace said. "You would just use it for criminal purposes." She removed the lock from the hasp and pushed the trapdoor open.

Marty shined the headlamp up through the opening, but did not start up the short ladder to the Skyhouse.

"What are you waiting for?" Grace asked.

"I'm not thrilled about sticking my head through a dark hole until I have a better idea of what's inside." He grabbed his cap away from Bo and tossed it through the trapdoor. Bo hooted, grabbed PD, and scrambled up the ladder.

"That was mean," Grace said.

Marty grinned. "Yeah." There was a dull thumping above them, then Bo stuck her head through the opening, wearing the cap. "Coast is clear."

Grace followed him up the short ladder.

"Whoa!" Marty said.

"What's that smell?" Grace asked.

Marty shined the headlamp on the ceiling. Dozens of upside-down bats stared back at them. He pointed to the wooden floor. "Bat guano," he said. "Better watch where you . . ." Something slithered just to the left of the beam. "Snake!" PD jumped into his pocket as he drew the machete and buried the blade behind the snake's head, removing it cleanly in one fluid motion. Grace screamed as the heavy body flopped around her feet, which upset the bats. They dropped from their roost and started a panicky flap around the dark room, which upset Bo. She jumped up to the back of an old overstuffed sofa and started batting bats out of the air, which upset PD. She jumped out of Marty's pocket and started attacking the stunned bats.

"Stop!" Marty shouted.

Grace stopped screaming, Bo stopped swatting, and PD stopped snapping. The bats continued swooping, but not for long. Most of them found the open trapdoor and disappeared into the rainy night, and the others returned to their roost.

"I'll figure out what to do with the rest of the bats tomorrow," Marty said.

"I'm more worried about snakes," Grace said. "What kind was it?"

"A green mamba."

"Venomous?"

Marty bent over and looked at the headless body, which had finally stopped writhing. "Not anymore."

"There might be others."

"I'll take a look around as soon as we get some more light in here." A tremendous gust of wind rocked the house, and the twins grabbed each other to stop themselves from falling down. "It's like being on a ship during a storm."

"How many sea storms have you experienced?" Grace asked.

"Plenty," Marty said, although he had never been to sea, and started looking for something to light the house. He found a kerosene lantern. "Now all we need is a match. Unfortunately . . ."

"You left them in the other pack," Grace finished for him. She opened a drawer and pulled out a Mason jar filled with matches. "Perhaps one of these will work."

Marty was too tired to ask how she might have known the matches were in that particular drawer.

He stuffed a handful into his pocket, lit the lamp, and began his search for deadly snakes.

The tree house was about forty by forty feet. A kitchen took up half of one wall and was equipped with a propane oven and a sink. Marty turned on a tap and watched brown ooze dribble from the faucet. "Don't drink the water," he said, and started opening cupboards. He found no snakes, but he did find canned goods, sugar, flour, rice, and various spices all sealed tight in mason jars. "We won't starve."

Running along the rest of the wall was a laboratory bench similar to the one in Wolfe's library, with a microscope, beakers, and test tubes. Next to the bench was a wall of books, most of which had been ruined by humidity. At the far end of the bookshelf was a door with an odd whistling sound coming from behind it.

"What do you think that is?" Marty asked.

"I have no idea," Grace answered. "But I think we should wait until tomorrow to find out."

Marty was ready to agree, but knew the sound would drive him crazy until he found out what it was. With his machete raised, he opened the door slowly and discovered a white toilet. He flipped the lid open with his foot and the whistling stopped. The bowl was empty except for the wind coming up through the hole. "Musical toilet," he said.

"I'm not sitting on that," Grace said. "Ever."

Marty kept the headlamp beam on the toilet.

"What are you doing?" Grace asked.

"I'm wondering why Wolfe would need a private toilet."

"Modesty?" Grace said.

Marty shook his head. "If you're alone there's no call for modesty. Which means Wolfe wasn't here alone. Who was with him?"

"Ted Bronson?"

"No way," Marty said. "Ted's a total recluse. He never leaves the island. It wasn't Ted."

"Next time we talk to Wolfe, we'll ask," Grace said. "In the meantime, let's continue the snake search."

Marty closed the door.

Along the last wall were more shelves filled with supplies. At the far end of the shelves was a ladder leading up to a second trapdoor.

"We'll leave that till tomorrow," Marty said. He was exhausted. In the center of the room was a sofa and two chairs with a table between them. He checked under all the cushions, pronounced the room snake free, and plopped down on the sofa.

Grace glared at him. "Excuse me?"

Marty had already closed his eyes. "What?"

"Where am I supposed to sleep?"

"The chairs look pretty comfortable to me. You can push them together."

"Some knight you are."

Marty sighed, got up, and helped her with the chairs.

Grace was tired as well, but too stirred up to sleep. She found a couple of blankets on the shelf—one for Marty and one for herself—then got her Moleskine out of her father's backpack and began to write.

Wolfe and Laurel were spending a miserable night huddled under a rain tarp.

"At least they've reached the Skyhouse," Wolfe said, massaging his stump. He had gotten brief glimpses through the Bo cam of them finding the ladder and climbing up the tree. "What I don't understand is why they don't answer my calls."

"Maybe there's a problem with the satellite," Laurel suggested. "Or perhaps Marty's Gizmo isn't working."

"I just had that video conference with Phil back on Cryptos," Wolfe said. "So it's not the satellite. But you have a point about the Gizmo. I suspect that Marty's a little rough on electronics. I'm just worried about Butch McCall. I went into the field with him once and it was a very humbling experience. I'm pretty good in the woods, but Butch is better than me—a lot better." He looked at Laurel in the dim light. "Speaking of which, you're pretty good in the woods yourself."

Laurel smiled. "Thanks."

When Grace and Marty made their unorthodox entry into the Congo, Wolfe had considered going after them by himself, thinking that Laurel would slow him down. But she turned out to be a better driver than he was. At the Liboko village he thought about leaving her behind again. Driving a Humvee was very different from struggling through the jungle. But he was glad he hadn't. She had an uncanny ability to pick the path of least resistance, even when that path looked like the least likely to take. He had let her lead the way most of the day. "We're making better time than I thought we would," he said.

Laurel nodded, and for a while they lay in silence, listening to the wind and thunder.

"Tell me more about this girl you met at the Ark," she said.

"Her name was Rose." Wolfe paused. "She was Noah Blackwood's daughter."

Subject: New Zealand
From: luther_smyth@xlink.com
To: marty@ewolfe.com

Marty, Old Mate:
    I broached the subject of spending the summer

with you in New Zealand with my parental units, leaving out the part about us fishing for Giant Squid and your uncle being a maniac. And they went for it hook, line, and sinker.

Oddly enough, my father owns a chunk of eWolfe stock, which has been very profitable for him over the years, and he thinks I'm finally moving in the right circles now. (Ha-ha. . . .)

I hope you and Grace are okay. I would hate to miss out on my New Zealand fishing vacation.

Selfishly yours,

Luther

Subject: Checking In
From: wolfe@ewolfe.com
To: marty@ewolfe.com

I've been trying to reach you all evening. I hope you get this. The storm has slowed us down, but we're still making good time. I see that you've arrived at the Skyhouse. Stay there! As I mentioned to you yesterday, you are not alone. Blackwood has sent a man to find Masalito. His name is Butch McCall. He's my size, bald, bushy mustache, and very dangerous. I don't think he'll find the Skyhouse, but if he does, lock the trapdoors and don't let him in. The house can be accessed from the roof along a series of cables strung through the canopy. There's a trapdoor in the roof and you'll need to lock that as well.

On the roof is a portable generator, water pump, and tank. The pump brings up water from the spring in the clearing. According to Dr. Lee it's in working order and there's plenty of fuel.

When you get up to the roof, find the *molimo* and use it to call Masalito. I'll feel a lot better when he's with you.

Again, stay inside the Skyhouse. We'll be there as soon as we can.

Love, Wolfe

Butch McCall was sitting in his gorilla-ruined shelter as the storm raged outside. A rare smile appeared on his face as he read the e-mail on the little computer he had found in the boy's pocket.

It was dark by the time he had gotten back to camp. The two men he had sent out were sitting in a lean-to made of palm fronds playing cards on a wet sleeping bag. In back of them lay the third man who was asleep or dead—Butch didn't care which. Neither man had seen any sign of Masalito, but one reported that he felt he was being watched. Butch thought this was probably true. He had sensed the same thing himself a couple of days earlier. In fact, he had been hoping that Masalito would follow him around the lake. This might have given him a chance to grab him.

But none of that matters now, Butch thought. The solution to everything lay in the palm of his big callused hand. He took the stylus and tapped out a response to Wolfe's e-mail on Marty's Gizmo.

Subject: Checking In
From: marty@ewolfe.com
To: wolfe@ewolfe.com

Dear Uncle Travis,

Sorry you haven't been able to reach us. It took us longer to get to the Skyhouse than we expected, but we're here now and this is where we'll stay until you tell us otherwise. Also, the pocket computer isn't working very well. The video conference function doesn't work at all, but the e-mail seems to be working, so we can keep in touch that way. I guess that's it for now.

Marty

Butch read the e-mail over and hit the SEND button. He then took the satellite phone and called Noah Blackwood, who answered on the first ring and said, "Did you find Masalito?"

"No," Butch answered.

"As I told you this morning, Butch. We're running

out of time. Wolfe is well on his way."

"I know exactly where Wolfe is," Butch said. "It will take him at least four days to get here."

"You've underestimated Wolfe before," Blackwood reminded him.

Not this time, Butch thought. He decided not to tell his boss about the little computer—for the time being anyway—but he did tell him about the two kids. When he finished, there was total silence on the other end of the line. It went on for such a long time that Butch thought their connection had been lost because of the storm. "Are you there?"

"I'm here," Blackwood said quietly. "What are they doing there?"

"I don't know."

"How did they get there?"

"I don't know."

Blackwood knew for a fact that Wolfe's niece and nephew had been on the jet with him. He also knew that they were not at the Liboko village. He had people all over the world feeding him information, most of which was very reliable.

"Wolfe must be at Lake Télé," Blackwood said. "That's the only explanation."

"The kids are alone," Butch said, although he didn't know this with certainty.

"That's preposterous!"

Butch had saved the best for last. He described the

223

girl. When he was finished, there was an even longer silence.

"Are you certain?" Blackwood finally whispered.

"Positive."

"I want her," Blackwood said.

"What about Mokélé-mbembé? What about the nest?"

"That's no longer a priority."

It was to Butch. Blackwood had offered a large bonus, and Butch was determined to collect it. He began to protest, but Blackwood cut him off.

"You can look for Mokélé-mbembé after you get the girl."

"What am I supposed to do with her?"

"Hold her until I get there."

"You're coming to Lake Télé?" Blackwood rarely went into the field anymore unless there was a television crew to film him.

"I won't leave until you tell me you have her," Blackwood answered. "But, yes, of course I'm coming. And Butch, I don't want her harmed in any way. Do you understand me?"

"Yeah."

"I mean it, Butch."

"I hear you. She won't be hurt. What about the boy?"

"I don't care about the boy."

*   *   *

Wolfe read Marty's e-mail out loud to Laurel with obvious relief. "I guess you were right about the Gizmo."

"I'm just glad they're safe," Laurel said.

Wolfe switched to the Bo cam, and a dim picture came on the screen. Grace was curled up in a chair with a blanket over her, holding the stuffed monkey. A tear ran down his cheek and disappeared into his dark beard.

"What happened to Rose?" Laurel asked.

Wolfe closed his eyes. "Mokélé-mbembé killed her."

rose 22

Noah Blackwood slept very little and was up before dawn, pacing the polished aisles of his dioramas in an absolute rage. He no longer cared that Wolfe was the best cryptid hunter in the world. "We don't need him to lead us to cryptids," he told Natasha. "We can find them on our own. Dr. Travis Wolfe is going to disappear. I should have taken care of him years ago."

Butch slept in.

When he finally opened his eyes, he did not get out of his hammock and rouse his men with the tip of his boot as usual. Instead, he lazily opened the little computer and checked on the girl and boy, smiling with satisfaction when he saw their blue and gray tags in the same spot as the night before. Next he checked on Wolfe and Dr. Lee. Their turquoise and yellow tags were moving, and he was surprised to see the route they were taking. It wasn't the most direct, but they were making remarkable progress just the same. He sat up and swung his long legs out of the hammock and pressed the Vid cam, which had been inactive the night before. The picture swooped through the trees at a dizzying speed, then suddenly stopped directly above a man and a woman. The man looked up and Butch saw his sweating bearded face.

Wolfe had gained a little weight, and the beard was new, but there was no mistaking the intense eyes. Wolfe was hunting.

But when you get here, Butch thought, your quarry will be gone. You won't beat me this time. He smiled at the thought and checked Marty's e-mail.

Subject: Important!
From: wolfe@ewolfe.com
To: marty@ewolfe.com

Marty,

I forgot to tell you what to do with the ladder. You need to pull it up into the tree behind you. If you leave it against the trunk it will be a dead giveaway for Butch McCall.

Also . . . You might want to check the clearing. Make sure you didn't leave anything lying around. After that go back up into the Skyhouse and wait until we get there. I can't emphasize

this enough. I don't care how bored you get. . . .
Stay in the Skyhouse!
　　Love, Wolfe

"I promise," Butch said.

He touched the Bo cam. The boy was up. He was cooking breakfast.

Marty was *trying* to cook breakfast, which was not easy with the primitive appliances and limited ingredients. His machete arm was so sore he was barely able to whisk the packet of freeze-dried eggs he was preparing. Grace was still asleep on the two chairs with her Moleskine and Monkey. PD was buried somewhere under her blanket. He suspected that she had been up most of the night, because the kerosene lantern was still lit and her pen was still in her hand. A sniff and taste of the spices revealed they had lost their pep and wouldn't do the eggs much good. "What I need is . . ."

Bo was fooling around with something on the floor. Marty slapped her hand and took the snake head away from her. "There are venom sacks in that head," he lectured. "If you had a cut in your mouth and bit into it, that would be the last snack you ever ate." He carefully dropped the head into the salt jar to preserve it, thinking it would make a nice souvenir for Luther.

He felt a slight breeze hit his face and heard the

toilet whistle. He turned and saw where the breeze was coming from. There was a broken window and torn screen above the laboratory bench.

Bat hole, he speculated. They must have stayed inside last night because of the storm. I'll board it up tonight after they leave. Where was I? Oh yeah, the eggs. He found what he was looking for—the six-foot-long green-mamba body. He gave it a sniff. It smelled a little odd, but not tainted. He sliced off a steak with his machete and tossed the rest of the body through the trapdoor.

Twenty minutes later he was finished with his breakfast masterpiece, which he called green eggs and mamba.

Grace felt someone or something shaking her awake. She opened her eyes in alarm, then breathed a sigh of relief when she saw it was Marty. It had been a revealing but terrifying night.

Her brother was holding a plate of food. In the center of the plate was a blue orchid, the same color as her eyes.

"It's beautiful," she said.

"The food or the flower?"

"Both. The whole presentation." She put the orchid in her hair.

"Look outside."

Grace looked through the windows over the

bench and smiled at the kaleidoscope of colorful orchids.

"If you discount the furry ceiling decorations," Marty said, "which I'll take care of tonight, this place isn't half bad."

Despite her weariness, Grace had to agree. With the morning sun streaming through the windows, the Skyhouse looked homey, cheerful, and . . . "I still can't get over how familiar it all seems," she said.

"That's because it looks like the house on Cryptos," Marty said. "I mean, if you've seen Wolfe's house on the island you would know that this was his place."

"You're probably right," Grace said, but she felt there was more to it than that. "What did you make for breakfast? It smells good."

"Eggs and . . ." Marty hesitated, "chicken." He didn't want to prejudice her taste buds before she gave it a try.

"Where did you get chicken?"

"Wolfe had a few cans in the canister," Marty lied. "They were in the bottom of your pack."

"So that's why it was so heavy."

"I guess. You'd better eat before it cools off."

Grace took a bite. "The chicken tastes a little odd."

"That's the spices," Marty explained. "They're pretty old and some of them have lost their flavor." He was looking forward to telling her the truth some-day. "How'd you sleep?"

"Not very well."

"The nightmare?"

Grace nodded. She wanted to tell him more, but she was reluctant to do so until she knew more herself. For the first time, she had remembered some of the dream.

"I don't suppose you want to hike over to the lake to pick up the pack with me," Marty said.

"I'm pretty tired," Grace said. "My legs are sore from last night. Maybe I should stay here and clean up. This place is a mess."

The place did need some cleaning, but it wasn't like Grace to offer to do it. Not that Marty was much of a housekeeper either. "I guess that would be okay," he said. "But you have to promise me something."

"What?"

Marty shook his head. "First the promise."

"All right, I promise." She squeezed Monkey's arm.

"You have to stay right here until I get back. No wandering off."

"Agreed. But I may go down to the pond to take a bath a bit later."

That hardly seemed necessary to Marty, considering the drenching they'd received the night before. "As long as you stay in the clearing."

"Okay."

Marty slipped his sneakers on and strapped the

machete around his waist. "See you later." Bo followed him out through the trapdoor.

As soon as they left, she retrieved her Moleskine and found the section where she had recounted what she had remembered of her nightmare.

I'm sitting by a pond surrounded by impossibly tall trees with a symphony of animals sounds coming from them. It's hot and damp, the air thick and still. I'm happy. Monkey is with me. Its arm is torn, but still attached. There are people around me, but I can't see their faces. They are laughing, enjoying themselves, and I'm the center of their attention. But something happens. . . . A voice calls from the trees. People scramble around, shouting, grabbing things. Monkey's arm is torn off as I'm picked up. I cry. "We'll fix it later," a woman says. "Don't cry. We'll fix it later." We're running through the trees. I'm still crying. I want Monkey. We stop, "Quiet, honey . . . quiet. We'll get Monkey later." I'm put on the ground near the base of a tree. There's a bright flash of light. A terrified scream. Deafening explosions. A man yells in agony. The sound breaks my heart. More explosions. Then . . .

That's all she remembered, but it was a start. She sat on the sofa with her eyes closed, her pen poised above her Moleskine, hoping to remember more, but nothing came. The sound of breaking glass shattered her concentration. Startled, she looked over at the laboratory bench. The parrot was back. It had squeezed through the torn screen and knocked over a beaker. PD ran over to the bench and started yipping and jumping in an effort to reach the gray bird.

"I'm not going to put up with this all day," Grace said, getting up.

The bird flew over to the ladder leading up to the second floor and began tapping on the trapdoor. Grace climbed the short ladder and pushed the door open. The bird flew through the opening.

She debated whether to follow, or to shut the door, trapping the parrot upstairs so she could have some peace and quiet. But her curiosity pushed her head through the opening. In the center of the room was a queen-size bed, unmade, as if the occupant had gotten up just that morning. On the floor next to the bed was a crumpled pair of pants and a pair of boots that were definitely too small for her uncle. Laurel had been to the Skyhouse with Masalito, she remembered. They must belong to her. But why would she leave them behind? She climbed the rest of the way up.

The parrot hopped over to a door and tapped on it with its black beak. Grace opened the door and found a closet filled with woman's clothes and shoes, including a beautiful red dress made of fine silk. This does not belong to Dr. Laurel Lee, Grace thought. Not her style. Who had been with her uncle?

As she turned to leave she saw an old trunk and several storage boxes pushed to the back beneath the clothes. She pulled the trunk out. Painted on the lid was a faded red rose. Grace's heart started pounding. She glanced over at the parrot. It had gone uncharacteristically quiet and was looking at her expectantly. She started to open the lid.

"Rose is back," the parrot said.

Grace slammed the lid shut and stared at the parrot in shock. "What did you say?"

"Rose is back," the parrot repeated clearly, then hopped over to a second door and started tapping on it.

Grace put her hand on the doorknob, but hesitated to turn it. She knew that on the other side lay something disturbing—something she wasn't quite sure she was ready to see. Maybe the door was locked. But it wasn't. The knob turned easily. She closed her eyes and pushed the door open. When she opened her eyes her knees buckled and she grabbed the doorjamb to stop herself from falling. It did no good. Her head hit the floor with a dull thud and everything went dark.

At first, Butch McCall thought the girl was dead—and if she was, he was dead too. Blackwood would make sure of that. She was slumped in a doorway on the second floor. He turned her over, felt her neck for a pulse, and breathed a sigh of relief when he felt blood pumping through the artery. There was an ugly bruise on her forehead.

One of his men came in holding his left hand, and reported that the Skyhouse was empty except for the crazy little dog, which had bitten him. Butch suspected as much. The pocket computer had shown the boy moving toward Lake Télé in a rather roundabout way. Probably to retrieve his pack, Butch thought. He'll be disappointed when he gets there.

"What did you do with the dog?" he asked in French.

"I put her in the toilet room," the man answered, looking at the girl. "What's the matter with her?"

"Bumped her head."

The man laughed.

"I didn't hit her on the head," Butch said. "She must have fallen."

The man didn't look as though he believed him.

Butch threw Grace over his shoulder and climbed down to the lower floor. He lay her on the sofa, then surveyed the room. He found what looked like a diary and a stuffed animal that resembled a monkey. He put them into the little pack she had been carrying the day before and gave it to one of the men. He wanted to make it look like she had gone out for a walk. But this time she isn't coming back, Butch thought.

The poodle was barking and scratching at the

door. He let her out and she immediately went for the man she had bitten. The man backed up to the wall like a lion was chasing him and pulled out his machete.

"No!" Butch shouted. "Leave it alone."

Reluctantly, the man put the machete back in its scabbard and tried to shake PD off his pant leg.

Butch went over to Grace, tore the tag from her neck, and kicked it under the sofa. "Let's go."

the molimo 23

Marty was having difficulties of his own.

The storm had washed away every trace of their footprints and all the dripping trees looked exactly the same. The night before there had seemed to be only one trail to the clearing, but in the daylight there were dozens, all crisscrossing one another, without any indication which was the right one. He wished he had spent more time paying attention to his surroundings and less time being irritated with Grace. And Bo was making the situation worse. She was stalking him, just as she had done back on Cryptos— no doubt waiting to rush in and steal his cap. At least he hoped it was Bo and not a clumsy man-eating lion. It was becoming so unnerving that he was tempted to sacrifice the cap so she would leave him alone. He looked at his watch and decided to give himself fifteen more minutes before giving up and heading back to the Skyhouse, providing he could find it, which he seriously doubted. About halfway through his allotted time he came across a partial sneaker print heading toward the Skyhouse. As far as he knew, there was only one pair of sneakers in the Lake Télé region, and they were on his feet. He followed the path a hundred more yards and was rewarded with another sneaker print.

"Okay, Bo," he said. "You can come out now." He took off his cap and waved it around. A bush rattled, but Bo did not show herself. "Last chance." Marty waited. "Fine."

He continued down the trail and a half hour later he came to the opening in the rock. He squeezed through and discovered to his dismay that Bo had gotten to the pack first. The contents were strewn all over the shore and she was helping herself to a package of beef Stroganoff. He charged her with his machete raised. Bo hooted and ran off with the package in her mouth.

"What a mess!" He started picking things up and stuffing them into the pack, periodically glaring at the seemingly unrepentant Bo, who was staying well out of his way. It took him nearly an hour to gather everything. When he finished, there was still one very important item missing. The Gizmo. He looked in Bo's direction and gave her his most charming smile. "Okay," he said with a cheerful voice. "All is forgiven. Come on over here, you thieving fur ball."

Bo hooted, but did not take a step toward him.

"All right." Marty removed his cap. "I'll swap you for the Gizmo."

Bo rushed forward and grabbed the cap, which was a very bad trade, because it turned out that she didn't have the Gizmo. Marty swore and spent the next hour looking for it, finally giving up because the insects near the lake were eating him alive.

His next problem was that the pack would not fit through the opening. He had to unpack everything again and make a half dozen trips back and forth to get all the supplies through.

It was late afternoon by the time he and Bo reached the clearing. Bo headed straight up to the Skyhouse. Marty dropped the heavy pack, stripped his clothes off, and jumped into the pond. He soaked in the tepid water for a half an hour, looking forward to spending the next several days doing absolutely nothing. When he finished, he lit a twig, sizzled eleven leeches off, then began the difficult task of hauling the pack up to the Skyhouse with a rope, one branch at time.

"Tarzan home," he said when he finally made it through the trapdoor. But there was no answer. "Grace?" He saw the second trapdoor was open and climbed up, surprised to find the queen-size bed. It looked very inviting, except Bo had discovered it too and was lying under the blankets. "This is not a chimp nest!" Marty grabbed the cap from her head. She threw the blankets off and started jumping up and down. "It's not a trampoline either. Get off!" Bo did a backflip, grabbed the cap off his head halfway through the flip, bounded to the ladder leading to a third trapdoor, flipped it open, and disappeared onto what looked like the roof.

"Grace?" Marty walked into the other room. He didn't faint, but he was just as shocked as Grace had been. He was standing in the middle of a baby nursery, complete with crib, changing table, playpen, and rocking horse. Why did Wolfe have a nursery? Did they have a cousin they didn't know about? He walked over to the playpen. Inside was a white soccer ball. He took it out and bounced it on the wooden floor, thinking about what all this meant. His musing was interrupted by a loud *bang . . . bang . . . bang . . .* overhead, which he thought was probably Grace. He was certain she was on the roof. He wondered what she thought about the nursery. *Bang . . . bang . . . bang. . . .* "I'm coming," he shouted, throwing the ball back into the playpen.

Grace was not on the roof and Marty began to worry. Grace had never broken a promise to him. And if she had to break the promise, the very least she would have done was to leave him a note. It's probably downstairs, he thought hopefully.

The banging noise was coming from Bo, who was

wielding what looked like a small log. She was hitting it on the steel guardrail surrounding the roof. Attached to the rail were several steel cables leading off into the green canopy, which he believed were there to stabilize the Skyhouse.

He walked over and took the log away from Bo and tossed it over the side. "I can't think with that racket." Bo retreated under a large tank and began chewing on Marty's cap. Next to her was a gas-powered pump. Marty turned the ignition and to his surprise the engine started and the tank began filling with water. He decided he was going to make Grace do the dishes as punishment for breaking her promise. On one corner of the roof was a gas-powered winch with hundreds of feet of cable attached to a stainless steel basket dangling over the rail. He started the engine and engaged the clutch. The basket started to descend. Bo ran over and jumped into it for a ride. He wished he had discovered the basket before hauling the backpack up through the limbs. Next to the tank was a storage shed. He opened the doors and found several cans of motor oil and fuel. Hanging above the cans were ropes, harnesses, helmets, goggles, gloves, carabiners, and other climbing gear. What's Wolfe doing with all this stuff? There isn't a mountain within a thousand miles.

"Wait a second!"

He took a harness over to one of the cables. Wolfe

wasn't using the gear to climb mountains, and the cables weren't being used to stabilize the Skyhouse. He was using them to explore the canopy—something Marty had always wanted to try. He revised his plan of doing nothing over the next several days. He was going to put on the climbing gear and crawl through the trees like Spider-Man. But first he had to figure out where Grace had gotten to. He glanced over at the winch and saw the cable was piling up. He put the clutch into reverse, then saw that the water tank was starting to overflow. He ran over and switched it off. When he turned back around, the basket was just coming up to the rail. Bo was inside, carrying the log he had tossed. He took it away from her and was about to throw it over the side again, when he noticed that it wasn't an ordinary log. It was hollow and there were holes on either end. He put an end to his lips, took a deep breath, and blew. A startling deep sound resonated through the canopy like a lion's roar.

"The *molimo*," Marty said, feeling a little sick to his stomach as Wolfe's entire conversation from two nights ago came back to him.

He raced down to the main floor and started searching frantically for a note from Grace. But there was no note. The Frankenstein monkey, their father's pack, and the Moleskine were gone.

He climbed quickly down to the clearing. In the

soft ground beneath the ladder were dozens of foot-prints. One set in particular caught Marty's attention. They were huge. Inside one of the prints was a crushed orchid the color of a robin's egg.

"Butch McCall," Marty whispered in mounting anxiety.

A movement near the spring caught his attention. Perched on the mound was an African gray parrot. He walked toward it, thinking it would fly away, but it didn't.

When he got within two feet, the parrot fixed him with its shiny black eyes and said, "Rose is back."

"Grace didn't say anything about you being able to talk," Marty said. He put his finger out and the parrot jumped up on it. "Who's Rose?"

"Rose is back," the parrot repeated.

The sound of the *molimo* brought Butch McCall out of his camp chair where he had been sitting the past two hours.

He looked over at his men, who had also gotten to their feet. All of them stood in silence, looking up into the trees long after the haunting call ended. Butch had no idea what the sound was, but he didn't like it. Something very strange was going on, beginning with the girl, who was still unconscious, lying on the hammock underneath his tarp. He had expected her to come to as he carried her through the jungle, but she hadn't. When they got to camp he tried smelling salts and even slapped her a time or two, but she still didn't come around. She didn't have a fever and her pulse was normal. It was as though she were in a coma, or something, and Butch was getting a little nervous. Blackwood would never believe that she'd gotten the bump on her head by falling down. His own men didn't believe it.

He sat back down and returned to his reading.

Grace was not in a coma. She was remembering. . . .

A woman with black hair and beautiful blue eyes sets her on the ground near a tree. "You'll be fine, Grace. I'll be back in a minute."

Grace watches her wade across a shallow stream and join a beardless and younger Wolfe and a dark little man half Wolfe's size wearing nothing but a loincloth.

"Masalito saw it go right through here," Wolfe says with excitement. "Not ten minutes ago. Look at this track."

The woman squats down and takes several photographs of the ground. The strobe lights up the jungle. There's a loud noise like a lion's roar, but higher pitched and more ferocious. Branches snap and a long grayish green neck shoots out of the bushes. A horrible roaring mouth grabs the woman by the waist and picks her up.

"Rose!" Wolfe shouts, firing his rifle from the hip.

The monster swings around and hits Wolfe and Masalito with its whiplike tail, knocking both of them down. Wolfe fires again from the ground. The animal shudders, stumbles a few steps, then falls over with the woman still in its mouth.

Wolfe gets to his feet and starts to run toward the woman, but before he reaches her, a second animal rushes out of the bushes—smaller than the first, but just as horrible. It grabs Wolfe by his right leg and flings him back and forth. He drops his rifle. Masalito runs in beneath the belly of the beast and comes up with the rifle, firing over and over again. The beast drops Wolfe and falls over. Its bloody head splashes into the stream not ten feet from the tree where Grace is lying.

Wolfe crawls over to the woman and gently pulls her from the beast's mouth. She talks to him very quietly for a long time.

"Bring Grace!" Wolfe yells.

Masalito crosses the stream and picks her up. He carries her over to the woman and puts her in the woman's arms.

"Someday you'll understand," the woman whispers. "I only wish . . ."

Wolfe buries his face in his hands. "Rose," he sobs. "My little Rose."

It's not a nightmare . . . it's a memory. All these years. Wolfe is not my uncle, he's . . . Grace opened her eyes, expecting to find herself in the nursery. Instead, she was beneath a filthy green tarp, lying on a sour-smelling hammock. The air was still and heavy. Where am I? Her head hurt. Very gingerly, she lifted it and saw the back of a very large man sitting on a camp stool outside the entrance of the crude shelter. He turned around. "You're awake," he said. "You had us worried."

"Us?" Grace sat up. "Who are you?"

"My name is Butch," the man answered. "Butch McCall."

It was the man Wolfe had warned Marty about. He had a bushy brown mustache and was completely bald.

"Where am I?"

"You're at my camp. We found you wandering in the forest. You were delirious."

Grace knew this wasn't true. "Where's—"

"Marty?" Butch interrupted. "We haven't found him yet, but we will. No worries there."

"How do you know Marty's name?"

"The same way I know your name, Grace. I was sent here to rescue you."

"By who?"

"Your grandfather," Butch said. "Noah Blackwood."

Grace felt as if her heart might burst. She closed her eyes, trying to rid herself of the dizziness coming upon her. "I don't believe you," she said.

Butch shrugged. "Suit yourself, but I'm telling the truth. You mother's name was Rose Blackwood— Noah Blackwood's only child. She ran away with Travis Wolfe fifteen years ago and was never seen again. It broke Noah's heart, I can tell you that. The only thing Travis told him about her death was that she died somewhere in Africa . . . until two days ago."

Grace opened her eyes.

"Travis called him," Butch continued. "Said you fell out of a jet and survived somehow. Dr. Blackwood flew us out and we parachuted in this morning. We were on our way to the Skyhouse when we found you."

"Why didn't you just take me back to the Skyhouse?"

"Because you were in bad shape and my camp was closer."

"I need to be alone," Grace said.

"Fine." Butch walked away with a smirk on his face. The conversation had gone much better than expected. He had to hand it to Blackwood. When he concocted a lie, it was effective. In fact, it was so plausible that Butch half believed it himself.

Just a few more errands to take care of, he thought with a smile. He joined his men to tell them what he had in mind.

*   *   *

247

Grace watched Butch walk over to the fire. *Noah Blackwood is my grandfather? I'm not a twin? I don't have a brother?*

This last thought shot an arrow of sorrow that entered her throat and quickly spread throughout her chest. She tried to stop the tears from coming, but there was nothing she could do. The tears flowed as if they would never stop. She wept for her fathers and mothers, she wept for herself, and she wept for Marty. It was a long hard cry, and when it subsided, she felt a little better—cleansed, as if she might be able to survive these terrible revelations. A warm breeze blew into the shelter and dried her tears. The sun was setting, casting an orange light on the camp. Butch McCall and two men were sitting near a smoky fire, talking quietly.

Grace could not imagine what Marty was going through right now, returning to the Skyhouse and finding her gone. She hoped he would stay there and not go out looking for her. At least Wolfe knows where I am, she thought, feeling for the blue tag that was no longer there.

masalito 24

When Marty climbed back up to the Skyhouse with the parrot on his shoulder, PD greeted him with Grace's blue tag in her mouth. The chain was broken, as if it had been torn from her neck. He was now certain that Butch McCall had taken his sister.

Bo, PD, and the parrot sat on the sofa, watching him frantically sort through his gear in the shadowy kerosene light. He had no idea how long it was going to take to find her, or how he was going to get her away from him, but he was going to get her back no matter what it took. He put a headlamp on his forehead, then tried the pack on for size. It was a little heavy.

PD barked.

"Don't worry," Marty said. "I'm going to take you with me. I'm just trying the pack to see . . ."

A head popped up through the trapdoor. And it certainly didn't belong to Grace. PD jumped into Bo's arms.

Marty was tempted to do the same. "Who . . ."

The man pulled himself up the rest of the way. He had gray hair, stood about four feet tall, and was naked except for a loincloth made out of okapi skin. He was carrying a long bow. Slung over his shoulder was an arrow quiver made out of the same material as his loincloth. His feet were bare. The parrot flew over to him and landed on his shoulder.

"Masalito?"

Without responding, the man walked over to the sofa and took a close look at Bo and PD, who growled, but didn't bark.

"My name is Marty."

Ignoring him, the Pygmy put the bow and quiver down and quickly climbed up to the second floor.

Marty followed him with the lantern, wondering if the man was a deaf-mute. He watched as the man checked under the bed and in the closet.

"What are you looking for?" Marty asked. "I'm here alone. My sister was . . ."

The Pygmy walked into the nursery. Marty tried a few awkward phrases in French, which was commonly spoken in the Congo, but the little man continued to ignore him. He finished whatever he was doing in the nursery and climbed up to the roof. Again, Marty tagged along and watched as the Pygmy looked under the water tank, over the rail, and in the storage shed.

"I know you don't understand a word I'm saying," Marty said. "But I don't have time to entertain guests right now. My sister has been kidnapped and I have to go out and find her."

The Pygmy picked up the *molimo*.

"Is that what you were looking for? I'm the one who called you." Marty pointed at it. *"Molimo."*

For the first time, the Pygmy seemed interested in what Marty was saying.

"Molimo," Marty repeated, then pantomimed blowing on it. He pointed to himself, then said very slowly. "My name is Marty. My uncle, Travis Wolfe, is a friend of yours." He pointed to the Pygmy. "Masalito?"

The Pygmy nodded.

Marty smiled. "Now we're getting somewhere."

Masalito carried the *molimo* down to the main floor and took a seat on the sofa next to Bo and PD. The parrot was still perched on his bony shoulder. The foursome looked like they were waiting for their favorite TV show to come on.

How am I going to explain the situation? Marty thought desperately. He looked around the dim room for something to help him, and saw his sketch pad.

The path Laurel had chosen was difficult, treacherous, filled with quicksand, swamps, snakes, and swarms of biting insects. But she assured Wolfe that it would get them to the Skyhouse at least a day earlier. They finally stopped just before dark. They were wet, hungry, and exhausted.

Wearily, Wolfe took the Gizmo out to see if Marty had sent another e-mail. He hadn't. He checked the tracking tags, which were all blinking in the Skyhouse, then reread Marty's last e-mail and shook his head.

"What's the matter?" Laurel asked.

"Marty's e-mail," Wolfe answered. "I've been thinking about it all day. There's something not quite right about it. For one thing, he called the Gizmo a pocket computer. I've never used that term and I've never heard him use it, either. Why didn't he just call it the Gizmo?"

"I don't know," Laurel said. "But I'm feeling uneasy too."

He turned on the Bo cam and saw Marty sitting on the floor, drawing something in his sketch pad. There was no sign of Grace.

He handed the Gizmo to Laurel. "Grace must be out of Bo's camera range. Maybe we should just rest here a few hours and push on before light."

"That might be best."

They ate some food without bothering to heat it, then climbed into their hammocks, but sleep did not come to either of them. Wolfe checked in with Phil back on Cryptos, then skimmed through his e-mail without enthusiasm, answering none of it. He no longer even cared about the Mokélé-mbembé and the possibility that they were still alive. The only thing that mattered was reaching Grace, Marty, and Masalito. "Are you awake?" he asked Laurel.

"Yes."

"Do you have any other shortcuts to Lake Télé up your sleeve?"

"I was just thinking about that," Laurel answered. "Masalito told me about one, but I haven't traveled it myself. It's flooded most of the year and impassable, but if the water's down we could be at the Skyhouse in a couple days. Maybe less."

"And if the water's up?"

"We would have to backtrack and that would add a couple days."

"What do you think?"

"I think it might be worth the risk. We need to reach those kids."

"I agree," Wolfe said.

They lay quietly for a long time, listening to the wind blow through the canopy and the night animals calling back and forth; then Wolfe broke the silence.

"I left a few details out last night about my last trip here."

"You don't have to—"

"No, I want to," Wolfe interrupted. "Just before Rose died, she made me promise to continue searching for cryptids. I promised her I would. And I made her another promise, which has been hardest to keep." He paused. "Rose and I had a child when we were here. Grace is my daughter."

Laurel sat up. "The nursery."

Wolfe nodded.

"I asked Masalito about it when he showed me the Skyhouse, but he refused to say anything."

"I asked him to be quiet about it."

"Grace has no idea."

Wolfe shook his head.

"Why would you let her and Marty think—"

"Rose insisted that Noah Blackwood must never know about Grace. Even if it meant giving her up for adoption."

"Why?"

"I'm not certain. There were a lot of things I didn't know about the Blackwood family. Things Rose refused to talk about—her father, her childhood. I knew Rose better than anyone in the world, but there were things she held back. And it wasn't that she distrusted me. There were just some things she wasn't allowed to share with anyone. I know this doesn't make sense, but I'm trying to explain why I made the decision to give Grace up.

"Rose knew that Blackwood would somehow gain custody of Grace. That he would corrupt and ruin her. I don't know how she knew this, but I believed her.

"When I was moved from the Liboko village to the hospital, I called my sister, Sylvia. She had given birth to Marty six weeks before Grace was born. She and Tim took her into their lives without question and raised her as their own. Giving her up was the hardest thing I ever had to do. The second hardest was staying out of her life all these years."

"Is that why you've been so distant with Grace?"

"Of course," Wolfe said. "How can I explain why I gave her up when I don't understand it myself?"

"That is a problem," Laurel said. "Why did your sister put them into a boarding school?"

"Sylvia wasn't exactly a stay-at-home-mom type. She and Tim actually wanted to take the kids with them on their assignments, but there was a problem. Grace looked exactly like Rose. Someone was bound to do a story on the famous O'Hara family. All Blackwood would have to do is to see one photograph of Grace in a newspaper or magazine, and he would know immediately that she was not their little girl. It was an agonizing decision for all of us, but in the end the boarding school seemed like the best alternative. As the years went by it became more and more difficult to reverse the decision." Wolfe sighed. "Looking back on it. I think it was a colossal mistake."

"What about now?" Laurel asked. "Won't Grace being with you expose her?"

"It's a risk," Wolfe admitted. "But what I do is done in secret. We don't talk to the press, publish scientific papers, or advertise what we're doing. I don't know if you've noticed, but I'm a little camera shy."

Laurel grinned. "I've noticed."

"Anyway, I think I'll be able to keep Grace away from Blackwood until she reaches legal age. At that point, Blackwood won't be able to touch her."

"Are you going to tell her about all this?"

"Yes," Wolfe said. "And that will be the third hardest thing I've ever had to do. I've been waiting for the right moment, and to be frank, the courage. I just hope she doesn't hate me too much when I tell her the truth."

Laurel reached across to his hammock and took his hand. "I think she'll understand."

Marty put the final touches on his masterpiece.

Despite the speed with which he had to work and his anxiety over Grace's disappearance, he couldn't help but be pleased with the results. Luther would love this, he thought as he sorted the pages into the right order. I just hope the Pygmy with the okapi underpants on understands it. He gathered the sheets and kneeled in front of Masalito and his three friends.

"This . . . is . . . a . . . comic . . . book," he said very slowly. "The difference is that everything in this story really happened. I . . . am . . . not . . . kidding." He showed him the first panel, which was a black-and-white sketch of his parents climbing into a helicopter. (He would have preferred to work in color, but there wasn't time.) The next panel was the most difficult for him to draw. The helicopter crash and his parents wandering off into the wilderness. The next several panels had been much easier to draw: a portrait of him and Grace at school. The flight to Cryptos. A portrait of Wolfe. Masalito being chased through the jungle by Blackwood's cutthroats. Their fall from the jet. He pantomimed each panel to help Masalito understand. When he got to the panels showing Grace's abduction, he had to make up the details. He started by showing several men storming the Skyhouse. Grace valiantly struggling to get away. A man tearing the tracking tag from her neck. And finally, his sister succumbing. The very last panel was of Marty on the roof playing the *molimo*.

"That's what happened," Marty concluded.

Masalito nodded as if he understood and said something that Marty didn't understand.

"I don't speak Pygmy," Marty said.

Masalito got up and started rummaging through Marty's art supplies.

"What are you doing?"

Masalito came back to the sofa with a fistful of colored pencils.

"We don't have time for this!" Marty protested. "We've got to find Grace."

Masalito smiled, then took the pad from him and sat down on the sofa and started drawing.

"We don't have time for this," Marty repeated, but with much less conviction.

Masalito knew how to hold a pencil and was making self-assured strokes on the pad. Marty started around the back of the sofa to get a look at what he was doing, but Masalito stopped him in his tracks with a Pygmy stink-eye.

"Just like Luther," Marty said.

Luther hated people looking over his shoulder while he drew. Of course, if I drew like Luther, Marty thought, I'd hate it too. He sat down in the chair and watched the bats drop from the ceiling in twos and threes and fly out through the broken window.

Masalito did not look up from his work.

doctor grace 25

Having gathered herself, Grace stepped out from Butch's shelter.

The first thing she noticed was the smell. It was terrible. The second thing she noticed was her father's pack, which was sitting next to a tree near the shelter. She had no recollection of taking it with her when she allegedly wandered away from the Skyhouse. She opened it and found the first-aid kit, the camp stove, Monkey, and the flashlight. The Moleskine was not there. She would have never left the Skyhouse voluntarily without it, which confirmed her suspicions about how she had arrived at Butch's camp.

The last thing she remembered was seeing the nursery and fainting.

Butch must have come along and simply picked me up, she thought bitterly. How convenient for him. My Moleskine was in the chair next to Monkey. He could hardly miss it. Everything he needed to know was there. Their arrival on Cryptos, the fall from the jet, the Skyhouse—more than enough for him to piece together what happened and make up a story. *Butch McCall read my diary!* She took a deep breath, trying to contain her anger. There was more at stake than her privacy. She knew that the only way she was going to get away from Butch was to act as if she were cooperating.

When she walked up to the fire, Butch and his two men stopped talking.

"I'm worried about Marty," she said.

"He's probably back at the Skyhouse by now." Butch nodded at the two men sitting across the fire from him. "They'll head over there tomorrow and bring him back here."

"Why wait until tomorrow?"

"Because it's going to be dark soon and it's not safe to wander around after sunset."

"You're well armed," Grace pointed out. The two men had shotguns laying next to them. "It's hard to believe that you would be intimidated by the dark."

Butch did not rise to her baiting. "We haven't slept in days," he said. "We'll rest up tonight and find him in the morning."

Undeterred, Grace tried a different approach. "The Skyhouse is a lot more comfortable than this place," she said. "And Wolfe is expecting us there. Maybe we should just move over there."

Butch stared at her. He and Blackwood had not discussed the possibility of Grace being headstrong. "We're already set up here," he said. "No point in moving everything."

"It smells here," Grace said.

"That's the dead gorilla."

"I beg your pardon?"

"A silverback came through and busted up one of my men," Butch answered. "We shot him."

"You shot a gorilla?"

Butch nodded. "Had to."

Grace looked at the two men. Neither looked injured. Nor did they look like members of a rescue team. In fact, in their filthy pants, rotting boots, and torn T-shirts they looked a lot like gorilla poachers. Butch was not dressed much better.

"We hated to do it," Butch said with a regretful expression, which did not look natural on his rugged face.

An agonized moan came from a lean-to behind the two men.

"What was that?"

"I told you the gorilla smashed up one of my men," Butch said. "That's another reason we can't move to the Skyhouse. He's in pretty bad shape, but you don't have to concern yourself with him. We'll take care—"

Grace ignored him. She took the flashlight out of the pack and walked over to the lean-to. The man inside looked as though he had been beaten. He was covered with ugly bruises and infected lacerations. The right side of his head was swollen to twice the size of his left. One ear was dangling by just a thread of skin. His right foot bulged out of his boot and was twisted at an unnatural angle. Grace felt pity for him despite his being a kidnapper and a gorilla killer.

She turned angrily toward Butch. "Why haven't you done anything for him?"

"I've been a little busy saving you," Butch said sarcastically.

"When did you say this happened?"

"This morning. Right after we got here."

Any doubt that Butch was telling the truth about how she'd arrived at his camp vanished. The bruising and infection indicated that the attack had taken place two or three days before, not that morning. Grace had not only read books on trauma injuries but had spent a week making rounds with a trauma nurse in a hospital.

"Help me get him out of this hovel," Grace demanded. "I'll need hot water, clean rags, and some decent clothes for him."

Butch was not used to taking orders from little girls, but he passed her instructions onto his men in broken French anyway. He hoped that playing doctor would distract her suspicious little mind. She has the same bossy personality as her mother, he thought.

Masalito stood in front of Marty and opened the sketch pad to the panel Marty had drawn of him and Grace at school, with one significant revision. Masalito had colored in Grace's eyes with the perfect shade of blue.

"You've seen Grace!" Marty shouted. This was the only way he could have picked robin's-egg blue.

Masalito flipped to another page. It was a drawing of a baldheaded man with a bushy mustache. The drawing was primitive, but quite good.

"Butch McCall," Marty said.

The next series of panels showed a camp with four men in it, a gorilla attacking a man, and Butch shooting the gorilla.

"They shot a gorilla?"

On the next page, Butch was leaning over Marty while he slept; he slipped something out of his shirt pocket, then stood and held it in his hand. Marty came out of his chair. "Butch stole the Gizmo! He knows every move we're making. No wonder he tore off Grace's tag. He wants Wolfe to think she's in the Skyhouse."

Masalito flipped the page. Butch was carrying Grace. He had a shotgun slung over his shoulder and so did the two men with him.

"Where did they take her?"

Masalito took a lantern and climbed up to the

second floor. Marty doubted his sister was upstairs, but followed anyway, and found Masalito digging through the closet. He pulled a storage box out and handed Marty a photograph.

A beautiful woman with black hair and startling blue eyes the color of robin's eggs stared up at him. She was smiling. Perched on her shoulder was an African gray parrot, and sitting in her lap was a blue-eyed baby girl with curly black hair. She was holding Monkey before he lost his arm.

"Grace," Marty whispered with trembling hands. Standing behind them, wearing shorts, was a clean-shaven Wolfe before he lost his leg. He sat down heavily on the edge of the bed. "I can't believe this. Wolfe is Grace's father? She was born in the Congo?"

Masalito sat down next to him and pointed at the woman in the photo. "Rose," he said, then showed him the next drawing in the sketchbook. A long-necked animal held a dark-haired woman in its mouth. "Mokélé-mbembé," Masalito said. "Rose."

The final drawing was a Mokélé-mbembé holding a man up in the air by his left leg.

"Wolfe," Marty said. "Excuse me." He scrambled down the ladder and barely made it to the whistling toilet before he threw up. His retching was not the result of seeing his uncle in the maw of a prehistoric animal, although that was upsetting. What caused his stomach to lurch was the knowledge that Grace was no longer his sister, that he was an only child.

When he came out of the bathroom he found Bo and PD sitting on the sofa. He started pacing. He hadn't felt this anxious since the night he and Luther smuggled Bill into their dormitory room. Why did Wolfe give Grace up? Why didn't Mom and Dad tell us?

Marty was upset that Grace was not his sister, but he wasn't surprised. There had always been more differences than similarities between them. And the fact that she was his cousin did not diminish his affection for her. He was still going to be her knight in shining armor, starting with getting her away from the men who had kidnapped her.

He checked the contents of the backpack again, then removed Bo's video harness and PD's and his own tracking tags. No point in letting Butch McCall know what we're up to, he thought. Then an idea occurred to him: he climbed back up to the second floor to get his sketch pad, but was sidetracked when he saw the trunk with the rose on the lid.

Unlike Grace, Masalito had not hesitated to open it, and was going through the contents as Marty walked up behind him. He had already taken out a stack of Moleskines. Marty picked one up and it made his heart ache. He missed Grace.

"What is all this?"

"Rose," Masalito said.

Marty squatted down next to him. "Her stuff, huh?"

Inside were books, files, and manila envelopes stuffed with papers and yellowed newspaper articles. Marty picked up an envelope, and a stack of photos dropped out. He was in a hurry to get going, but something in one of the photos caught his eye. He put it under the lantern and took in a sharp breath. The girl in the photo was about Grace's age and looked exactly like her, except for the braces on her teeth. (Grace's teeth had never needed straightening.) She was sitting in front of a birthday cake with eleven candles. But the thing that really surprised him was the man standing next to her. He was younger, but there was no mistaking who it was.

Noah Blackwood was helping her blow the candles out.

He quickly went through the other photos. There was another photo of Rose holding Grace. He turned the photo over. GRACE'S FIRST BIRTHDAY was written on the back. Along with a date.

Grace gave the man a sponge bath, set his ankle, wrapped his cracked ribs, treated the lacerations, snipped off his ear (reattaching it was beyond her abilities), then made him swallow an antibiotic and pain pill. Butch and the other two men sat next to the fire and watched her work.

Butch's satellite phone rang. He stepped away

from the fire to answer it, then returned, holding the phone out for Grace. "It's for you," he said.

Grace tentatively took the phone.

"Grace?"

She didn't answer.

"Can you hear me?"

It was the distinctive and soothing voice of Noah Blackwood.

"Yes," Grace said.

There was a long pause, then Noah Blackwood said, "I cannot tell you how relieved I am that you're safe. Beyond that I cannot describe the joy I experienced when Travis informed me that I had a granddaughter and that he needed my help to save her."

Grace didn't know how to respond. The short speech sounded rehearsed, as if he were in front of a teleprompter reading the words for a television show. Was he in on the lie with Butch McCall?

"They killed a gorilla," Grace said.

Blackwood sighed. "Butch told me. Unfortunately, it was unavoidable. It was either them or the gorilla. Sometimes difficult decisions have to be made in the wilderness."

"There's an injured man here," Grace said. "They didn't do a thing for him."

"Butch has many talents," Blackwood said. "But medical skills are not among them. He's grateful for what you're doing for him. Despite what you think,

Butch is very upset about the whole incident."

Grace glanced at Butch. "He doesn't look upset."

Blackwood chuckled. "I know Butch's appearance is a little off-putting, but I can assure you beneath his rough exterior lies the soul of an angel—a guardian angel—your guardian angel, Grace. He's there to help you. He's there to make sure you get home."

"What about Marty? What about Wolfe and Laurel Lee?"

"We'll get everyone out," he assured her. "But my primary concern right now is you. At this very moment I'm in my private jet. I'll be in the Congo in the morning. We have a helicopter standing by. I'll have you out of there by tomorrow evening."

"And the others?" Grace asked.

"If we've found them by then, yes."

"And if you haven't?"

"We'll fly you out and continue looking. The Lake Télé region is vast. It won't be easy to locate them, but we will find them."

This was not the answer Grace wanted to hear, and she was about to object, but stopped herself. "I was told you sent Butch and his men out here to find a Pygmy named Masalito," she said. "That you're looking for a dinosaur called Mokélé-mbembé."

"Good Lord!" Blackwood exclaimed. "I see that Travis has not given up on his fantasies. No wonder he didn't tell me how you happened to do a free fall into the Congo. I suppose he told you that I'm interested in the pursuit of so-called cryptids?"

"Yes, he did."

"Well, I'm not," Blackwood assured her. "And I never have been. I've dedicated my life to the preservation of endangered wildlife. Unlike your father, I do not spend my time gallivanting around the world chasing mythical creatures, wasting valuable resources. I was always fond of your father until . . . until he lost your mother. He's a brilliant man, but misguided, and quite frankly, unstable. What kind of man would deny an old man the company of his only granddaughter—his only blood relative? What kind of man would allow two children to fall from a jet? I can tell that you are very perceptive, Grace. And you have no doubt figured out by now that your father needs psychiatric help."

Grace hung up on him, which surprised her as much as it surprised Noah Blackwood. It was all right for her to think Wolfe was crazy, but it was not all right for someone else to say it. Especially now that she knew Wolfe was her father. She didn't have all the answers to Blackwood's questions, but she was certain Wolfe would provide them when she saw him next. She gave the phone to her "guardian angel" and went over to check on his fallen helper, who seemed to be improving. His color was better and the swelling around his face had gone down a little. The phone rang again, as Grace knew it would.

"Just a minute," Butch said, annoyed at being a little girl's receptionist.

Grace had hoped to use the injured man as an excuse not to speak to her grandfather, but the man was sound asleep. She took the phone.

"I guess our connection got interrupted," Blackwood said. "I don't know what kind of nonsense your father has told you about me, but I can assure you that none of it's true. I'm going to make up the years we've lost. I promise you that. I can't wait to meet you. I love you, sweetheart."

Blackwood hung up and Grace felt ants dancing on her neck.

"You can sleep in my hammock," Butch said. "I'll bunk out here with the men."

Grace wasn't about to crawl back into Butch's stinking hammock. "I think I should sleep out here with . . ." She pointed to the injured man.

"His name is Jean-Claude," Butch said, and pointed to the other men. "And that's Philippe and Jacques."

Grace doubted that Butch had used their real names, but it didn't matter. She wasn't planning on staying around long enough for it to make any difference.

"I don't think Jean-Claude will need any more doctoring tonight," Butch said.

"I still think I'll stay out here," Grace said sweetly. "Just in case."

Butch let out an exasperated sigh, then turned to the two men. "The girl's going to sleep out here," he told them in French. "Make certain she stays here. If she gets away I'm not going to pay you a single franc. And keep your hands off her. If either one of you touches her, I'll kill you both. Do you understand?"

The men gave him a surly nod. Butch glanced at Grace. She was sorting through the first-aid supplies and didn't seem to understand a word he was saying. Satisfied, he turned back to the men. "At first light you'll be heading out to intercept the man and the woman. I know exactly where they are and where they're going, thanks to that little computer of theirs. . . ."

He's been following us, Grace thought with alarm. He must have taken the Gizmo when Marty was sleeping by the lake. That's how he knew I was alone at the Skyhouse. He knows . . .

". . . and make sure it looks like an accident."

Grace stifled her gasp of surprise and quickly started tending the injured man. She felt Butch staring at her. "I'll need some fresh water," she said in the steadiest voice she could manage, still bending over the man. "He's dehydrated. I'll have to give him water through the night. And I'm hungry. I have

some freeze-dried eggs. There's enough for everyone, if you're interested."

After a few agonizing seconds, Butch said, "Yeah,
okay." He turned back to his men and switched back
to French. "They'll be wearing colored tags around
their necks. Bury the tags deep."

The men nodded and Butch walked off to get the
water.

Grace pretended to be going through her pack, not
daring to look up at the two men. She had to do
something to warn Wolfe and Laurel. And what
about Marty?

That's when saw the bottle of sleeping pills. She
hoped Butch and his men were hungry.

Subject: Air Cav
From: phil@ewolfe.com
To: wolfe@ewolfe.com

We're on our way.
Phil

"Finally, some good news," Wolfe said, handing
Laurel the Gizmo with Phil's e-mail, the first he had
ever gotten from him. He handed the Gizmo to
Laurel as they waded across a waist-deep swamp.
Laurel's shortcut had been grueling, but it looked like
it was going to work. If they didn't get stuck in quick-

sand they would arrive at Lake Télé in less than twenty-four hours.

"Did you check the Bo cam?" Laurel asked.

Wolfe nodded. "Grace and Marty weren't in the picture, but they're still in the Skyhouse. He looked at Laurel in the beam of his headlamp, still amazed at her stamina. The rough going seemed to have no effect on her. In fact, if anything, she looked stronger than she had before they crossed the Ubangi river. "I have a feeling that I'm slowing you down," he said.

"Don't be ridiculous," Laurel protested. "I'm as tired as you are."

"You don't look it."

Laurel laughed. "Looks are almost always deceiving."

Marty was putting the finishing touches on his final sketch when Masalito finally climbed down the ladder and picked up his bow and quiver. The parrot flew off the Pygmy's shoulder, flew over to the laboratory bench, and squeezed through the opening in the screen.

Marty put his pack on, then looked down at PD. "Change of plans. You and Bo are staying here. I've put food out and it should last you a day or two if Bo doesn't hog everything."

He followed Masalito down through the trapdoor and slipped the lock through the hasp.

escape 26

Grace lay on the edge of Jean-Claude's green tarp, pretending to be asleep.

Through half-closed eyes she watched Butch walk over to his shelter and crawl into it like a bear returning to its den. The two men sat by the fire quarreling about who would take the first guard duty. They finally settled it by cutting cards. Philippe lost with a three of diamonds to Jacques's jack of hearts. Soon the night animals' sounds were mingled with Butch and Jacques's snores, and Philippe's shuffling the deck of cards over and over again. If he didn't stop shuffling and fall asleep soon, Grace knew her plan was doomed. An hour passed and the monotonous shuffling continued. She had put enough sleeping-pill powder into their eggs to put three gorillas to sleep. But now she was worried that the powder hadn't mixed evenly, and Philippe hadn't gotten his share.

She lay perfectly still, using Laurel's gaze-anchoring technique to help pass the time and dull her terror. At the end of the wire she saw herself safely back on Cryptos with Marty, Wolfe, and Laurel. They were gathered in the living room, looking out the window at the Pacific Ocean. Oddly, boarding school was no longer in the picture. She couldn't imagine going back there now that she knew that Wolfe was her father. She recalled the first time he had seen her and his look of astonishment. And the following morning when she caught him crying on the sofa in the library. How was he going to explain everything that had happened? No wonder he had been so awkward around her.

The shuffling finally came to a stop. Very slowly she turned her head and breathed a sigh of relief. Philippe was slumped over, sound asleep.

Grace got to her feet and started toward Butch's crude shelter.

Masalito moved through the jungle like a ghost, ducking under branches and clambering over fallen trees without a sound.

Marty followed like a derailed locomotive engine, breaking branches, tripping, cursing, and hoping Masalito was leading him to Grace. He still wasn't sure if his guide understood the big picture.

After nearly an hour of this, Masalito stopped and waited for Marty to catch up. Masalito pointed to his pack and motioned for him to take it off. At first Marty thought that he was offering to carry it for him, which he didn't think was a good idea. The pack was nearly as big as Masalito. But that wasn't what Masalito had in mind. He took the pack and scraped it along trees and vines and pointed to his ear.

"I get it," Marty said. "It makes too much noise."

Masalito hung it on a branch, then pointed to Marty's machete.

Marty shook his head. "No way! I need it to get through the jungle."

Masalito made wild slashing movement with his arm and again pointed to his ear.

Marty sighed and hung the machete next to the pack.

Masalito squinted at him, then covered his eyes in mock pain as if he were being blinded.

It took Marty a while to realize that he was referring to the headlamp he was wearing. "It's the only way I can see where I'm going!"

Masalito continued his blind man charade.

"Okay, okay. I'll compromise. I'll turn it off, but I'm leaving it on my forehead." Marty turned it off, wondering how long it would take him to smack face-first into a tree. He wished he had brought along a climbing helmet from the Skyhouse. "If you ask me to strip down to my underwear, I'm not doing it. And I'm taking this with me." He opened the pack and took out the small sketchbook he had brought along. "I have a feeling I'm going to need it to talk to you later."

Masalito said something, then scrambled up a tree like a gecko and disappeared.

"Where are you going?" Marty called up after him, but Masalito didn't answer.

Marty sat down and leaned against the tree. As he swatted insects he thought about Noah Blackwood. He still found it hard to believe that he was Grace's grandfather, or that Wolfe was her father for that matter. There must have been an important reason for his parents to have kept this a secret all these years, but he couldn't for the life of him think of what it was.

Twenty minutes went by and he began to wonder if he was supposed to have followed Masalito up the tree. After another twenty minutes he started to think that Masalito had ditched him. He stood up and was about to start climbing, when Masalito dropped to the ground right in front of him.

"You scared me to death!"

Masalito smiled, then squatted down in front of him and started pounding what looked like a chunk of vine with a rock. A terrible smell filled the air.

"What's it for?"

Masalito looked up from his work, then made a buzzing noise and waved his hands around his head.

"Bugs?" Marty looked around and saw that there

wasn't an insect anywhere near them. "Wow!"

Masalito took the ball of smelly pulp and started smearing it all over Marty's body. Despite the stink, Marty didn't resist. Not only was the juice keeping the insects away but he felt instant relief from the itching that had plagued him for the past few days.

Masalito pantomimed that he wanted Marty to follow him closely through the woods and to do everything that he did.

At first Marty had a hard time even seeing Masalito in the dim moonlight, let alone mimicking him, but after a while his eyes adjusted to the dark, and the shadowy pantomime became easier. And he noticed something else. The farther they went and the faster they moved, the better he felt.

Grace was experiencing the opposite feeling.

She was in Butch's shelter, so close to him she could smell his breath. She had quietly searched his pack and every square inch of the shelter's floor, including the insides of two pairs of boots, and still had not found the Gizmo. The only place she hadn't looked was in his pockets, which was why she felt so anxious. Twice he had stopped snoring, and Grace had held perfectly still until the terrible noise resumed. She knew Marty would approach this delicate operation much differently from how she was handling it. He would simply hit Butch in the head with a large rock, find the Gizmo, and walk off with it. Grace had undergone a lot of changes in the past few days, but she could not do that.

Butch was lying in the hammock, his shotgun resting across his chest. She surveyed the pockets she would have to search, trying to determine which would be most likely to contain the Gizmo. He was wearing army fatigues and a baggy shirt.

She reached for the first shirt pocket. The top flap was buttoned. With her heart in her throat she gingerly pushed the button through the hole and slipped her fingers inside. Butch stopped snoring. She froze and held her breath. There was something in the pocket, but it was too big to be the Gizmo. After what seemed like an eternity, Butch resumed his snoring and Grace carefully pulled the object out. It was her Moleskine, which she was glad to have back, but disappointed it wasn't the Gizmo. The next pocket contained Butch's wallet.

She moved down the hammock to Butch's cargo pockets. In the first she found a folding knife, which she took. And in the second pocket, to her great relief, was the Gizmo. Unfortunately, as she was pulling it out, Butch turned over, pinning her arm. When she tried to pull it free the hammock swung toward her and Butch stopped snoring again.

She now wished she had that rock, and went so far as to feel around for one with her free hand.

Butch started snoring again, and her arm started going to sleep. She did not find a rock, but she remembered the knife. She opened a blade with her teeth and started cutting the hammock mesh, one square at time, careful not to stab Butch, and hoping the whole thing didn't unravel and dump her "guardian angel" on the ground.

The hammock held, and with tremendous relief, she took the Gizmo and her Moleskine back to the campfire. Philippe was still slumped over his spilled cards, Jacques was snoring away in his hammock, Jean-Claude had not moved, and to her dismay, the gray parrot had flown into camp and was hopping around the sleeping men. What if it started its terrible screeching? She prayed it wouldn't.

Her immediate goal was to keep Butch and his men away from Wolfe and Laurel. That's all that mattered right now. After that she didn't know what she would do.

She slipped the pack over her shoulders, then turned the Gizmo on, relieved to find Marty's gray tag at the Skyhouse along with Bo's and PD's. For once in his life he hadn't rushed to her rescue. She thought about contacting Wolfe and telling him what was going on, but then thought better of it. There would be time for that once she was safely away from the camp.

But as she started to leave, two hands clamped on

her ankles and pulled her feet out from under her. She hit the ground and the Gizmo went flying. Apparently, Jean-Claude was feeling much better. His hands felt like iron shackles.

"Let go of me, you ingrate!" Grace hissed in French. "I saved your life."

Jean-Claude was surprised that she spoke French, but he did not let her go. The girl may have saved him, but the only way he was going to make it out of Lake Télé alive was if Butch McCall deemed him worthy of being dragged out of the jungle. He tightened his grip.

Grace kicked and clawed at the ground, but could not break free. She glanced in Philippe and Jacques's direction and saw they were both awake now, although moving very slowly. Her plan was coming apart before it had even started.

The parrot let out a loud screech, then hopped over and sunk his sharp black beak into Jean-Claude's remaining ear. Jean-Claude screamed and let go of Grace's ankles. Grace rolled away and got to her feet. There was a roar from Butch's shelter. He came stumbling out, but didn't make it very far. His leg was tangled in the torn hammock and he fell flat on his face. Grace looked around for the Gizmo but didn't see it.

She ran.

Wolfe had removed his prosthetic leg and was working on it with a special tool kit he kept in his pack.

"Can I help?" Laurel asked.

"No, this is a one-person job. I just need to tighten
the screws and make some adjustments to the hinges.
It's a prototype that Ted made for me. This is the first
time it's been in a swamp and it's a little gummed up."

"We'll be on relatively dry ground from now on,"
Laurel said.

"I'm glad of that," Wolfe said. "There is one thing
you can do." He handed her the Gizmo.

Laurel found the blue, gray, pink, and purple tags
at the Skyhouse. "They all seemed to be tucked in for
the night." She hit the Bo cam button. "Marty left us
a message."

Wolfe grabbed the Gizmo. On the screen was a
drawing of Bo and him sitting on a log. Beneath it
was a note:

Wolfe,

Butch has Grace and the Gizmo. No sign of Masalito. I'll wait for you here.

Marty

Wolfe swore. "I knew something was wrong! If Butch so much as . . ." He let the rest of the thought go, closed his eyes, and took a deep breath. When he opened them he looked back at the screen and studied Marty's drawing. "It looks like they're sitting on the *molimo.*"

Laurel nodded in agreement. "What's it mean?"

"I think he's telling us Masalito *is* there. And look at this." He pointed at Bo. "He's drawn her with all the tracking tags around her neck." Wolfe switched back to the tracking mode and zoomed in on the four colors. They were right on top of one another, moving around the Skyhouse at the exact same pace.

"Marty and Masalito aren't there," Laurel said. "But why did Marty leave the tags at the Skyhouse?"

"Butch has a Gizmo," Wolfe said. "Give me your tag."

Laurel took it off. "What are you going to do?"

"Take a page out of Marty's book." He hung his and Laurel's tags on a tree branch.

Philippe was blabbing on about how the gray parrot had bewitched him; Jacques was yelling about how

Philippe had had guard duty; and Jean-Claude was holding his bleeding ear, moaning about how he was the only one alert enough to grab the girl.

"All of you shut up!" Butch shouted. He picked up the Gizmo and checked the tags in the Skyhouse—they were all there. Next, he clicked on the Bo cam and saw Marty's note and drawing. "Oh, that's just perfect! Wolfe knows we have the girl!" He checked Wolfe and Laurel's tags and was shocked to see how close they were. The only good thing was that the tags weren't moving. He got the map out of his pack and walked over to Philippe and Jacques.

"Change of plans. Our friends are making better time than I thought. I want you two to head out immediately and wait here." He pointed to a spot on the map. "It's a narrow land bridge over the swamp. They have to cross it to get here—unless you think it's beyond your capabilities to dispatch a woman and a one-legged man."

Philippe and Jacques assured him that it wasn't.

"While you're taking care of them, I'll retrieve the girl. We'll meet here," he pointed to the map again. "A helicopter will pick us up this evening."

"What about me?" Jean-Claude asked.

Butch looked at him for a long time, then nodded and turned back at Philippe and Jacques. "After you take care of Wolfe and Dr. Lee, come back here and pick up Jean-Claude." He looked at Philippe and shook his head in disgust. "We weren't bewitched by a parrot. We were drugged by a little girl."

Grace had gotten much farther than she thought, and she was worried. The whole point of her escape was to get them to follow her. As she collapsed on her hands and knees with her lungs on fire, there were no breaking branches or shouting men. The only thing she heard was her breathing and the jungle creatures awaking in the gray mist of another dawn.

Where are they? She sat up and saw that the parrot had followed her. He was perched on the lower branch of a tree, calmly preening his feathers. I have no idea where I am, she thought. And with the Gizmo gone, no way to find out.

She looked up at the preening parrot. "I don't suppose you know the way to the Skyhouse?"

The parrot stopped preening and made a gurgling noise.

"That's what I thought." Grace stood and brushed the damp leaves from her pants. If I can find Lake Télé, I can find the Skyhouse. She started forward, but stopped when she discovered that the parrot was not following.

Then he started to fly in the opposite direction.

She nodded. "Okay, I'll follow you," she said. "But I hope you know where you're going."

*　　*　　*

Marty lay next to Masalito at the edge of Butch's camp.

There wasn't much to it. A couple of crude lean-tos (both empty), a green tarp near a smoking fire, and a smell that made Marty want to retch. The camp looked as though it had been abandoned. "Where are they?" he whispered.

Masalito stood, strung an arrow, and motioned for Marty to stay where he was. Without making a sound he walked toward the fire. When he got there he kicked the green tarp. Someone screamed, the tarp flew, and the man beneath backed up like a crayfish being pursued by a bobcat. Masalito followed him with his arrow pointed an inch from his eye.

The man began speaking in terrified French, which was a little hard for Marty to follow, but he was able to pick up enough to hear something about Grace and Butch. The man was a wreck. Marty gently put his hand on Masalito's taut forearm. Masalito nodded grimly and relaxed the bow, but kept the arrow strung. Jean-Claude visibly relaxed.

"What happened to you?" Marty asked in French.

"Gorilla," Jean-Claude answered.

"Where's Grace?"

"She ran away. Butch has gone after her."

"And the others?"

"They have gone after the one-legged man and the woman."

"Wolfe and Laurel?"

Jean-Claude nodded.

"Why?"

Jean-Claude did not answer.

Masalito pulled the arrow back again.

"To kill them," Jean-Claude said.

Butch McCall had not caught up to Grace.

Following her tiny footprints was easy, but he was surprised at how much ground she had covered in the short time she had been gone.

His satellite phone rang. He cursed himself for putting it in his pack, and considered not answering, but if he turned it off, Blackwood would know it and go into a rage. Noah did not tolerate being out of touch with his people, no matter where they were.

"Butch?"

"Yeah."

"How's everything going?"

"Good."

"We'll be landing in a couple of hours. The helicopter is waiting for us. How's the weather?

"Good."

"How's Grace?"

Butch hesitated. "She's fine."

"Let me talk to her."

Butch winced. "Well, she's . . . uh . . ." No one, not even Butch McCall, lied to Noah Blackwood.

"She slipped away early this morning."

"Are you telling me that a little girl escaped from four grown men?" Blackwood shouted.

"We couldn't very well tie her up," Butch defended himself. "That would have blown our rescue story."

"Obviously, she didn't believe your story."

Butch wanted to point out that it was Blackwood's story, not his. "No, sir, she didn't," he said.

"Do you have any idea how important she is to me?"

"Yes."

"What are you doing about it?"

"I'm on her trail right now," Butch said. "She won't get far."

"And our friends?" Blackwood asked.

"They won't be a problem."

"When you find Grace, call me," Blackwood said. "Immediately."

Marty explained the situation with the aid of the sketch pad. Masalito nodded as if he understood and began looking at the ground. He found the footprints of the two men and pantomimed that they should follow them.

"Forget it." Marty was not about to leave Grace in the forest by herself with Butch McCall after her. He pointed at Butch's big boot prints. "I'm going after Grace."

Masalito shook his head.

"I have to find Grace," Marty insisted. "I'd just slow you up." He squatted down and drew a quick sketch of the Skyhouse. "We'll wait for you here."

Masalito stared at the crude drawing for several seconds before finally nodding in agreement.

They started off in separate directions just as daylight began filtering through the canopy.

Butch arrived at the spot where Grace had fallen to her hands and knees to catch her breath. He touched the faint impressions in the soft ground and smiled. She wasn't far, and with the sun up, tracking her would be easy now. He checked the location of Wolfe and the boy. The boy was still at the Skyhouse and Wolfe and the woman were in the same place they had been when he left camp. He shook his head. Something wasn't right. He checked the Vid cam. The bird was flying above the canopy—no sign of people in the picture. What are you up to, Wolfe? he thought.

There was a way to find out, but before taking that path, he unlaced his boots and took off his socks. He always carried several spare socks in his pack. Wet socks kill feet. He wondered how the girl's feet were doing. As his feet air-dried he took the Gizmo out and pushed the VIDEO CONFERENCE icon.

*   *   *

Wolfe and Laurel had been virtually jogging through the forest since seeing Marty's message. Wolfe's stump hurt, but he ignored the pain. The only thing that mattered was reaching Grace and Marty. If Blackwood got his hands on them Wolfe would never see them again.

At first he didn't hear the Gizmo's call above his labored breathing and the heavy pack slapping against his back, but the sound finally filtered through, and he stopped and touched the video conference button.

"Butch," he said.

"Long time no see," Butch said. "Caught any great whites lately?"

Wolfe did not answer. It was obvious Butch had not gotten over the fact that he had failed to bring Blackwood his prized shark. And that was just the beginning of their rivalry. What Butch had really wanted to catch was Rose. Wolfe could see by his expression that his hatred had not dimmed over the years.

"Where's Grace?"

"This little pocket computer is really something," Butch said. "I've got to hand it to you and Ted."

"Where's Grace?" Wolfe repeated. Laurel joined him.

"The old man is very upset with you," Butch said. "First you take his daughter and get her killed. Then you neglect to tell him that he has a granddaughter. I wouldn't want to be in your boots."

"I mean it, Butch. I want her back. And if you so much as—"

"Harm her?" Butch interrupted. "Not likely, pal. You forget who I work for . . . who you used to work for. You know, I can't get over how much she looks like Rose. Brings back memories."

"Let me talk to her."

Butch shook his head. "No way. You've had twelve years to talk to her. It's her grandfather's turn now. And he's a pretty smooth talker."

Wolfe stared at the screen, wishing he could jump through it and throttle him.

"How's the stump?" Butch asked. "I imagine it's getting pretty sore. Doesn't seem to have slowed you down, though. And by the way, nice try on the tracking tags. Did you hang them in a tree? Did you think that would throw me off? You've always underestimated me. Serious mistake. The only reason your sweaty face is still talking is because Noah had some use for you. But not anymore. I wouldn't be surprised if he puts your carcass in one of his dioramas."

"At least let me see her," Wolfe pleaded. "I just want to make sure she's okay."

Butch smiled. "No can do, pal. She's uh . . . indisposed at the moment. But I'll tell you what I will do. We're out here looking for Mokélé-mbembé and we're having a little problem finding it. I mean, you'd think a sauropod would stick out like a sore thumb. Anyway, the rumor is that you might know where we can find it."

"An exchange," Wolfe said hopefully.

"I wouldn't go that far. Blackwood has his heart set on showing Grace the wonders of the world. No, what I had in mind is letting you have a final conversation with her if you could give me an idea of where I might find the beast. You know I'll find it anyway."

"I don't know where it is," Wolfe said.

"Too bad. But of course I don't believe you. It would be out of character for you to mount an expedition to the Congo for the fun of it. This isn't Disneyland."

"The only reason I came here was to find Masalito before you did."

"You came here so he wouldn't tell us where to find Mokélé-mbembé."

"How much is Blackwood paying you?"

"A lot more than you can afford," Butch answered. "Look, I'd better get going. If you change your mind about that conversation with Grace, give me a call back. And because I'm a generous guy, I'll pass on some more information. It will save that stump of yours some wear and tear." Butch looked at his watch. "By the time you get here we'll be long gone. I gotta go. Call me sometime."

The screen went blank. Wolfe stared at it for a long time before looking up at Laurel. "How long before we get there?"

"Three or four hours. Maybe a little longer."

Wolfe started walking. And oddly, the pain in his stump had gone away.

Marty had overheard most of the conversation between Butch and Wolfe.

He was hiding behind a fallen tree not twenty feet from where Butch was now massaging his bare feet. He knew he wasn't going to get another chance like this. He crept forward, carrying a large stick, which snagged on a vine, alerting Butch, who reached for his shotgun a little too late. The blow to his bald head wasn't hard enough to knock Butch out, but it gave Marty enough time to scoop up one of his boots, the Gizmo . . . and run.

Butch yelled.

There was a gunshot.

Marty didn't look back.

He ran for at least a mile, coming to a stop near a pond. He threw the boot into the water and watched the crocodiles fight over it, while he caught his breath and figured out what he was going to do next.

Will Butch continue after Grace? Marty asked himself. Try to catch me? Or will he head back to camp to get another pair of boots? Providing he has spares, which I hope he doesn't. He listened for the sound of pursuit, but heard nothing. Satisfied that Butch had taken option number three, he switched the Gizmo on and called Wolfe.

Wolfe's face appeared immediately, and the scowl on it changed to shock when he saw who it was. "How did . . ." he stuttered. "I just talked to—"

"I swiped it from him," Marty said. "Along with his right boot, or maybe it was his left."

"Butch is nobody to be fooling around . . ."

The picture and sound started to break up. "What?"

The picture came back on. "My battery's getting weak and I don't have any spares. We'll have to make this brief."

"Butch sent two guys to kill you and Laurel," Marty said.

"When did they leave Butch's camp?"

"I don't know. Masalito is on their trail."

"You mean he's not with you?" Wolfe raised his voice in alarm.

"Not anymore."

"And Grace?"

"She got away from them sometime this morning. Butch was following her when I got his boot."

Wolfe sighed. "You'd better start from the beginning."

Marty quickly explained what had happened.

When he finished, Wolfe stared at the screen for a while before responding. "I think I know where they're going to set up their ambush."

"Can you go around them?"

Wolfe shook his head. "It would take too much time. Don't worry about us. You need to find Grace."

"I'll find her," Marty said.

"Do you have that silent whistle?"

Marty took it out of his pocket and held it in front of the Gizmo.

"Good. Call Vid in to you. He's closer to you right now than he is to us. If he sees you, we'll know where you are. He also might spot Grace, and you can track to his signal. If he spots Butch, stay away from him. "

"I will."

"When you find Grace I want you to go directly to the Skyhouse."

"Okay." Marty was about to turn the Gizmo off, but found himself hesitating. "Are you Grace's father?"

"I am," Wolfe said.

"And Noah Blackwood?"

"He's her grandfather."

Marty nodded. "Be careful."

Reunion 28

Grace was disheartened. Her plan had failed miserably.

For the past hour she had been making as much noise as she possibly could, hoping to draw Butch and his men away from Wolfe and Laurel. But none of them had appeared. They were either the worst trackers in the world, or they had decided to take care of Wolfe and Laurel first, knowing then they would have all the time they needed to find her.

On top of this, she had no idea where she was. She continued to follow the parrot. She didn't know what else to do.

With great caution, Marty worked his way back to where he had hit Butch on the head. As he'd hoped, it looked like Butch had returned to camp for fresh footwear. In the muddy trail there were clear imprints of a left boot and a right sock heading in that direction.

Following Grace's path through the forest was not easy. Her step was much lighter than Butch's, and Marty would sometimes lose the trail for hundreds of yards before picking it up again. Grace was heading roughly toward the Skyhouse, but in a crazy way. She would follow a clear trail for a while, then inexplicably leave the trail, breaking through thick foliage for a time, then pick up another trail, and repeat the process. If she was trying to throw Butch off her track, this was not the way to do it. When they got back to Cryptos he was going to give her some lessons in how to ditch a tracker. The subject had been thoroughly covered at survival camp.

Every few minutes he stopped to check the Vid cam and blow the whistle. The raven was flying above the canopy, but so far he hadn't spotted Grace or Butch.

Marty heard Grace before he saw her. She was talking to someone. He wondered if Butch had tricked him with the footprints heading back to camp. Silently, he crawled forward. Grace was talking to a tree. At least that's what it looked like. He stepped out into the open.

Grace screamed in delight, ran over, and threw her arms around him. "They're going to kill Wolfe and Laurel," she said breathlessly. "We have to warn them. Noah Blackwood is on his way to pick me up. Butch is—"

Marty managed to separate himself from her iron grip and held her at arm's length. "You look pretty good for someone who's been kidnapped."

"Did you hear what I said about Wolfe and Laurel?"

He took the Gizmo out. "I already warned them."

"How did you get that?"

Marty explained what had happened since Butch had taken her from the Skyhouse, leaving out the trunk and photos of Rose. He didn't know if she knew that Wolfe was her father and he wasn't exactly sure how to broach the subject.

When he finished, Grace explained what had happened to her, leaving out the reason she had fainted, her nightmare that was actually a memory, and the parrot who was still perched in the branch above them. Marty hadn't noticed him yet.

Their updates were followed by an awkward silence, something neither of them had ever experienced with each other.

"What's the matter?" Grace finally asked.

"Nothing," Marty answered innocently. "I was just thinking we should get moving toward the Skyhouse. It won't take long for Butch to lace up his boots and get back on our trail."

He was right about Butch, but Grace didn't believe this was what he was thinking. "Did you happen to go up to the second floor of the Skyhouse?"

"Yeah," Marty admitted.

Grace's blue eyes began to well with tears. "So, you saw the nursery."

Marty turned away. She gently turned him back. He had begun to cry as well. She told him about the dream. When she finished, she said, "It doesn't make any difference, Marty. As far as I'm concerned you're still my brother."

Marty wiped his tears away and grinned. "Older brother," he said.

"What?"

He told her about the photographs he had found in the trunk. "One of them was you celebrating your first birthday. You'll be thirteen, two weeks . . ." He checked the date on his watch, "from yesterday."

Butch McCall was in a foul mood.

His head hurt where the boy had cracked him with the branch. His right foot was on fire from the vicious thorn he had stepped on on his way back to camp. And he was still groggy from the sleeping pills. When he arrived at camp he kicked the sleeping Jean-Claude awake.

"Why didn't you grab the boy?"

"What boy?" Jean-Claude said innocently. "I've been unconscious since you left. I'm not feeling—"

"Give it a rest! The boy was here. Along with the Pygmy. Their tracks are all over the place."

"What happened to your head?" Jean-Claude asked.

Butch didn't answer. He limped over to his lean-to and put on his boots, then started following the Pygmy and the boy's tracks. He came to the place where the Pygmy had gone after his men and the boy had followed Grace. He swore and tried to reach the men on the walkie-talkie, but there was no answer. They were too far away. His brain told him to follow the Pygmy and make sure he didn't interfere with his plan for Wolfe and Laurel. His battered pride told him to go after the kids who had duped him. His pride won out.

"Where are Wolfe and Laurel?" Grace asked.

"I don't know. They took their tags off. Wolfe said they would be at the Skyhouse this afternoon. Why were you talking to a tree when I got here?"

"I wasn't." She pointed up. "I told you there was a parrot."

"We've met," Marty said. "It's an African gray parrot, sometimes called a Congo gray parrot. And you didn't tell me that it talked."

"I didn't know till yesterday. What did it say to you?"

"'Rose is back,'" Marty answered.

"That's what it said to me," Grace said. "It seems to want to show me something."

"We're not going to follow the parrot," Marty protested. "Wolfe was very specific about us going directly to the Skyhouse."

"Aren't we going in that direction?"

"More or less."

"Aren't you curious?"

Marty looked up at the parrot. "A little," he admitted. "I've been following your tracks, and the bird does seem to have something in mind."

Grace smiled.

"We'd better call Wolfe." He handed her the Gizmo.

It was the first time Grace had seen Wolfe since learning he was her father, and a stream of emotions filled her when she saw his tired face on the little screen. She felt concern, fear, and affection for the man looking at her. "Hi," she said shyly.

"Hi," Wolfe said. "I'm sure glad to see you. Marty's a good man to have around."

"Yes, he is." She glanced at Marty, who was beaming at the compliment.

"How did you get away from Butch?"

She told him about the sleeping pills. Wolfe laughed, then asked if they were headed to the Skyhouse.

"More or less," Grace said. "We'll be there soon. Noah Blackwood is on his way here in a helicopter."

"A helicopter," Wolfe said. "That might come in handy. Bertha . . ."

The Gizmo screen blinked off.

"His battery's going dead," Marty said.

The Gizmo came back on. "What about Butch?" Wolfe asked.

"We haven't seen him."

"You've got to keep moving."

"We will."

"My battery is just about gone, so I can't explain everything, but things are looking up. Just get to the Skyhouse and we'll be there soon."

"What about Butch's men?"

"Don't worry about them. I have a pretty good idea of where they're going to be waiting. We'll get around them."

"How's Laurel?"

"I'm about a hundred and fifty yards behind her and I'm afraid if I don't catch up soon, she'll leave me behind. In other words, she's doing better than I am."

"I know you're my father," Grace said. "And it's okay." The words had just slipped out, and they weren't exactly the words she wanted to use, but it was too late to take them back.

Wolfe stared at the screen for several seconds, then his face broke into a broad grin, which completely transformed his appearance. "Okay is absolutely wonderful," he said.

the stream 29

Grace and Marty had been following the parrot for half an hour.

"I think this parrot's crazy," Marty said.

He looked at his watch. "Fifteen minutes, then we head to the Skyhouse on our own. I'm starving."

Grace did not argue, she was getting hungry too.

Five minutes later Marty said, "Do you smell that?"

"Yes." The stench was impossible to ignore. "It smells like Butch's camp."

"We're a long way from there," Marty said.

They walked a little farther and stopped at a small stream. Marty pointed to a tree on the other side with several well-fed vultures perched in it. "I think there's a snack bar open somewhere around here."

Grace was not interested in the vultures. She turned around. The parrot was perched in a tree about ten feet to their left. She walked over to it. The parrot ruffled its feathers and started preening.

Marty joined her. "What's going on?"

"This is the tree," Grace said.

"What are you talking about?"

Grace sat down next to the tree and told him how her mother had been killed and how Wolfe had lost his leg. "All these years I thought it was a nightmare, but it really happened. My mother set me in the branches of this tree. She crossed the stream there." She pointed. "A Mokélé-mbembé came out of those bushes to the right. I think it was the flash from her camera that made it mad. It picked her up . . ." Grace covered her face and began to sob.

Marty held her hand for a while, then stood up. "Let's cross over and take a closer look."

Grace shook her head.

"You've come this far," Marty said. "You might as well finish it. We're not going to be back here anytime soon. If you don't look now you'll regret it."

Reluctantly, Grace followed him across the shallow stream, with the vultures looking on.

"This is far enough," Wolfe said, taking his pack off and sitting down. Laurel sat down next to him.

Wolfe consulted his Gizmo. "If Marty's information is accurate, they're waiting for us here." He pointed to the land bridge. "It's the only way through this area."

"We could go around," Laurel said.

"That would take at least another day, which we don't have. Blackwood's on his way. And I'm worried about Masalito. He didn't follow these guys for the fun of it. He'll try to take them out and he might get hurt in the process. The original reason for this trip was to protect him. I suspect he's somewhere on the other side of the gap trying to figure out what to do."

"What do you suggest?"

"Actually, Grace gave me the idea." He took a leather case out of his pack and unzipped it. Inside was a pistol.

"You can't fight them with that," Laurel protested.

"I don't intend to fight them," Wolfe said. "I'm going to put them to sleep. This is a tranquilizer gun."

"Why did you bring a tranquilizer gun?"

"Mokélé-mbembé."

"I was under the impression that you didn't believe—"

"Not entirely," Wolfe confessed. "A cryptozoologist can't afford to be completely skeptical." He patted his pack. "I also brought along everything a veterinarian might need to treat an ailing dinosaur."

"What do you want me to do?"

"If they start firing, I want you to run through that gap as fast as you can."

"And leave you by yourself?" Laurel protested.

"One of us has to get through. And I hate to admit it, but you're better in the woods than I am. You have the best chance of reaching Grace and Marty. Also, I don't speak Pygmy . . . you do. You're the only one who can explain what's going on."

Laurel held his gaze for a moment.

Uncomfortable, Wolfe looked back down at the Gizmo and checked the Vid cam. He swore.

Butch was looking at the ground, his bald head in sharp contrast to the greenery surrounding him.

"He's tracking them," Wolfe said grimly, and quickly checked Vid's location. "And if he's close to Grace and Marty, they're still a long way from the Skyhouse."

Almost as if he could hear, Butch looked directly up at Vid and gave him a broad smile, waved, then walked out of the camera's view.

"This is where Mokélé-mbembé came out?" Marty asked. He was on his knees in front of the wall of vines Grace had pointed to.

"Yes," Grace said. "And you're making me a little nervous sitting in front of it like that."

"Nothing bigger than a duiker has come through here in years. It's all overgrown, but this is where the horrible smell is coming from. At least it's a lot stronger down here than it is anywhere else."

The Gizmo rang. He took it out of his pocket.

"What are you doing?" Wolfe asked. "You should be at the Skyhouse by now. Butch is on your trail!"

"Where is he?" Marty asked with alarm.

"I'm not sure, but we just saw him on the Vid cam."

"Vid isn't—"

Quark . . . quark . . . quark . . .

Vid landed right next to him and looked up at the vultures with suspicion.

"Gotta go," Marty said, stuffing the Gizmo into his pocket. He stood and listened. He didn't hear anything unusual, but that didn't mean Butch wasn't close. The parrot flew from the tree on the other side of the stream, landed next to Vid, and bit him. Vid flew away.

"We have to get out of here."

"Which way?"

Marty looked down at the vines where the smell was coming from. "We'll hide in here until the coast is clear. After you."

A few days earlier there was no way Grace would have gone first. She squeezed through the vines on her hands and knees.

Grace had a much easier time wriggling through the brush than Marty did. She emerged from the tangle several minutes before her cousin, and found herself in a sculpted tunnel of vines and branches. Light filtered through the domed ceiling like sunlight

307

flowing through cut glass in a cathedral. The ground had been packed hard and was clear of growth, as if it had been weeded. It was so beautiful that she nearly forgot the terrible stench.

Their father's backpack came through the vines, followed by Marty's arms, head, and shoulders. Grace took his hands and helped pull him free. The parrot hopped through right after him.

"This wasn't one of my better ideas," he said, brushing a spider off his face.

"I don't know," Grace said. "At least we're safe from Butch in here."

Marty stood and was just as impressed with their surroundings as Grace. "I've never seen anything like it. In fact, I've never *heard* of anything like it." He looked up at the domed ceiling. "I guess the tunnel was made by Mokélé-mbembé. After all these years you'd think it would be a little more overgrown."

"A lot more overgrown," Grace said nervously.

Marty put the pack on. "At least big M hasn't used this as an exit in a while."

"What should we do?"

"I wish Bo were here," Marty said. "This is a perfect job for a scout."

They started down the tunnel.

* * *

"This is where we part company," Wolfe whispered.

He and Laurel were hiding behind a fallen tree. He pointed to the narrow land bridge. "They're up there somewhere. I'm going to go straight ahead. I want you to swing to the right and wait. When you hear the commotion, run through the gap."

"I still think—"

"I'll be fine," Wolfe interrupted. "They expect us to come pounding through here like a couple of elephants. I'll have the tranquilizer dart in them before they know what happened. As soon as they're out, I'll catch up with you and Masalito."

Laurel gave him a hug, then began working her way to the right.

Wolfe took his pack off and began filling the darts with tranquilizer. The dart pistol was virtually silent, but he knew he would only have a chance for two shots, perhaps three. He wished that tranquilizers worked like they did in the movies, with the animal collapsing as soon as it was hit. But the truth was that it took time—ten to fifteen minutes—for the drug to take effect. This meant he would have to stay concealed, or run, until the men were down.

His preparations were interrupted by the loud roar of a jet passing overhead.

"What was that?" Grace asked.

"Sounded like a jet," Marty said, hoping that's all it was.

"It was loud."

"Yeah." Marty's voice was a little shaky. "Do you remember what Mokélé-mbembé sounds like?"

"Yes," Grace answer. "But it didn't sound anything like that."

Marty breathed a sigh of relief. "Where's the parrot?"

"Up ahead somewhere."

They continued down the twisting vine tunnel, which was much longer than they thought it would be.

Wolfe crept forward. Every twenty feet he stopped for several minutes to watch and listen. The closer he got to the bridge, the more he worried. What if they were waiting on the other side? What if they were hiding in the swamp waiting for them to cross? If they were on the other side he wouldn't be able to reach them. The effective range of a tranquilizer pistol was only about thirty feet. And what about Grace and Marty? Had Butch caught up with them? He was tempted to check in on them, but now wasn't the time. Why hadn't he thought to bring more batteries with him? He closed his eyes and took a deep breath. He knew better than to let his mind wander during a stalk. He crawled forward a few more feet, then stopped. At first he did not recognize the sound. It came from his left, subtle, but persistent. Cards, he thought. Someone is shuffling a deck of playing cards.

He crawled toward the sound very slowly and picked up the faint smell of cigarette smoke.

"Just deal," a man said in French.

"When they're shuffled," a second man responded.

They were sitting across from each other with a flat rock between them.

Wolfe was too far away for a clean shot. He worked his way around toward a large moss-covered log to their right, taking his time, stopping every couple feet to make sure they hadn't heard him. Their guns were leaned up against a tree, out of easy reach. The pistol only held one dart at a time. He would have to reload between shots. He hoped he would have time before they got to the shotguns.

He finally reached the log. Beneath it was an opening just big enough for him to stick the pistol through. He slipped a dart into the breech and held the other dart in his teeth.

Quark . . . quark . . . quark . . .

Butch looked up irritably at the raven and the vultures, then squatted in front of where Marty and Grace had crawled through the tightly packed vines.

It would take me hours to cut my way through there. He sniffed the air. Something dead. Big and dead. And it didn't get in there the same way the brats had crawled. He glanced back up at the vultures. Four of them. Where there are four there are dozens.

Butch set off to find the rest of them.

Philippe jumped up and screamed. His cards went flying.

"Quiet!" Jacques hissed. "They'll hear us."

"I've been bitten by a snake," Philippe screamed.

"Where?" Jacques started looking around in a panic. A snake could bite two people as easily as it could one. He started toward his shotgun, but stopped when a searing pain erupted from the back of his thigh. He reached down and ripped the barbed dart out.

"It's not a snake," he said, holding the aluminum shaft out for Philippe to see.

Philippe stopped jumping around and stared at the shaft, then reached back and pulled the dart out of his butt.

As enjoyable as the scene was, Wolfe did not stick around to see any more. As soon as they got over the shock, they would come looking for him. He backed away from the log, hoping the distraction had been enough for Laurel to slip over the bridge.

the nest 30

Grace and Marty came to a stop about ten feet from the end of the tunnel. In front of them was an open area lit by bright sunlight and scattered with engorged vultures.

"I don't think Mokélé-mbembé would tolerate vultures," Grace said hopefully.

Marty didn't think so either. "Let's go see what's on the menu."

They stepped out into a clearing nearly fifty feet across, roughly circular, surrounded by dense trees. Directly across from them was a second opening, identical to the one they had just stepped through. The parrot was picking at the ground.

"What is this place?"

Marty barely heard her. He was looking at the forty or so vultures to their left, fighting over the last scraps of what had once been a very large animal. "Mokélé-mbembé," he said.

This time Grace did not laugh or disagree. There

was enough skin and bone left to see what that animal had once been, and it was clear that it was unlike anything they had ever seen before.

The skin was the color of green olives, dappled with purple splotches. Its tail was as long as its body, thick at the base, tapering down to a fist-sized nodule at the tip. Its legs were the size and shape of an elephant's, but on the feet, instead of toenails were three large claws. Its neck was nearly as long as the tail, topped by a large skull with two rows of sharp teeth that had been exposed by the hungry vultures.

Grace shuddered at the memory of what those jaws had done to her mother and Wolfe. "Do you think it's the last one?"

"Has to be," Marty answered. "You overheard Laurel tell Wolfe that the male died, but the female was still alive. This must be her, and she hasn't been dead very long." He took the Gizmo out and started taking digital photos. "Wait till Luther sees these photos. He's going to flip."

"Marty!" Grace shouted. "Over here."

Grace was on her knees at the far end of the clearing, holding what looked like a deflated soccer ball. "I think it's an egg," she said. "One of the vultures must have dug it up."

Marty took it from her. It was nearly torn in two. The shell was leathery and pliable—nothing like the brittle egg Laurel had brought to Cryptos. He turned around and looked at the clearing again.

"This must be why Mokélé-mbembé attacked your mom and Wolfe."

"What are you talking about?"

"We're standing in the middle of a dinosaur nest. Your parents got too close." Marty began digging in the soft soil. "We've got to see if there are more eggs."

"What about Butch?"

"I bet you a dollar I find an egg before you do."

Grace started digging.

Wolfe had a bird's-eye view of Philippe, stumbling, dropping his shotgun, then collapsing on the ground. Jacques glanced back at his partner for a moment, then continued forward, stopping directly below the tree Wolfe had climbed.

Keep going, Wolfe pleaded silently. Don't look up.

Jacques looked up, grinned, brought his shotgun to his shoulder, and fell over backward. The shotgun went off, peppering the branches and leaves all around Wolfe's perch, but none of the pellets found him. Wolfe breathed a deep sigh of relief and climbed down.

He threw Jacques over his shoulder and walked back to where Philippe lay. He had never tranquilized a human before and was a little worried they might have an adverse reaction to the drug, but their pulses and respirations were normal. The men would be out for at least two hours before they could walk with any coordination. That would give him plenty of time to reach the Skyhouse.

Before he left, he checked the Gizmo.

Subject: Delivery
From: phil@ewolfe.com
To: wolfe@ewolfe.com

Package delivered. We'll be waiting on the tarmac. Good luck.
   Phil

Wolfe smiled. Two e-mails in as many days. Phil hated computers, e-mail, cell phones, two-way radios, even regular phones, preferring to communicate face-to-face. He wrote him back, then checked the Vid cam.

Butch had moved about two miles from where he had last seen him. He was standing behind a tree looking at something.

Vid flew off and started circling above the trees. A small clearing came into view.

"I don't believe it!" Marty said.

Grace turned around from where she was digging. Cupped in Marty's trembling hands was a perfectly formed white egg.

"There's two of them," he said. "And you owe me a dollar."

Grace hurried over. He handed her the egg and carefully dug the second egg out.

"Do you think they're fertilized?" Grace asked.

"Depends on how long ago the male died."

"Maybe we should put them back."

Marty shook his head. "And let the vultures eat them?"

Quark . . . quark . . . quark . . .

Vid landed near the carcass.

The Gizmo rang. Marty set the egg down and answered.

"What do you think you're doing?" Wolfe shouted. "Butch McCall is less than two hundred yards from where you two are sitting."

Marty had just about forgotten about Butch in his excitement over finding the eggs. "We . . ." he stuttered. "Hang on." He handed Grace the second egg and pointed the Gizmo at their find.

"Where are you?" Wolfe asked in awe.

Marty turned the Gizmo back on himself. "We're sitting in the middle of Mokélé-mbembé's nest."

Wolfe stared at him in silence as he went over the possibilities and decided what had to be done. "Do a three-sixty with the Gizmo," he said. "I need to see where you are."

Marty stood and started turning in a very slow circle.

"Hold it," Wolfe said. "What's that?"

"Mokélé-mbembé," Marty said. "Or at least what's left of her. I took a bunch of photos and downloaded them to the Cybervault."

Wolfe stared at the carcass. It had taken Rose and him nearly two years to find Mokélé-mbembé. And they never did find the nest. Grace and Marty had found both in a matter of days.

"How did you find it?"

"A little bird told us." Marty pointed the Gizmo up at the parrot.

"His name's Congo," Wolfe explained. "Rose . . . Grace's mother named him. He adopted us the day we arrived at Lake Télé. They were inseparable. I'm surprised he's still around after all these years." He shook off the sad memories. "Continue panning."

Marty completed the circle. "What do you think?"

"Two entrances," Wolfe said. "Which one did you come through?"

Marty told him about the blocked tunnel.

"You'll have to go back through the same one. Butch is waiting for you outside the second entrance. At least he was a moment ago. I . . ."

The picture on Marty's Gizmo went blank, but he could still hear Wolfe.

"The battery's going," he said hurriedly. "Before you leave I want you to set Mokélé-mbembé on fire."

"You're kidding."

"Do you have matches? Maybe some kind of fuel?"

Marty felt in his pockets and found the matches he had put there the night they arrived at the Skyhouse. "Yeah, but I don't understand why—"

"Mokélé-mbembé's DNA," Wolfe said. "She has to be destroyed so that Blackwood doesn't get his hands on it. As soon as you set the fire, get out of there. Go directly to the Skyhouse. I mean it, Marty. No more side trips. When you get there, bolt the trapdoors from the inside."

"What about the eggs?"

"Take them with you. Be careful with them, but remember, they're not nearly as important as you and Grace. If they slow you down, destroy them. Bertha . . ."

The Gizmo went dead.

Marty looked at Grace. "Bertha?"

Grace shrugged her shoulders.

"Do you want to torch a dinosaur or pack eggs?" Marty asked.

"I'll pack the eggs."

Butch was beginning to wonder if he had made a mistake by waiting outside the second entrance for the kids. It was the most direct route to the Skyhouse, but they rarely took the most direct route to anywhere.

Quark . . . quark . . . quark . . .

The raven came flying through the opening, followed by half a dozen hopping vultures, too heavy with food to fly.

Butch stepped out from behind the tree expecting the kids to come out next. Instead, a gray parrot flew out, followed by a cloud of smoke the same color as its feathers.

"Hurry!" Marty shouted. "Smoke's coming up behind us."

Marty's head was bumping into the bottom of Grace's boots. "I'm going as fast as I can," she said. They had reached the end of the tunnel and were crawling out the same way they came in. Before Marty had lit the dinosaur, Grace put the eggs into the pack, cushioning them with moss and Monkey so they wouldn't be damaged. The only problem now was that the pack was three times larger than it had been. It was like pushing a beach ball through a thorn hedge.

"If you hadn't used the camp stove fuel on the dinosaur we might have had more time to get through here," Grace said.

"If you had let me use your Moleskine to light the fire I wouldn't have had to use the fuel," Marty said, although he probably would have had to use the fuel anyway. (Marty always enjoyed a good fire.) He had covered Mokélé-mbembé with branches and moss, but it wasn't dry enough to light with a match. Grace had emptied the pack to make room for the eggs and discovered the fuel, which Marty had liberally applied to the carcass. When he dropped the match, Mokélé-mbembé didn't light—it exploded. Marty was blown backward, his hair and eyebrows were singed, which was nothing compared to what had happened to the handful of vultures that had refused to give up control of the carcass. Two of them lit up like torches. The others fled down the nearest tunnel.

Grace had stopped again.

Marty twisted around to see behind. All he could see was smoke. At least I have the satisfaction of knowing Blackwood isn't going to get his hands on Mokélé-mbembé, he thought. Unless he likes his DNA charbroiled. A vulture came up behind him and pecked at his sneaker. "We're not on the menu yet." He kicked it away. "If you don't get moving, Grace, those eggs are going to be poached and so are we."

"I'm almost there," Grace said. "Just a few more feet."

They stumbled out of the vines, coughing, followed by several vultures with smoking feathers. While Grace scooped water from the stream to wet her parched throat, Marty checked the eggs, which seemed to have survived their smoky crawl.

Grace joined him.

"Where're Vid and Congo?" Marty asked.

"They flew off when you blew up the dinosaur."

"I didn't blow it up!"

Grace smiled. "You know, you look better without eyebrows."

Butch had to wait for the smoke to clear before entering the tunnel.

What he found in the scorched clearing made him very angry. There was only one reason the kids would burn Mokélé-mbembé—Dr. Travis Wolfe—which meant that Philippe and Jacques had failed to get rid of him. He tried them on the two-way, but there was still no answer.

There was just enough left of the beast to figure out what it had been, but not enough to collect usable DNA.

He walked around the clearing and came to the spot where Grace and Marty had been digging. What were they looking for? A flash of white caught his eye. He stooped down and picked it up.

Eggs. They were looking for eggs. And by the look of this ground, they might have found one or two.

Wolfe stopped in the middle of the land bridge and threw one of the shotguns into the murky water. He looked at the ground and saw Laurel's tiny boot prints, which reminded him of Rose's. He thought about Grace and Marty. When he had brought them to Cryptos to live with him, he had had no idea how challenging it would be.

I forgot what I was like at their age, he thought. What his sister, Sylvia, was like, too. Wild. We all have that Wolfe blood running in our veins, drawing us to risk like a moth to a flame. If these first few weeks are any indication of what it's going to be like, the next several years are going to be very interesting for me.

He could still hardly believe they had found Mokélé-mbembé's nest and two eggs. Until Laurel had shown up on Cryptos, he was convinced the beast was gone, extinguished forever at his and Masalito's hands. In the past eleven years not a day had gone by when he hadn't relived, second by second, the two minutes it had taken to kill Mokélé-mbembé. Could he have done something different? Could he have saved Rose? Could he have saved Mokélé-mbembé? Those two terrible minutes were the driving force behind his search for other cryptids. But now Grace and Marty had the eggs. The last deposits of prehistory. And perhaps more important, a way for him to look forward instead of backward.

His reverie was interrupted by the sound of branches cracking. He stopped and listened, relieved when he realized the sound was coming from in front of him and not behind, where he had left Philippe and Jacques. A moment later, Laurel and Masalito broke through the brush to his left.

"We heard the shots," Laurel said, out of breath.

Wolfe put his hand on Masalito's shoulder. "It's good to see you, old friend."

Masalito looked at Wolfe's leg and grinned.

The juice Masalito had given Marty had lost its potency, and the insects were attacking him with renewed vigor. He looked back at Grace. The parrot had found them again and was sitting on her shoulder.

"I was just thinking of that delicious omelet you made yesterday," she said. "Is there any more of that canned chicken left at the Skyhouse?"

"The place is crawling with it," Marty mumbled.

Grace caught up with him. "What did you say?"

"I said that if I don't get something to eat soon, I'm going to take one of these eggs I'm *hauling* and fry it."

"How far are we from the Skyhouse?"

"We'll be there soon."

"Do you have Grace?" Noah Blackwood asked.

"Not yet," Butch said.

"We'll be there in less than half an hour," Blackwood said, raising his voice. "What's going on there, Butch?"

"Mokélé-mbembé eggs."

There was a long pause followed by a much calmer voice. "How many eggs?"

"I don't know."

324

"So you don't have them."

"No, but I will by the time you get here."

"Are the eggs viable?"

Butch thought about the broken egg he had found in the nest. "There's a good possibility."

"And Mokélé-mbembé?"

"Dead."

"You saw it?"

"What was left of it."

"Any recoverable DNA?"

"Not a chance." Butch took his map out as he walked. "I've got an alternative landing spot for you. It will be tight, but I think the pilot can put it down there." He gave Blackwood the coordinates.

"What about Wolfe and Dr. Lee?" Blackwood asked.

Butch had just tried again to reach Philippe and Jacques on the radio without success, which could not be good.

"I have to go." Butch hung up and quickened his pace.

grandfather 31

By the time Grace and Marty reached the Skyhouse clearing, they could barely walk. The activities of the past twenty-four hours and lack of food and sleep had just about done them in.

"We made it," Marty said dully. The first thing he was going to do when he got into the Skyhouse was eat everything he could swallow, then lie down on the bed—no, the sofa. He didn't think he had the strength to climb to the second floor.

They walked toward the aluminum ladder in a daze.

"When did Wolfe say he was going to get here?" Grace asked.

"He didn't. At least not before his Gizmo conked out." Marty started up the ladder, then hesitated.

"What's the matter?"

He stepped back down to the ground. "I'd better check this out before we go sticking our heads up through the trapdoor. I don't think Butch beat us here, but you never know." He took the Gizmo out and punched the Bo cam. It was not in the same position as before, but that wasn't surprising, with Bo and PD running around, which they were in fact doing at that very moment. Bo lumbered in and out of the picture, followed a moment later by the dainty PD. The camera was pointed toward the kitchen area. Every cupboard was open and stuff was strewn all over the counter and floor.

"Looks like they've been having fun," he said, looking at Grace. She was sitting on the ground with her face in her hands. "Are you okay?"

She raised her head and said, "I'm just . . ." She was too tired to say tired.

"You don't look too good." She was sunburned; dirt and leaves had pulled all of the curl out of her hair; and there were dark half-moons under her eyes. Marty didn't tell her so, but she looked like a blue-eyed raccoon. "I'll climb up and make sure things are clear. Then I'll send the elevator down for you."

"What elev—"

"You'll see." Marty started up the ladder.

Bo and PD were excited to see him when he climbed through the trapdoor. PD did circles around his legs and Bo handed him his cap, which was covered with something sticky and smelly.

"At least you made an attempt to clean up your

mess," he said. "But I wish you hadn't used my cap to do it." He threw it down.

He hadn't thought about where the animals were going to poop while he was gone. And by the look of things they hadn't thought about it much either. He made a quick search of the Skyhouse, then climbed up to the roof and started lowering the lift down through the canopy. Bo grabbed PD and jumped into the bucket.

"You're not coming up the same way," he yelled down to them. "The return trip is reserved for my cousin."

Bo hooted and PD barked.

Grace had dozed off and was startled awake by the sound of breaking branches, hooting, and high-pitched barking as the lift came down through the canopy. She found herself smiling in spite of her exhaustion. It seemed like an eternity since she had seen the two occupants. Bo jumped out with PD in her arms before the bucket reached the ground.

They started chasing each other around the tree, but Grace didn't have time to enjoy their antics. As soon as the bucket touched the ground, Marty started it back up. She quickly but gently put the pack in it, and was about to climb in herself, when she was pulled backward. At first she thought it was Bo playing one of her tricks.

"What's your hurry?" Butch asked.

Still holding her around the waist, he made a lunge for the pack.

"No!" Grace managed to get her legs tangled in his. Butch stumbled and fell. The elevator rose out of his reach.

"I've had just about enough of you." He threw her on her stomach and wrenched her arms behind her back.

Congo latched on to his hand. "You little . . ." He tore the parrot off and threw it against a tree.

Grace felt her hands being tied, then her feet. When he finished, he flipped her over. He was covered in sweat and dirt and there was an ugly gash on his head.

"Where's the parrot?" she shouted, struggling against the ties.

"Your grandfather has a thousand lousy parrots," Butch shouted back. "Were the eggs in the pack?"

"I don't know what you're talking about."

Butch smiled. "I guess I'll just have to go up there and check it out for myself." He touched the gash on his head. "I'm looking forward to it."

"Watch out, Marty!" she screamed. "He's coming up after you!"

But Marty couldn't hear her above the sound of the winch engine.

The bucket came up to the rail and he was dismayed to see that it only contained the pack. Grace must have thought there wasn't enough room for her and the pack, he thought irritably. If there was enough room for a chimp and a poodle, there's enough room for a girl and a pack. What was she thinking? He took the pack out and started the bucket down again.

Suddenly, the trees started blowing, accompanied by a loud roaring. Loose debris from the canopy started raining down on him. A white helicopter passed a few feet above the tree. "Blackwood!" He checked the cable. It was only a third of the way down. He didn't think it would reach the ground before the helicopter landed.

Butch left Grace where she lay and stepped out into the clearing to help guide the pilot down. Noah Blackwood jumped out before the helicopter touched down.

The two men talked for a few moments, then Blackwood walked over to Grace. He was dressed immaculately in a crisp safari suit, the same outfit he wore on every television show Grace had ever seen him on. He was smiling.

"It's a miracle," he said to her. "After all these years.

"Untie me," Grace said.

Blackwood shook his head, still smiling. "Butch

tells me that you've had quite an adventure the past couple of days. He says that you're under the impression I'm trying to hurt you. I can assure you that nothing could be further from the truth. I would never hurt my own flesh and blood."

"What about Marty?" Grace asked. "What about Wolfe and Laurel Lee?"

"I'll admit that I'm a little cross with Travis," Blackwood said. "But I certainly wouldn't cause him harm."

"What about the parrot?"

"What parrot?"

"The one Butch threw against the tree."

Blackwood glanced at Butch.

Butch shrugged. "I told you she was delirious. I had to tie her up for her own good."

"And I'm glad you did," Blackwood said, then looked back at Grace. "I understand you came across some rather unusual eggs while you were running around out here. Remarkable! Are they up in the tree house?"

"If that's what Butch told you, then he's the one who's delirious," Grace snapped. "And I don't believe that my *real* grandfather would leave me tied up."

"There is nothing I would like more than to untie you," Blackwood said. "But in your current state that would be far too dangerous. I'll untie you as soon as we're on our way back to civilization."

"And Marty?" Grace asked.

"Of course," Blackwood said, turning to Butch. "Perhaps you should go up and get the boy so we can be on our way."

The bucket came down through the trees again. Butch rushed over to see if the pack was in it. It wasn't. "It will be my pleasure to get the boy," he said, and started up the ladder.

"Don't be such a scaredy-chimp," Marty said. "It was just a helicopter. Get out of my way!"

He had gotten halfway down the tree when he encountered Bo clutching PD in one hand and clinging to a handhold with the other. She was blocking his way.

"I mean it, Bo! Either climb around me or climb down. I've got to help Grace."

Bo looked below her.

"That's right," Marty encouraged. "Climb down."

But that was not why Bo was looking down. A shiny head appeared about ten feet below her.

"The game's over," Butch said. "All I want are those eggs. I promise, nothing will happen to you."

For some reason Marty didn't believe him. He scrambled back up to the Skyhouse.

"I know this is difficult." Blackwood was on his knees in front of Grace. "But I can assure you that in a couple weeks all of this unpleasantness will be a distant memory. You're going to be a princess, just like your mother was. Losing her was the worst thing that ever happened to me. And finding you is the best."

"I'm not going with you," Grace said. "I'm waiting here for Wolfe."

A flash of anger came into Blackwood's eyes, but disappeared almost as fast as it had appeared. "Travis Wolfe is responsible for all of this. Can't you see that? How you survived the fall from his jet I'll never understand. He killed my daughter . . . your mother, Grace."

"He didn't," Grace said. "Mokélé-mbembé killed her. He nearly died trying to save her."

"Is that what he told you?"

"I was there!"

"You were too young to remember anything that happened," Blackwood said soothingly. "Travis has filled your head with lies. He's a menace. I must protect you, Grace, just as I've dedicated my life to protecting animals all over the world."

Butch virtually launched himself through the trapdoor, fully expecting the boy to be waiting for him with some kind of club. But the blow did not come. The boy wasn't there.

He quickly searched the room, then climbed up to the second floor, then to the roof, where he found the chimp and dog. But the boy was nowhere to be seen. Nor were the eggs.

Marty was sliding through the canopy, with branches and leaves whacking him in the face. He hadn't taken the time to put a helmet or goggles on, but he wished he had. The cable ended at a small platform a hundred yards from the Skyhouse tree.

He unclipped the harness and started down.

dinosaur eggs 32

Butch stepped off the ladder.

"Well?" Blackwood asked.

"He's not up there and neither are the eggs. There are canopy cables on the roof. He must have used one of them to slip away."

Grace smiled.

"It's going to be dark soon," Blackwood said. "If we don't leave, we'll have to spend the night out here."

Butch shrugged. "Go ahead. I have some other things to take care of before I leave. I'll get the eggs, and you can send the chopper back for me."

"That would probably be best," Blackwood agreed. He pointed at Grace. "Bring her to the helicopter."

Butch picked her up and threw her over his shoulder. Grace struggled, but it was hopeless. They started across the clearing.

"Put her down!"

Butch and Blackwood stopped and turned around.

Marty had stepped out into the clearing about thirty yards behind them. He was holding a large egg in each hand. "I said, put her down."

Butch smiled. "Nice try."

Marty tossed one of the eggs into the air and caught it.

"For God's sake," Blackwood shouted. "Do what he says."

Reluctantly, Butch set Grace on the ground. "Now what?" he asked.

"Cut her loose."

"Forget it," Butch said.

Marty tossed the egg into the air again and nearly missed catching it.

"Be careful with that," Blackwood said. "That's not an egg, it's a prehistoric relic. It's worth millions of dollars. You're going to be rich, son."

"Big deal," Marty said. He tossed both eggs into the air and caught them, then brought his arm back like he was going to throw one.

"He's bluffing," Butch said.

Marty threw the egg. It hit a tree trunk with a sickening splatter.

Blackwood moaned. Butch brought his shotgun up and pointed it at Marty's chest. "What are you going to do now, sport?"

Marty held the remaining egg with both hands. "One to go. If you shoot me, I swear to you that the last thing I'm going to do is crush this thing."

"Be reasonable," Blackwood pleaded.

"Cut her loose," Marty repeated.

Blackwood got down on his knees and cut the ropes with his own pocketknife.

Grace got up, rubbing her wrists, and ran over to Marty.

"All right," Blackwood said. "You have the egg. You have Grace. Where are you going to go?"

Marty didn't answer. He hadn't figured that part out yet.

"They're coming with me," Wolfe said breathlessly, stepping into the clearing, pointing a shotgun at Butch. Laurel stepped out behind him.

"Travis," Blackwood said, giving him the most hateful look Grace and Marty had ever seen.

"Put the gun down," Wolfe said. "I mean it."

Butch started to lay it down.

Blackwood gave a scornful laugh. "He won't shoot you. That's Travis Wolfe."

Butch hesitated.

"His father used to tell me stories about how his son couldn't finish a hunt. The man's a pitiful coward."

Wolfe seemed unfazed by the insult. "You have a point, Noah. And my friend standing over there has a point, too."

Masalito stepped out into the open with an arrow strung.

"And if that doesn't convince you," Wolfe continued, "this will."

Another person stepped out of the trees, wearing a full set of camouflage army fatigues and carrying an automatic rifle.

"Bertha?" Marty said. "How did you get here?"

"Same way you did," she answered, with her eyes and rifle fixed on Butch. "And I would have been here sooner, but I got blown a little off course. Then my chute got tangled in the canopy. It's been a long time since I've made a jump."

She walked over to Butch without the slightest trace of fear. "Are you going to put your gun down, or am I going to have to take it away from you?"

"You?" Butch smirked.

Butch was on the ground so fast with his arms pinned behind him that Marty and Grace didn't see how she had done it.

"Yeah, me," Bertha said, securing his wrists with plastic manacles. When she finished, she jogged over to the helicopter and climbed in. A few seconds later the pilot came flying out the door.

Grace, Marty, Wolfe, and Laurel stood in front of the mound of rocks near the stream. Marty was holding the egg. Grace was holding Congo. Vid flew overhead.

The parrot was alive, but his wing was broken in two places. Wolfe had set and bandaged the wing, and said he would pin the bone when they got back to Cryptos. Masalito had climbed up to the Skyhouse with Bo and PD to retrieve his precious *molimo*. Bertha was guarding Blackwood and the others at the edge of the clearing.

Laurel pointed to the rocks. "Is this where Rose is buried?"

"Yes," Wolfe answered quietly.

They all stared down at the grave for several moments.

"I wish you all could have known her," Wolfe said.

Grace took his hand. "I guess we'll just have to get to know her through you."

Wolfe rubbed a hand over his eye.

"I'm sorry we lost one of the eggs," Grace said. "Marty threw it so that Blackwood would let me go."

"The only thing that matters is that you and Marty are safe," Wolfe said. "Although, it would have been nice to get here a little sooner to—"

"You got here in plenty of time," Marty said. He handed Wolfe the egg and shrugged out of his father's backpack. He unzipped the flap and pulled the second egg out.

"But I saw you throw the dinosaur egg against that tree." Grace pointed to it.

Marty grinned. "*Alleged* dinosaur egg." He jogged

over to the tree and came back with the egg, which was actually the ball from the nursery. "I filled it with motor oil so it would make a good splat when it hit the tree."

"You *are* a good man to have around," Wolfe said, shaking his head in admiration.

Marty grinned. "What are we going to do with the eggs?"

"Let me borrow your Gizmo," Wolfe said. "I need to e-mail Ted and have him build us a dinosaur incubator."

Grace, Marty, Wolfe, Bertha, Laurel, and Masalito rose above the clearing in the white helicopter. Along with them were Bo, PD, Congo, Vid, two dinosaur eggs, and a trunk with a rose painted on the lid.

Over Blackwood's protests, Wolfe had convinced Blackwood's pilot to fly them to the airport. Marty was the last to get into the helicopter. He had to retrieve his mamba head in the mason jar and his soiled cap. He looked out the window as they rose above the clearing. Blackwood ran over to where Marty had dropped the alleged dinosaur egg and picked it up.

"I didn't do it!" Marty said.

home 33

Subject: 8th Try!
From: luther_smyth@xlink.com
To: marty@ewolfe.com

Hey, Marty,

Now that you're back on Cryptos, safe from enraged television personalities, baldheaded thugs, and hungry crocs . . . Why haven't you responded to my last seven e-mails????

The hurried e-mail you sent from the hijacked helicopter was not nearly enough to satisfy my curiosity.

Have you forgotten that I'm still imprisoned here?

I know that I'll be pardoned in a few days to join you in your island paradise, but I need news before I get there. You can't imagine how boring it is here without my partner in crime and comics.

Write me.

Worriedly yours,

Luther

Subject: RE: 8th Try!
From: marty@ewolfe.com
To: luther_smyth@xlink.com

Dear Worried,

Sorry for the delay. I have several excuses . . .

1) Wolfe gave my Gizmo to Laurel. We stopped at the Mokélé-mbembé nest before we left Lake Télé. Wolfe filled some bags with soil from the site, thinking it would be best to incubate the eggs in the same stuff they've been setting in. (He also wanted to make sure there wasn't a trace of Mokélé-mbembé DNA. There wasn't. I wish you could have seen that fire!) Laurel and Masalito stayed behind to monitor the nest. (Boring!) They'll send hourly data to Ted Bronson to feed into the controls of the incubator. So, I'm Gizmo-less. Now, you might be thinking I could have just borrowed a Gizmo. Nope. When we got back, Ted confiscated all the Gizmos on the island. He's making some modifications to them. I'm in the Wolfe Den, using one of Wolfe's desktop computers. He's only letting me use it for twenty minutes, though. He

needs to keep all the data lines open.

2) When we got back to Cryptos, I stumbled up to my room and slept for three days. They were worried about me. Thought I'd been bitten by a tsetse fly and had sleeping sickness. They flew in a tropical disease specialist to check me out. After being poked and probed by the scariest doctor I've ever seen—believe me—I was no longer in the mood for sleep. (Dr. Grace thought this guy was great. After he decided that I was going to live, she spent several hours bending his ear, which had an amazing amount of hair growing out of it.)

3) And last but not least . . . I've been making preparations for your imminent arrival. Depending on when the eggs hatch, and what comes out of them, we should have a couple weeks on the island before we set sail for New Zealand. I have several things planned for us before we ship out.

Now for the good stuff . . . I don't want you to feel left out. So, below is an update since we swiped the chopper at Lake Télé.

I already told you that Grace and I aren't twins, Wolfe is her dad and got his leg bitten off by Mokélé-mbembé, blah, blah, blah . . . What you don't know is that Grace is still 12 years old. (And we always thought she was so mature. Ha!) As it happens, her birthday falls on the same day you arrive here. You might want to think about a way we can really surprise her. Make her 13th "special," if you know what I mean. But I warn you, she's not going to be so easy to scare. The Congo toughened her up. She hasn't fainted since Butch nabbed her from the Skyhouse, and believe me, there were things that made me a little faint after that. In other words, a snake in the bed won't do the trick anymore. You'd better get creative.

But enough about Grace . . .

When we got to the airport, Phyllis and Phil flew us directly to Cryptos. Ted Bronson invented a dinosaur egg incubator, and I fully expected him to be waiting for us when we arrived. The incubator was there, surrounded by three geeks to explain how it worked, but no Ted. They said that he was already working on another project in the QAQ. Which brings me to one of our missions when you get here: we need to get at least a glimpse of this guy.

Anyway, we set the eggs in the Wolfe Den, which is this incredible room on the top floor of the house. It's filled with TV monitors, computers, FAX machines, printers, and a bunch of other electronic stuff I've never seen before. Phil calls it the "heart" of Wolfe's cryptid operation.

They have these animal scouts all over the world, flying, running, swimming with their video cameras, streaming pictures into the Den and the QAQ. People monitor all this stuff 24/7. If they see something unusual the data is fed into this big computer, where it's cataloged and used for what I don't know exactly. This is how they are keeping tabs on the search for my parents. (No word on them, but we haven't given up hope. If anyone can find them, Wolfe will.)

Everyone is still concerned about what Blackwood is going to do about Grace and the eggs. Wolfe has implemented some extra security measures, but it's all very hush-hush. I don't even know what they are. He's convinced that Blackwood has a spy on the island, so he's being tight-lipped about what he's doing. Which brings me to another one of our missions: I think you and I should be able to put our heads together and figure out who the spy is. I've been looking into it and I have some likely suspects.

Anyway . . . this is what you'll encounter when you finally get here.

See you soon . . . Marty

P.S. Grace paid me the dollar she owed me from the egg bet. I have it pinned to the wall above my bed.

I divide my time between the library and the den, where Wolfe stares at the eggs hour after hour. If they hatch, the babies will be raised on Cryptos, then moved to a deserted island he owns that has a similar environment to the Congo's. No press release or television news. He'll keep it all very quiet. "If the word gets out," he said, "Lake Télé will be overrun with scientists, collectors, adventurers all trying to make a name for themselves and in the process destroying the flora and fauna that have lived there in peace for tens of thousands of years."

He's discussing the preservation of the Lake Télé region with government officials. "It could take years, decades, or it may never happen. But if it does, with enough safeguards in place, we'll take Mokélé-mbembé back home one day."

I've filled nearly two Moleskines since I've returned to Cryptos. . . . The blank Moleskines I've received since I was a child were not sent by my uncle Timothy as I thought—they were sent by Wolfe. My mother used Moleskines for her journals and field notes. After she died, her yearly order continued to arrive on the island. Wolfe did not have the heart to cancel the order. He said it would be like canceling one of his memories of her. So, he had the order transferred to me.

Marty told me that my mother's Moleskines are in the trunk, which I have not opened . . . yet. I thought I had left my fears behind in the humid air above the Congo, but I guess some still remain.

The eggs have helped me get to know my father . . . and my mother. Without the eggs, Wolfe would be down at the Coelacanth, *getting ready for New Zealand. But the eggs have confined him to a single room like a brooding hen. We've been able to talk. He's not the fierce pirate I thought he was on the first day we met. He's kind, shy, funny, and knows a great deal about many things . . . except for children. He has no idea how to go about raising us.*

He's told me a lot about my mother, but it's painful for him. I can see it in his eyes and hear it in his voice, which goes very quiet when he talks about her.

"Your mother was not only beautiful," he said today, "she was the smartest person I've ever met. When she left the Ark she bloomed. She woke up happy and went to bed happy. She devoured each day like a hungry wolf."

I asked him what I was like when I was a baby.

"A lot of trouble," he said. "Fearless. We couldn't leave you alone for a second. You crawled into the spring when you were four months old, nearly drowned. The next day, I glanced away for a second and you were back in the water. We had to put a fence around the water to keep you out of it.

"You started to walk when you were ten months old . . . run, actually. We kept a rope tied around

your waist, but of course you figured out how to untie every knot I tried."

I'm still practicing on the high wire. I've raised it a foot more and . . .

Marty walked into the library where Grace was writing. "How's the parrot?" He walked over to Congo's perch and offered him a peanut, which Congo refused.

"He's been a little off all day," Grace said, putting her pen down. "I told Wolfe. He said he'd come down later and take a look at him."

Marty raised his eyebrows. "And leave the eggs?" He wandered over to the squid and coelacanth tanks, imitated the occupants for a few moments, then looked at his watch. "I'd better get into the kitchen and give Bertha a hand with dinner."

"That reminds me," Grace said. "I was talking to Wolfe last night and he said there was no canned chicken in the canister they dropped."

"Really," Marty said innocently. "Bertha must have put a few cans in without him knowing." He turned to leave.

"Marty?"

He turned back to her.

"What did you feed me that morning?"

Marty grinned as he backed toward the door. "Green eggs and mamba," he said, then ran.